DAD
TO
THE
FUTURE

Copyright © 2024 Miles Hamer

The right of Miles Hamer to be identified as the author
of this work has been asserted.

All rights reserved.

This is a work of fiction. Except in the case of historical fact, names, characters, places, and incidents are the product of this author's imagination or are used fictitiously. Any resemblance to actual persons, living or dead, events, or locales, is entirely coincidental.

You may not sell or reproduce any part of this book, except in brief quotations embodied in reviews or articles, without written consent from the copyright owner.

Consent can be obtained from www.mileshamer.com

First paperback edition August 2024

Cover design by Daniel Morgan

Edited by Shaun Baines

Published by Amazon on behalf of St Brannocks Books

PROLOGUE

1984

Barely thirty seconds after waking, Ruth wondered how on earth she'd ended up here. She'd been at a low ebb, sure, but never quite to *this* level of under-achievement. She deftly lifted the crusty bed sheets to get a better look at the man who'd somehow wooed her into this predicament the night before.

He was a thin strip of snoozing piss. A gangly frame dominated the mattress. Bare, blackened feet dangled over the edge of the bed. His legs were less limbs than they were gnarled truncheons of ham. His sallow, pale skin looked like a warning from a medical textbook about the dangers of vitamin D withdrawal. Dusty eyebrows crowned a pair of sunken eyes, above a bulbous, alcohol-sodden nose and a cruel open, thin-lipped mouth. With no teeth.

No teeth.

Where the fuck were his teeth?

Oh, that's ok, they're over there in that smudged jar of dirty water by the bed.

His teeth are in a jar.

Great hair though.

She spied his denim jeans and matching shirt. They were flung over the chair the previous night in his hurry to get naked. If it weren't for the clothes, Ruth would be calling the police. It felt like the smooth-talking charmer at the pub had done a runner out the fire escape and left her to share a bed with Gollum here. Her vagina shuddered at the thought of what she'd put it through during last night's mercifully brief encounter. She might treat it to a week's worth of her cosy period knickers to try and make up for it.

Ruth reached for her jeans at a glacial pace, careful not to make a sound. There was no chance she was risking rousing, or even worse, arousing him. With painfully slow deliberation, she teased her feet into the waist of her jeans and lifted herself up gently to allow her legs through. That was the hard part over with. She stretched across for her blouse, just beyond the reach of the bed. She held her breath as she fastened nimbly each button with surgical precision.

Please god don't wake up!

As she leant to grab her handbag, a small murmur piped through his nostrils. A streak of fear catapulted through Ruth's spine, as a string of snot spattered onto his upper lip. She didn't move for a full ten seconds, making sure he was definitely still unconscious.

When she was double-confident he wasn't anywhere near awake, she trod lightly towards the bedroom door. She just needed to make it to the bedroom door. Once she was on the other side, she could run as fast as her heels could carry her.

"Morning flower." came a baritone rasp.

Fuck!

She froze, forced a smile, then pivoted on the spot to face him.

"Hey there," Ruth replied, with as much begrudging enthusiasm as she could muster.

"Looking for the bathroom?"

"Erm..."

"Only, if you need a shit, the flush hasn't quite got the punch at the moment. I've left a message with the landlord about getting a plumber round. Depends how your guts are, really." His gums flapped hypnotically as he spoke.

Every last milligram of sexiness Ruth had ever experienced died immediately.

"No, thanks. I've just, well, I must have drunk a lot last night, which isn't usually, erm..." She trailed off, unsure how to tell him that his morning patter needed, let's say, a little work. She straightened her jeans. "I've got places to be."

A glimmer of rejection flickered across his face for the briefest of milliseconds, before he sat up in bed and reached across for his teeth. Holding firm eye contact, he flailed for the dentures, accidentally upsetting a cracked saucer full of fag butts on the way. He pulled the grinning falsies from the jar. Without warning, he hawked up a gobful of phlegm, spat on them, wiped it off with the duvet sheet and popped them in. He then flashed a toothy smile at his latest sexual conquest. Ruth instantly vowed never to have sex with anyone ever again as long as she lived.

"I better be off." she stammered, and headed for the door. The lovely door that granted sweet release.

"Hang on a minute, I never got your name!" he cooed, optimistically.

"No," confirmed Ruth. "No, you didn't."

And with that, Ruth turned and left the worst place she would ever wake up in.

"I'm Nigel" came a muffled, slightly desperately cheerful voice from the other side. "Nigel Stanton!" And with that, he farted.

Out on the street below stood a middle-aged man in a fancy long coat with floppy collars. Keeping watch on the flat, he witnessed Ruth's pelt from the front door, almost losing her heels as she stumbled swiftly out of danger and into the cosy familiarity of the town's morning hubbub. The man narrowed his eyes and felt his fists clench as they dug into his pockets. He gave a withering sigh to no one in particular. Not for the first time that week, he regretted digging up his past.

Ten minutes later, Nigel rummaged through his goolies loosely in the shower, lazily rinsing off last night's athletic conquest. His mind flashed back to the evening's shenanigans, the music, the pints, the laughter, the bonking. (He especially enjoyed the bonking.) Perhaps she was a keeper? Maybe *she* was the one? He couldn't just ignore the bonking, after all. Should probably learn her name first though.

Nigel placed the hardened stump of grubby soap back into the stained plastic dish, and let the scalding hot water pour down on him a little more. He turned off the shower, grabbed an already damp towel, and left the room before he gave the mirror a chance to clear. He wasn't always proud of what he saw. His wife even less so.

As he patted himself as best he could with a soggy bit of cloth, Nigel tried to recall his carnal encounter with Ruth. Just as he was trying to determine her bra size by miming grabbing her breasts, a sharp knock on the door downstairs interrupted his thoughts.

Shit! What if it was the landlord? Perhaps he actually did call out a plumber even though he owed two months' rent? Even better, what if it was that girl back for a second helping of the Stanton? Either way, he was getting a shit or a shag. Result!

He threw on a pale blue denim shirt and darted downstairs for the front door.

"Coming! Coming!" he brayed cheerily, hoping that would be disgustingly true in a short amount of time. Nigel flung open the door and flashed a wide smile of yellow-stained falsies.

There on the doorstep stood neither his landlord nor last night's lay. Nigel's smile faltered. The hand whose knuckles had knocked on his door belonged to a man not entirely unlike Nigel himself. In fact, he was oddly familiar. The same dusty eyebrows, thin mouth, pale, hollow eyes, and great barnet of thick wavy hair. The man looked Nigel up and down, then sighed in conclusion.

No sooner had Nigel managed to croak a startled, "What?" then the knuckles formed a fist, pulled back as far as the owner's arm would go, and ploughed straight into his astonished face.

CHAPTER 1

2019

James Harpman decided that his car needed to be looked at by a proper man, as his Mum used to say (and wife still did).

Frankly, it hadn't been a difficult decision. He stood in his drive, fruitlessly inspecting the smoking bonnet. He ran his hands through his lustrous wave of hair and hoped the engineering knowhow might magically come to him. It didn't. He phoned the garage and tried to explain the symptoms.

"Well, there's black wisp billowing out from the grill. A bit like archive footage of a fighter plane downed from enemy fire in World War II. Or is it the First World War?"

James heard a slow exhale on the other end of the handset.

"Mr Harpman," asked the mechanic. "Do you know as much about cars as you do about global conflicts?"

"What's your point?"

"Just bring the car in, ok?"

"Shall do, boss. I'll chance the mile journey in, save on recovery costs, eh?" James thought he was doing *excellent* bloke chat. "At the very least, if the car explodes en route, I might look a bit like James Bond. Or possibly Mr Bean. A movie star, either way. Anyway, I really need to get these clothes for my children's nativity and prove to my wife that I'm not just a feckless…hello?"

He popped quickly back into the house to change from the three-quarter length fancy coat with the ostentatious floppy collars in exchange for the un-showy practicality of his combat green jacket. His kids called it his 'Dad coat'. James knew that garages could smell an amateur man a mile off, and he didn't want to come across as some sort of fey dreamer who knew sod all about motors.

Ten minutes later, he handed over the keys to a mechanic sipping a mug of coffee. Shakin' Stevens' *Merry Christmas Everyone* strained against the tinny speaker of a small radio on the reception desk.

"My car's, erm…" James struggled for the right word. "…injured?"

The mechanic offered a little pity smile, and promised to let him know, 'the damage' within the hour.

"Thanks, dude," James replied, regretting instantly using 'dude' instead of the more universal 'mate'.

"If it's a cracked radiator it's not going to be cheap," warned the mechanic.

"A radiator? In my car? Really? It's electric air heating, isn't it?"

The mechanic stared ahead at his customer, his expression undimmed by James' ignorance.

"No, a car radiator. To cool the engine."

James' face faltered slightly, as his mistake dawned on him.

"Right, yes. Sorry, of course. OK, cheers. Bye." He turned to leave, reasoning that he might as well have handed his bollocks over the counter as well.

He began the short walk into Hartnell town centre and popped his earphones in, as the howling guitar din drowned out the feelings of his own inadequacy. And more importantly, the garage mechanic's laughter.

Bill Lambert texted his best friend James, then tried not to notice that his bedroom *really* needed a tidy. Or a decorative re-think. Perhaps even setting on fire. But something to make it look more outwardly human and approachable and less like a foetid crack den. As he paced slowly around the room, phone held against his head, he accidentally kicked over a small pile of empty Pot Noodle cups. He cursed, then spoke confidently into his phone's memo recorder.

"I, Bill Lambert, am on the verge of fine-tuning the greatest scientific discovery in all of history. The next evolution in human achievement. The wheel, fire, and gravity all rolled into one." He paused, quizzically. "No, wait, that makes it sounds like a stunt car show." He pressed pause, took a deep breath, and hit record again.

"I, Bill Lambert, have made the most significant scientific discovery this world has ever known. History is about to be made!"

He was happier with that. More concise, straight to the point.

"First of all though, I'm busting for a number two. Oh flapjacks! Disregard that last comment." He hit the off button and strode purposefully to the bathroom.

Out of desperation, James found himself walking reluctantly to a giant sportswear store. For his young son's imminent nativity play, he had been tasked with finding a pair of red or white plain shorts, and/or a red and white striped t-shirt, but not a plain red t-shirt. Frankly, the order's specificity gave him a headache, and no other shop had stocked any plain clothes. It was all Marvel or Minions and suchlike these days. Even Marks

& Spencer had joined in on the act. He celebrated briefly when he thought he'd found a pair of red shorts, only to find a cartoon firefighter beaming back at him from the left leg.

"Oh, piss off Fireman Sam," James exclaimed in disappointment. A nearby elderly lady retorted with a disapproving glare. Being angry reminded her to complain again to her daughter about foreigners in the NHS. Even though James was white.

Unaware of the future racist tirade his profanity had triggered, James trudged on to the giant leisurewear warehouse. He stared listlessly at rows upon rows of ugly, chunky trainers of mildly variant design. A shining white gleam of footwear that would likely never see sporting action, he wondered idly whether a legitimate athlete had ever stepped foot across the threshold of JD Sports? He turned to see the only other customers: three obese women vaping heavily whilst thumbing through a rack of giant grey joggers.

Failing to find any of the items his wife had written out carefully for him, he turned to leave. He apologised inwardly to his so far costume-less son. His face exploded in happiness at the mere thought of his boy Jude, who had just this morning babbled excitedly about 'not doing real lessons' for at least a week.

James' phone rang. He scowled at the caller ID. It was his editor.

"Hey," he greeted, meekly.

"James," began Jacqui. "When are you going to get that *Fear of Beans* review in? You're overdue by three days, we go to print at the end of the week. It's only 1,000 words. I'll give it to Gary if you can't deliver."

"Yes, sorry, no please don't give it to Gary. I'll have it your way shortly, promise."

"Thank god you said that, Gary couldn't review a teaspoon. Plus, his byline photo looks like he won a trolley dash round Mencap. Now come on, it's just a middling indie rock band. In fact, there's your piece. Just add some shit to that. OK get it done, bye."

"Bye?"

"I share your concern Mrs Agnew, really I do."

Susan Harpman paused to let her concern hang momentarily. She continued. "And we have taken all the necessary health and safety precautions; we will be extra vigilant about headcounts and observing the correct procedure." She paused again before delivering the stupidest caveat she would hopefully ever state. "But you must understand that in the event of a terrorist attack, I cannot guarantee the safety of the children."

Mrs Agnew puckered her face up to a tight ball of flesh, and tutted so loudly it knocked a small pile of children's drawings onto the floor. As Susan scrabbled to pick up the papers, Mrs Agnew leaned back in the miniature plastic chair and exhaled forcefully. Her discontent reverberated around the classroom, mocking the bright bunting and illustrated timetables. The walls' kaleidoscope of cheerful colour was losing the mood battle with the black hole of bellicose currently squeezed beneath the child's workspace.

"Are you telling me my boy might die?" Mrs Agnew asked.

Mrs Harpman swallowed back a flash of anger. "No, I'm just saying that despite our best efforts, a terrorist attack is a random, freak occurrence and incredibly unlikely. In this most improbable of scenarios, I will of course do my utmost to protect the children, but I can't say with absolute certainty that my efforts will be successful."

Mrs Agnew narrowed her eyes and tightened the lips around her gums.

"I simply cannot believe what I'm hearing – that you're not prepared to guarantee the safety of my Callum from Islamic Muslims. It's disgusting, is what it is."

"I am sorry you feel that way. You are, of course, perfectly entitled to withhold your son from the day trip to Uncle Rusty's Petting Zoo if you think he is in danger."

The only danger he encounters is chronic obesity, thanks to your terrible parenting.

"Of course, the school will open specially on the day if he wishes to attend. But it'll be the usual school hours. All the pupils on the trip won't be returning home until 8:30 that evening."

Mrs Agnew broke out in a smile. It was eerie.

"8:30pm?"

Got her!

Mrs Harpman knew mentioning the return time would reel her in. If there was one thing Mrs Agnew loved more than her chip-gobbling grunt of a son, it was not spending much time with him (both teacher and parent had at least that in common). Casually mentioning that she could gain an extra five hours bereft of his company would easily be enough to overlook the likelihood of a bomb threat from ISIS in the meerkat pen.

Mrs Agnew capitulated swiftly.

"You say this is on the syllabus?"

Susan nodded and ignored the fact that in the three years her son had attended Hartnell Primary Mrs Agnew had not once concerned herself with the syllabus. (The only school policies she objected to were the PE lessons and healthy options on the menu.)

"Well then," began Mrs Agnew's tactical withdrawal. "As long as they're learning something and you say you'll do everything you can to protect the kids, I suppose he can go."

"Thanks for coming in Mrs Agnew. I'm sure Callum will enjoy the day and learn a lot!"

With that she ushered the belligerent parent to the office door with an overly gracious motioning. She hoped her gesture didn't appear too sarcastic.

A safe thirty seconds later a small voice piped up.

"Has she gone?"

"Off the premiscs completely, thank Christ," replied Mrs Harpman. "You can come out now, Barbara."

A short, young female colleague crept nervously into the office from the adjoining staff room.

"I thought she'd never leave," said Barbara.

"*You* didn't?"

"Fair enough, you took a bullet for us there. Thank you."

"No bother, at least I convinced her to let Callum on the trip."

Barbara grimaced in agreement.

"Yeah, better than opening the school all day purely for one pupil. Good work."

Susan Harpman smiled thinly. It was the most minor of victories really.

"I don't know, beyond the blubber and bluster, maybe he's a good kid at heart." Susan trailed off and stared to the back of the classroom. "But I wouldn't put it past him to try to eat some of the animals."

At 11 am sharp as instructed, James sat at Harry's Rock n Roll Cafe, waiting impatiently for his friend, Bill. His eyes darted about the room manically.

Where was Bill?

He wasn't sure why they still came here: a retro fifties diner whose faded decor made it look older than the era it represented. The walls displayed poorly rendered line drawings of barely-remembered rock stars such as Gene Vincent, The Big Bopper, and Buddy Holly. The chequered flooring was only just visible and the formica tables cracked and creaked with the decades of dining gone by. The restaurant's one concession to the festive season was from the might-as-well-not-have-bothered school of Christmas decorations: a lone silver piece of tattered tinsel wrapped scarf-like around a life-size plastic statue of Elvis.

James thumb-drummed on the table nervously and noticed a few customers shoot dirty looks his way. Which he felt was a little unreasonable, given that the place was already bursting at the decibels with the loud surf guitar music, the clattering of the kitchen, and roller-skating waiting staff.

James' petulance melted away as soon as Bill flung open the door of the café, and offered his apologies to the entire building for his lateness. He ordered a takeaway cappuccino and muffin from Harry, the granite-faced owner, then motioned to James' table and made his way over.

"Bill, you adorable human, how are you? But also, where have you been, for crying out loud?" James was rubbish at not sounding annoyed.

"You wouldn't believe me, mate. So, I've…"

"I've just finished a bowl of beef soup," interrupted James.

"Erm, ok. How was that?" Bill responded, a lilting deflation in his voice.

"It was delivered by a waitress on roller skates, how do you think it went? And honestly, you'd get more meat by letting a cow fart on your plate. Worse still, I completely failed to get my son's nativity costume."

"Oh, what does he need?"

James repeated the strict orders he had committed to memory.

"What? Who's he playing?"

"A candy cane," replied James.

"How's that a nativity costume?"

"No idea, but at least my daughter's wearing something more reasonable."

"Which is?"

"A bale of hay"

Bill screwed his face up in confusion.

"Eh?"

"There's about eighty kids in her year alone and this was the nearest they had to a character part. It was that or chorus line and she wanted to stand out a bit." James shrugged, attempting to absolve himself of the whole process.

"Can't Susan get them better-dressed parts?" enquired Bill, feigning interest.

"She works at the primary, they're at the juniors. My eldest has been there for nearly four years. Do you ever listen to me?"

Bill chuckled apologetically. Children really weren't his thing.

"So come on then," asked James, eagerly. "You texted that you had massive news. What is it?"

Bill took a bite of his muffin, spraying a mouthful of crumbs at his friend.

"Come on," repeated James. "Tell me what it is now, or you can kiss my big, black ass goodbye."

"What? You're whiter than David Bowie's foreskin."

"Whatever, just get on with it you big sciencey man you."

"Sorry, it's just that I thought the best person to tell you this news would be, well, me."

And with that, the man with his back to the couple removed his baseball cap, then turned to face the two. To James' utter astonishment, he appeared to be an exact copy of the man already sitting opposite him. It was Bill.

Both Bills smiled back, eerily.

CHAPTER 2

2019

James said nothing for ten achingly long seconds, as he took in the scene of two identical Bills in front of him. He blinked several times to check that his eyes simply hadn't malfunctioned. He tried mouthing, "holy balls!" but the words simply wouldn't form. He tentatively reached out his left hand and lightly pinched the left Bill on his chubby cheek.

Eventually, the Bill that James had just spoken with piped up.

"Weird, isn't it?"

The punctuated silence was enough for James to let leash.

"You're a twin? We've known each other since we were four. You never told me you had a twin." he stammered, addressing the second Bill.

The second Bill responded.

"How long have we known each other?"

James put his hands up in surrender.

"I don't know, since forever. Since you used to come round just because you had a mega crush on my babysitter, Sophie Davison."

Bill 1 winked.

"*Everyone* had a crush on Sophie Davison."

Bill 2 blinked gently in agreement.

"In all that time James, have you ever known we were twins? No, because we're not, James. We're not twins, we are both Bill."

James furrowed his brow further. It was in danger of collapsing off his face entirely.

"You're both Bill?"

Both Bills nodded in unison.

"Your parents gave you the same name? How shit and unimaginative of them."

The first Bill leant forward.

"James, I'm Bill, and he's Bill. We're the same Bill."

James narrowed his eyes and surveyed each Bill. He studied each in rapid succession. The Bills were right. They were exactly the same; slightly plump, stubby fingers, and both sported a mop of unruly curls. Each was utterly indistinguishable from each other, hair by hair. An utterly identical pair of Bills, right down to the tiny scar beneath his right eye; the result of James' compass making contact during a Maths lesson fight decades ago.

"How?"

The second Bill took a sip of his doppelganger's drink.

"Time travel. I'm Bill from an hour in the future,"

James laughed.

"Yeah, good one." His smile faltered. "You're serious?"

"As serious as I can be, whilst sitting next to myself."

"That's death-of-a-Royal kind of serious," affirmed the second Bill.

"Holy shitballs!" exclaimed James. James mouthed, "sorry" to owner Harry for his language. The inscrutable proprietor hadn't noticed. James lowered his voice. "You mastered time travel. How?"

The second Bill glanced over at his double, who took this as a cue to explain.

"James, do you remember doing art class together?"

James shrugged, confused where this was going.

"Oh, for crying out loud, a bit. What's that got to do with time travel? Oh my god - is time travel powered by poster paint?"

Both Bills sighed in unison.

"No James, but it's that sort of ignorance I'm getting at. You remember that time in art where we had to invent our own characters, and I asked you that really stupid question?"

James grinned.

"You mean, 'Does the moustache come below or above the nose?' Christ yes, I'd forget my own name before I let that beauty go!"

Bill 1 shuffled a little, still embarrassed by the memory. The second Bill merely smiled, smugly.

"Well," he began. "That's kind of where I think you'd be if I even began to start trying to explain the scientific miracle of time travel."

James' face fell a little at the explanation.

"Yeah, good point. I wouldn't have a clue. Got Ds in science."

Bill 1 nodded, encouragingly.

"Didn't you draw a little puzzle for the examiner?"

James' face brightened instantly.

"'Which way to the pie?'! Yes! It had three intersecting fishing rod lines and a pie at the end."

"Why would you be fishing for pie?"

"Erm..."

Bill 2 sat up attentively.

"Look I know this is time travel, but time is something we ironically don't have much of. Or at least, you don't. You've got to be off shortly."

James snapped out of his pie reverie.

"Why? And why me? Shouldn't you be sharing this with New Scientist? Or, you know, your parents?"

Bill 1 bowed his head and scratched his nose.

"You've met my parents, yes?"

James thinned his lips and sucked back his teeth.

"You know," James began. "I've never quite understood how you came from those two."

Both Bills raised their unkempt eyebrows in unison.

"Eight years of studying the universe's mysteries at CERN, yet still the biggest puzzle to me is my Mum and Dad," sighed Bill 2. A grim hush descended upon the table for just a little too long.

James slapped the table to break the uncomfortable silence.

"OK then, you - or rather he," he pointed to Bill 1, "stay here and tell me how the bollocks you can do this. Or at least, what we're going to do now that we can."

Bill 2 shook his head.

"I, or rather he, will do that, whilst you travel back in time to meet me. Or rather, him."

"But!" protested James.

"Please James," insisted Bill 1. "I'll explain as we go."

James exhaled in submission.

Bill 1 stood up to leave and grabbed his drink. James knocked back the contents of his mug and reached around for his wallet.

"Don't worry," began Bill 1, "I'm getting those in about an hour." He nodded at Bill 2, who smiled back.

James sighed, shook his head, and waved goodbye to his friend's doppelganger. He motioned to Harry.

"He's paying!" he yelped, pointed to Bill 2, and shrugged, nonplussed. Harry nodded in bafflement as the men left.

The pair walked briskly back in the direction of Bill's flat. James' body tingled with delight and wonder, as he tried to comprehend what he'd just witnessed.

"So, what are we doing now? Where are we going? Oh, my trousers, this is the best thing that's ever happened to you!" James paused. "Second for me."

"Hang on, what's the best thing that ever happened to you?"

"Use your imagination." James winked lasciviously.

"You had sex with a dinosaur?"

"Alright, use less imagination."

"You had some lovely sex?"

"Obviously!"

Bill thinned his lips and gave a curt nod of acknowledgment. He had learnt to accept grimly his friend's rampant libido, even if he still didn't approve. James caught Bill's distaste.

"Don't give me that look Mary Shitehouse, it's not like you don't still masturbate!" They strode past a gaggle of carolling pensioners, who's hearing suddenly improved.

"Thanks mate," Bill hissed. "Next time take an ad out in the local paper, eh?"

"Like anyone reads that now I'm not writing for it," scoffed James. "So, are we going to Victorian times or something? Are we going to the far-flung future? Will I have to wear a bodywarmer? I've always secretly wanted a bodywarmer."

"James, stop talking and keep walking. We're not going to Victorian times or space times or dinosaur times or any of that lemon drizzle. We're going one hour into the past."

"An hour? One hour? Whoop-de-bastard-do. You invent time travel and you're using it to - what - defy Greenwich Mean Time?"

"Not quite. We've got to make sure the last hour happened exactly as it did for us."

James' face crumpled in confusion.

"Run that past me again."

"We've just met my future self. I've now got to fulfil that role by being my future self in the present. It's perfectly simple."

James nodded unconvincingly and kept walking.

"We just met you?"

"Correct," confirmed Bill, with the timbre and patience of a kindly school nurse.

"And now you are going back to be the other Bill we just met in the cafe?"

"Give that man a toasted teacake, that's right!" beamed Bill with delight.

James' phone rang, startling the pair.

"Ooh, the garage!" exclaimed James, with a jaunty squeal. His smile soon turned south however, as he assured the mechanic he would come get his vehicle for which he would hand over an extraordinary amount of money. He felt fairly certain the cost was higher than the actual value of his car.

The pair arrived at Bill's flat, a first-floor apartment in a Victorian former family home. Set opposite a church, it was, at first glance, a pleasant enough dwelling from the exterior; deceptively spacious inside and fronted by a privacy-guarding evergreen bush. A gardener stood at the front, shearing spindly branches with aggressive abandon.

"Good day!" greeted Bill, with a broad smile. The gardener grunted in response.

"Why's he trimming a bush this close to December?" whispered James.

Bill shrugged, heading swiftly into the building. James followed and stepped over the threshold.

It was an unusual property. The faded decor of decades past haunted its halls, whilst new fixtures sat uncomfortably next to original fittings: an avocado bathroom suite squatted ungainly within pearly white tiled walls as a carved, ornate ceiling rose conspicuously above; a grand oak door with brass fittings lead to woodchip paper painted walls peeling from top to bottom; a feature fireplace of gleaming marble was blocked awkwardly by hardboard with a swiftly typed, "NO - NOT YOUR USE!!" in comic sans taped to the front; assortments of badly-fitted plug sockets, phone points, and wiring from across the decades jumbled haphazardly in small pockets of chaos all over the apartment. It was the blended history of furnishings poured over an architect's blueprints. With a light dusting of fag ash for good measure.

It didn't help that Bill, whilst not exactly dirty, didn't adhere to any level approaching order when it came to his possessions. A few smudged framed photos placed wherever they could find a space, various abandoned clothes, stained coffee mugs, and, of course, books.

Not just books.

But *BOOKS*.

So many books. Volumes of authors piled to the ceiling. Spines jutting out at irregular angles, yellowing pages curled from a good thumbing, and entire walls providing a backdrop to shelves groaning at the weight of the printed word. James didn't understand how anyone had the time or inclination to read so much. He hadn't read a tenth of what was in the flat, yet *he* was the writer.

James could see how this might have once been a proud family home. But over the decades, as the place was divided messily into flats, it had gradually become a revolving door for sole male tenants. A living shrine to lonely masturbators; high on Kleenex, but low on deodorant. He shivered inwardly, sat down next to a bin stuffed entirely with tissues, and tried to shake the feeling.

"So, where is it and how does it work and when are we going?" he barked, excitedly.

"Here, hold this," Bill replied, and tossed James a combination bicycle lock. Nearly dropping it, James fumbled with the device and stared in amazement at its distinctly non-amazing presence.

"Kick a badger, is this it?" he asked in astonishment. His face lit up. "Oh, I see! We put the date here as the combination and then you - what - unlock it? Is that right?" He simpered inanely. "It is, isn't it? Fuck my pants Bill, you're a genius. A bike lock!"

Bill frowned.

"No James. That's a bike lock. I use it to keep my bike safe."

James' entire body crumpled in disappointment, like a marionette whose strings had been severed.

Bill continued.

"I just didn't have anywhere else to put it, and It was on top of this…"

He pointed to a grey metallic box, from which an upright arm extended, that led to a bulky rectangular mirror a foot above the body below. From what James could make out, it was one of those overhead projectors they used to use at schools.

"Is that one of those overhead projectors they used to use at schools?"

Bill flashed a mischievous smile.

"Was!"

"No, it is, I can see it is," replied James. "Are you going to do a slideshow? Really?" You're not a Bond villain, Bill. Are you?"

"Villain? No. Time traveller? Yes. This seemingly ordinary box of secondary education days gone-by is, as we've just witnessed, the most advanced piece of technology this world…" Bill hesitated suddenly. "No - the universe! - has ever seen! This, my friend, is time travel. Projected."

Bill left his proclamation hanging, hoping for awe. James' face broadcast his disappointment.

"Oh. Right." James muttered. The bitter sting of underwhelming exhaled from both syllables.

Bill took offence at this ennui.

"Oh, sorry to disappoint James. Invented something better, have you? Invisibility ring you're waiting to show me? Perhaps a clockwork sandwich or a self-fellating penis?"

"Alright, sorry! Don't shit yourself, I just thought it'd be more, dunno, time machiney. But yeah, of course, amazing achievement."

Bill evaporated the frosty air.

"Thanks, friend. Let's get back to an hour ago!"

He grabbed a nearby remote control and fumbled with its buttons. An LED readout flared up as Bill's pudgy fingers smeared instructions into the screen. He motioned to James to stand up. James leapt to his feet and flashed a nervous smile.

"This better not be an elaborate prank."

Bill ignored the comment.

"Ready to travel in time, my friend?"

"Holy shit yes!" replied James, unsure of what might happen next.

"Get in front of the projector," instructed Bill. James tripped over several small piles of books. "Make sure *every* part of you is covered by the beam!"

"What will happen if I'm not?" asked James, shuffling on the spot, his wands waving manically.

"Just make sure you are."

James realised that both had been almost shouting over the white noise of the projector. Its volume was now closer to the din of a jet barrelling down a runway, rather than a wheezy bygone appliance. The thunderous roar elevated in pitch to an almost indecipherable squeal of decibels. Several nearby dogs yelped in confusion. James thought his ear might perforate. The beam's brightness intensified, and a gleaming, blinding burst of white exploded onto an increasingly concerned-looking

James. Bill smashed more buttons on his remote, flicked a small switch onto the side of the box, then leapt into the beam.

The cochlea-shattering squeal stopped.

The light suddenly stopped.

A small cloud of air puffed from the rear of the box.

Bill & James disappeared in time.

CHAPTER 3

2019 - one hour ago

James thought his head might explode; it was as if his skull and brain had declared war against each other and moved immediately to nuclear conflict. A swirling mass of colour and light pinned his eyelids back. A cacophonous choral groan drowned out his own screaming. He looked across to Bill, who didn't seem nearly so concerned. He merely wore the daft smile of a man being gently fellated. James could swear his ears were bleeding. A violent pain surged through his cerebral cortex. He thought it would never end.

It ended.

"Fuuuuuuuuuck!" he screamed. His knees buckled as he collapsed to the floor, cradling his head. Bill blew some imaginary dust from his knuckles and glanced at his remote control.

"Here we are, dear boy," he began. "We've time travelled!"

James breathed deeply and steadied himself to his feet.

"Three things, Bill," said James. "Firstly, we always travel in time. Generally though, just one second at a time. That's just being alive."

Bill raised his eyes at the facetiousness.

"Secondly," continued James. "Where's the proof? I'm just in bastard agony. Feels like I've given birth to a drum kit."

"Proof?" snorted Bill in derision. "Check the clock."

He pointed theatrically to a gaudy teapot-shaped timepiece on the wall. James followed Bill's finger. He was right. It was an hour before they left. He double checked his own watch: still an hour ahead. He couldn't be sure Bill hadn't set the clock as part of this elaborate hoax; it's not like he'd taken any notice of it before they left. He ran to the front window and peered out to the street below. Not only was the gardener not there, but the bush completely intact from its clumsy savaging just moments ago. The hairs on his arms stood to attention, and his whole body convulsed with a crackle. He felt intrinsically that somehow, this was all very real. He froze in wonderment and not a little horror.

"Shit, Bill. Have we *really* gone backwards in time?"

"Well," said Bill quietly. "It sure looks like it. Probably explains why the universe seemed to be screaming at us for daring to do it."

"Yeah. I mean, I don't know much about cosmic forces, but it did feel like we'd punched Father Time in the balls and he was properly pissed off about it."

Bill chuckled, danced on the spot, punched the air, then pocketed his remote control.

"Time! Like I mentioned, we don't have a lot. We need to get to the cafe and see me and you before we leave there and get here and be us."

James was starting to follow the logic.

"Hang on. If we simply stay here, won't we meet ourselves?"

Bill strode over to his mantelpiece and started fiddling with a penknife.

"We're not going to do that."

"How do you know?"

"Because it's already happened."

"No, but..."

"We've already met me at the cafe," interrupted Bill. "We have to proceed with exactly the same plan. I was there, for past me to meet."

"OK," said James.

"Oh, and what was the third thing?" demanded Bill, pointing the small dagger accusingly at James.

"What?"

"You said there were three things."

"You called me 'dear boy'! We went to the same comprehensive. Where'd you pick up that public school boy shit?"

Bill shook his head.

"Unbelievable," he lamented. "We shatter the fourth dimension and you're more bothered about - what - my colloquialisms?"

"I just worry about you sounding like a dick, mate."

"And I thank you for that, James. Now let's get freaking you out from an hour ago."

Bill and James promptly left the flat fifty-five minutes before they were due to arrive.

The pair walked briskly back towards town. Bill unfastened a shirt button, and wafted air into his clammy paunch. James peeked backwards and smiled smugly at Bill. Bill *knew* that look.

"I know what you're going to say, but I'm too busy. The gym, quite frankly, can go fudge itself."

"Hang on!" exclaimed James in a sudden burst of excitement. "Can we do that?"

"Can we do what?" asked Bill, puzzled.

"Can we fudge ourselves? Can I meet and shag me? I've always tried to give myself a blowjob, but never been quite able to reach. I could go back or forward an afternoon and me and other James can suck ourselves off."

Bill stopped, disgusted. James' eager smiling face turned ashen in an instant.

"No time travel self-blowies?" he whimpered.

Bill shook his head.

The pair kept walking.

James and Bill turned a corner and approached Harry's.

"Right, where are you off to?" asked Bill.

"What?" spluttered James.

"You can't come in. The past version of you is due here shortly. This version of you wasn't here."

"Suppose I could go and pick up my car?"

Bill's eyes widened in alarm.

"For Garibaldi's sake, don't do that! They haven't finished fixing it yet. That phone call was one hour in the future."

James screwed his face up as his brain shifted rusty gears over the very simple calculation.

"So, why bring me on this escapade at all?" he asked.

"Well, I need a witness, you're my best friend, and besides, who else would I ask - Harry?" Bill pointed to the elderly cafe owner.

"Fair enough," agreed James, and offered his friend a weak thumbs-up.

"Right, disappear quickly, and don't bump into you!"

"Or suck myself off?"

"Especially that."

Bill disappeared into the cafe.

James walked in the opposite direction, and idly wondered what craziness he might be able to get up to in the whopping thirty minutes of history his body had already lived through. He could go back into the newsagents again and finish the mags he'd started reading. Hardly any value in that, he decided. Besides, if he wanted to support the very industry for which he was working, he should probably buy at least one on occasion.

He wandered off through the high street, rueing the fact that Bill hadn't at least transported them back to last week, when an angry scaffolder had taken a dump onto a ticket inspector from the second floor of an office building. He'd only seen poorly filmed YouTube footage of the aftermath and would love to have seen it live. He reasoned, quite correctly, that what with his desire to suck himself off or watch a tradesman shit onto a civil servant just doing her job, that perhaps time travel was wasted on him.

Not wishing to confuse anyone by seeing him in two locations at once, he headed off to the library. It was a building he visited so rarely, he wasn't sure if they even lent books anymore. Wasn't it all downloads now? His only resolve was to take a short journey to Hartnell Library to find out.

James shuffled suspiciously through the library's gliding doors. He took a moment to take in the view of the inner building. He'd brought his children here many times over their formative pre-school days, but to his shame, hadn't visited in at least three years. How had he and literature become so estranged? He blamed Netflix and laziness, before realising it was just the latter, which had only become easier due to the former.

He was startled to see how *modern* the place was. It wasn't the stuffy, muted thrum of study and dark oak architecture his mind conjured up whenever he thought of the word 'library'. With all the garish wall displays, rows of PCs, and cliques of yummy mummies fussing over toddlers, the building felt more like the offspring between an internet start-up and a creche. The sort of place that normal people who have regular sex come to. They probably don't come *here* for that. But James thought it not unreasonable that some of the racier members probably have a book club which covers as a front for a weekly orgy or something. He'd put money on the guy with the glasses and ponytail having recently indulged in a threesome. (And from the way he was checking out the young librarian with the nervous laugh, was clearly planning another.)

James noticed a couple signing out books using checkout machines, like they do in supermarkets. Surely he'd done that with his children? Why couldn't he remember? Casting his mind back, he could only recall trying to make sure that his son and daughter were enjoying themselves by reading out chapters in funny voices, or occasionally building and hiding in towers using the perennial stack of Enid Blytons that no one ever seemed to borrow. Also, when they were a little younger, he had the safeguarding job of making sure they didn't kill or maim themselves on any sharp corners or particularly vicious paper edges. Or lured away by opportunistic paedophiles. He guessed his wife must have done all the necessary administration. That, or he was off thumbing through the Batman comics, which was also fairly likely.

Ruminating on the exorbitant cost of the garage, he strode to the hobbies and crafts section. If he could teach himself about engineering and cars and all that mechanical stuff in which he had zero interest whatsoever, perhaps next time he could fix the car himself? Perhaps if his stupid Dad had been around, he might have known that a car has a radiator. (Or so the garage man told him anyway. He could have told him his car needed an atomic banana and a cuddle to sleep every night and he'd have believed him.)

Cars were as much a mystery to him as time travel. Dirty, oily confusing mesh of machinery, cogs, and sharp things. A dangerous, boring clump of metal. Something that inexplicably takes you from one place to another if you press a few buttons with your feet and grip a big wheel with your hands, trying not to hit things. It baffled him why anyone found any joy in driving. It was a laborious necessity. You might as well get excited about brushing your teeth or opening an umbrella. He cursed his dad and reached for a large hardback on classic 1970s sports cars. Its lurid green cover and promises of "full colour photos" looked marginally less like evoking suicide than its shelf-sharing brethren. James leafed idly through five dog-eared pages of ugly hatchbacks and decided that was quite enough. He was back in time, technically. He should be *in* the 1970s, not staring at it through a page. He'd ask Bill for a slightly more reaching journey into the past. Or, hey, the future. At least hover cars would be more interesting than normal cars, plus almost definitely sex robots. (He wouldn't use one, but he'd love to watch a few YouTube reaction videos to them malfunctioning.)

Bored of his own thoughts, James decided he'd killed enough time and began to return the book to its shelf. As he went to close the page, a figure in one of the photos stopped him dead in his tracks. He opened the book fully and stared hard at the page, agog. He blinked several times, trying to take in the image. He even doubted his own eyes. Because in the photo next to a sludge brown Triumph Dolomite, stood the unmistakable sight of James Harpman, giving a goofy thumbs-up to the camera.

The realisation dawned on him. He was a time traveller. And he was clearly going to be one in the future.

CHAPTER 4

2019

James' legs pummelled furiously through the high street, smashing hard against the asphalt as his mind tried to keep up. With *Car Classics: The 1970's* clutched tightly to his chest, it looked like an incredibly low-level shoplift had gone disastrously wrong.

He pelted to the door of Harry's, but skidded to a halt as he caught sight of Past Bill and Past James heading out in the opposite direction. He paused to consider how odd and frankly alien the back of his head looked. Sure, his big wave of hair looked great, but the bulbous shape was completely off. It reminded him of one of those parochial, "grow a massive vegetable" competitions, where a ruddy-faced pensioner would coo delightedly over a peculiarly big aubergine he's spent all year cultivating. From inside the cafe, Bill coughed loudly, distracting James from his sudden urge to plant tomatoes. He headed inside, still breathing heavily from his run.

"How did it go?" asked James, needlessly. Bill's face pained, almost sympathetically.

"You know exactly how it went. You were here an hour ago! Remember?"

"Good point," replied James, still only half understanding. "Anyway, never mind those two sexy imposters from the past. Check this."

James opened the book on the page that featured him giving a dopey thumbs up. Bill gasped as his eyes met with his friends' on the printed page.

"What have you done?" cried Bill.

"I just went to the library, for crying out loud!" James protested. Bill's head did several mathematical leaps.

"Of course, sorry. It's not happened yet. Bloody time travel." he muttered, flustered. "Right, well, that's given me more to think about than I wanted. Let's draw up a plan then."

"Do we have to? I hate planning. It's just listing things I haven't failed yet."

"My friend, that's not the attitude. Just one hour into the past and we already know that we're going to travel again! We have a lot to do and you're clearly going to be in the past in the future. Let's get back to our timeline, research that book, get back in time, then suck ourselves off!"

James' eyes lit up.

"Really?"

"Except the last bit, yes."

They handed Harry a fistful of loose change and headed back to Bill's grotty apartment. The pair kept a slow pace so as not to catch up with themselves headed in the same direction.

As they reached the flat, James needed to clarify the situation.

"So, us two from the present just went back into the past again? Is that right?"

Bill opened the door and ushered in James.

"Yup, they are us an hour ago going back to the hour we've nearly used up," he assured, as they both clambered over a hazardous jumble of clutter leading into the living room. Bill picked up several baffling gadgets of unknown purpose and began fiddling with each in swift succession.

"Righto," brightened James. A puzzled query suddenly etched across his face. "So why didn't we just go with them then?"

Bill grimaced in frustration. No wonder he only taught undergraduates.

"Because we didn't go with us before!" His arms shook as he spoke, exasperated.

Slightly put out, James simply mouthed a disingenuous, "Oh!"

He gingerly moved some boxes of clutter and sat lightly on the sofa. Sensing the unease, Bill relaxed into a smile.

"So!" he beamed. "Any more thoughts?"

"Well, do we now go back to our timeline? We've just re-lived an hour. Can we carry on or do we have to move forward an hour to appease the Timelords or whatever?"

Bill sucked his gums in thought.

"Actually, not a bad question for once. I think you're right. We better get back to our…" Bill hesitated, "timestream, for want of a better word."

"Fair balls," concluded James. "Let's get your time gizmo pissing minutes then, or whatever it is it does."

The pair straightened their clothes and positioned themselves in front of the projector.

"Remember," re-warned Bill. "Every bit of you must be covered by the beam. Every last bit."

James nodded.

"Scout's honour, boss."

Bill punched some numbers into his remote control and stood rigid. The low thrum of the projector started again as before, slowly turning to a sharp pitch. The retina-puncturing glare of the projector glowed a migraine white. Bill pressed some buttons on the device before thrusting it back into his pocket.

James suddenly jerked with an epiphany.

"*Car Classics: the 1970s!*" he shouted, waving the tome in Bill's face. "Do I leave it in the flat or take it forward in time? Does it matter?"

Bill simply opened his mouth, dumbstruck for a response. Panicked, James flung the open book out of the overhead projector's beam. Bill let out a gasp of panic. A dazzling burst of white flashed onto the pair, amidst a small explosion of sparks and orange flames. James' hand jolted back, dropping the book. As it fell to the floor, Bill swivelled from his spot to stare at the crumpled mess.

"James, no!"

Startled, James stared at the book on the floor. It had been completely bifurcated right down the centre from the beam's ray. One half was missing entirely. The remainder sizzled lightly away, almost mockingly.

Bill bent down to cradle the book and brushed off the live embers. He gave James a grave look, who returned the grimace.

"So," began James, clutching his aching head. "That's why we stay in the beam, yeah?"

Bill nodded, and smiled gently.

"Yes mate."

James plumped down onto a sofa arm and sighed loudly. He raised a hand nervously.

"I do have more questions."

"My friend, ask away."

"Right, we came back to your flat in the past. So, we used the time machine in the past to get back to the right hour. How does that work?"

Bill thinned his lips and pocketed his controller.

"James, this was a maiden voyage, I'm still thinking things through. I'd like to make it more portable so we can take it with us next time. Save us having to come back here and avoid bumping into other versions of ourselves."

"What do you have in mind - Police Box? DeLorean?"

"Bit cliched, but basically, yes - a vehicle is definitely the way to go. Speaking of which, your library book is fudged." Bill held up the remaining pages.

"That's your scientific conclusion?"

"Pretty much. We've still got most of the back cover, index, and erm, some ghastly looking heaps from yesteryear, but the crucial pages featuring you are missing. Now we'll have to buy a copy."

"Soz."

"No bother. Did you get a ticket for it?"

"Sure," answered James, and pulled from his pocket a library card and a small paper receipt the self-service machine had issued when he scanned the book.

"Leave it with me," assured Bill, and pocketed the ticket.

The two sat motionless for a few seconds, simply staring ahead. The only sound was the swish of James' incessant leg-jiggling. Both turned to face each other. Finally, James laughed.

"We've time travelled!"

"I know!" Bill clasped his hands together, cracked his knuckles, and jumped to his feet. "Thanks for coming with me today, James."

"Dude, no bullshit but it's an absolute honour, I swear. This is *amazing*!"

An affectionate glow enveloped Bill. "My friend, I don't know what to say. Leading the world in scientific discovery is one thing…"

"Just the world?"

"Alright, *universe*. But really, your genuine praise is touching. Thanks man."

James raised his eyebrows and gave his pal a clumsy thumbs-up.

An awkward hush descended on the pair.

"Shall I put the kettle on?" suggested Bill, breaking the silence.

"I should probably head off to pick up the car. Hang on, what the fuck is that?"

James pointed sharply towards the floor.

Bill peered over for a better look. A photograph nestled between two scorched pages of the book. James picked it up and brought the picture into view. He recognised it instantly. To the left, wearing a fake white beard so thin it was barely perceptible, and a fur trimmed red cloak, was a middle-aged man gurning at the lens. On his knee, a young girl with an ear-reaching smile clutching a small neatly wrapped Christmas present. James' mouth dropped.

"Oh, for crying out loud," said James. "It's Nina and…" James paused, unable to finish the sentence.

"That's your dad?" asked Bill, softly.

"Nigel," spat James. "Why the fuck is that picture in the book?"

"Still time before the school run for you to find out," suggested Bill.

"Yeah," agreed James with a sigh. "I'll grab the car then go over now. This must be there for a reason. Coming round tonight?"

"Sure."

"I'll text Susan, let her know."

Bill agreed with a curt nod. He needed space and time to document the morning's activities, draw up his findings, and make plans for his next journey. Also, *much* more importantly, he had decided to tidy up and get the vacuum out.

The two said their goodbyes. James stuffed the photo into his pocket then started his journey back to the garage to pay an eye-watering sum of money to fix a problem he didn't even understand.

Bill flipped the kettle's switch and sat down at his kitchen table. He pushed aside a scattered wad of unopened utility bills and dog-eared documents, to create a small amount of surface space. He slapped his laptop down in the centre, pulled the library ticket from his pocket then google-searched the title: *Car Classics: the 1970s*. The search engine spat out over seven million results in an instant. Bill scrolled lazily through the hundreds of books listed, yet none matched the exact title he had on the receipt. *Cars We Loved in the 1970s, A-Z of Cars of the 1970s, Great British Cars: 1970's* and so on. All bore similarity to the title. None were identical. Bill brought up images. Again, lots very similar, but nothing that bore resemblance to the ugly if memorable toxic green of the cover. He scanned the remains of the book by his side. Despite losing the front, there must be some more clues as to the book's origins? He scrutinised the battered and battle-scarred rear cover. Oddly, there was no barcode. Just a badly assembled collage of poorly photographed motors, with a short, baffling blurb that Bill thought would benefit from a proofreader or twelve. Bill read it, slowly.

"Travel back in time! Would you drift into this book? We project you will travel back in time! Vehicles! Colour photographs! Hurry up, for crying out loud."

Bill re-read it several times, before the realisation surged through him. The penny didn't just drop, it plummeted through to the earth's core. He knew exactly what it meant. James wasn't just in this book. He had published it.

Bill burped in bewilderment as the kettle boiled.

CHAPTER 5

2019

James pulled up outside his sister's house. A lurch panged away guiltily in his stomach. They lived barely twenty minutes by car, yet he hadn't visited in over six months (and that was only to drop off some cat food for reasons he couldn't even remember).

Partly, it was because of where she lived. Nina had never strayed from their hometown, Alfred's Valley. It was a place James did everything he could to avoid. A Victorian seaside resort whose winter had lasted a century, the town bore its crumbling buildings and cracked paintwork like the symptoms of neglect they patently were. Alongside the occasional modern buildings stood burnt out hotels, boarded up once-popular grockle shops that sold unearthly plastic tat, and migraine-inducing amusement arcades. The queasy, uneasy mix of wear and sheen made for a chaotic aesthetic; like a child had just built itself a brand-new Lego town then immediately took fistfuls of shit to it.

James locked the car and gave the neighbourhood a furtive glance for feral, school-dodging kids on the prowl. Finding none, he took the short few steps up to the front door and knocked loudly, ignoring the broken doorbell. He gave it a few seconds before knocking again, this time followed by a volley of swearing and the clattering of objects.

"Piss! I'm coming, the doorbell's not working."

"Nina, it's just me," he deadpanned to the frosted glazing, as his sister's silhouette came into view. She flung open the door, welcoming in her brother with a comically wide hug.

"James! How lovely! Come in!"

James' curmudgeonly facade melted slightly at his sibling's excitement: he felt instant remorse at not making more effort than, well, none at all.

James followed her through to the kitchen, past racks of tumbling shoe clusters and stacked cages of unidentified rodents nibbling at stale bread. He could barely tell it *was* a kitchen, thanks to the sheer mountains of clutter piled up on top of the surfaces and floor. Clothes, blankets, toys, empty cigarette cartons, DVDs, games, boxes, and all manner of useless junk obscured almost every inch of the cupboards and appliances. It was as if a charity chop had burst its banks and flooded the neighbourhood.

The hopeless chaos of the jumble pained James, who had always maintained an almost obsessive tidiness around him. With Bill's laissez faire attitude towards order, and his sister's utter disregard for anything even hinting at neatness, he wouldn't mind visiting someone with a nicely stacked row of books for once.

"Cup of coffee?" offered Nina, looking around for the kettle.

James declined politely, reasoning that the effort to make it would eclipse the enjoyment he might take from drinking it.

"Have you seen what I'm making?" asked Nina.

James frowned a little, before he realised, to his horror, a solitary hob was burning away with a saucepan nestled on top. The flames were perilously close to a pile of unironed t-shirts and unread newspapers. Nina pointed delightedly at the pan. James peered inside at a bubbling smear of brown, boiling rapidly to a crust of jagged matter. He thought for a brief moment that a dog had crapped into a Tefal.

"Guess what I'm cooking?"

"Exhibit A?"

Nina's smile didn't falter, although her eyes betrayed confusion. James regretted making the joke. (Not because she would take offence; she simply never understood them.)

"No," she said with absolute sincerity. "Chilli con carne!"

"That's great Nina, good job!" enthused James, idly hoping that one compliment might undo a lifetime of neglect.

"Kids at school?" he asked, pointlessly, knowing full well that they were.

Nina smiled, as James dug his hand into his pocket. His fingers caressed the photo of Nina and their dad.

James clapped his hands together to break the silence. He found talking with Nina impossible. Like trying to juggle vapour.

"Hey!," said Nina, beaming. "Do you remember when Dad…"

"No," cut in James. "I don't remember 'Dad anything'. Nigel was barely there at all, and then he wasn't there at all."

James found himself lightly screwing up the picture in his fist.

"James, you're going to have to…"

"If you're about to ask me again to let go of this anger for *Nigel*, I just can't do that. We've both been parents for over a decade now. We put in the hours, we're not neglectful."

"Well, Susan was telling me about how you can't even get round to buying them nativity costumes, so maybe you're not the Super Dad you think you are?"

"Jesus, Nina!"

The room soured instantly, as both siblings stared ahead, neither looking at the other. Nina sipped her coffee slowly. The slurp cut through the silence, but the thick tension suffocated the air. Nina put down her mug and folded her arms defiantly.

"James, I don't want to fight over Dad."

"Good, because Nigel is not worth it."

Nina threw her hands up in a flurry of frustration.

"Do you see James? I think you would benefit from talking about it, but you just keep burying your head in the sand. For Christ's sake put down the spade!"

James let out a giggle at his sister's clumsy metaphor. Nina didn't laugh. James sighed deeply.

"I'm sorry."

"So am I."

Both accepted the other's apology with a weak smile.

"I know you thought he wasn't any good," began Nina. "But we only heard Mum's side of things. Now they're both gone I don't see what good it does dredging up the past and being bitter about it."

"Well, sure, ok. When you put it like that," lied James. He was still bitter. Lemon orchard bitter. He left the picture in his pocket. He couldn't face this talk right now.

The front door opened, and a shaven-headed teen traipsed through to the front room. An untucked, scruffy shirt hung over black school trousers, above a pair of expensive but definitely not school-approved trainers. An unzipped backpack slung over one shoulder with such a casual nonchalance even James was envious of the clear disregard in which his nephew held school.

"Sid!" welcomed James.

"Hey Uncle James," smiled Sid.

"How's school?" queried James.

Sid merely shrugged insouciantly. "How's writing?" he asked back.

"Good question. One to which I wish I had a good answer. In short, it's alright. Got some copywriting bits on, and a band review of *Fear of Beans*. You might like or hate them, dunno. Then some corporate businessy stuff and management bollocks and the like…" James trailed off, noticing that Sid had started to tug absent-mindedly at the bag straps, his eyes glazed over entirely.

"Any video games things?" wondered Sid.

"Actually yes, an old school Nintendo vs Sega thing." He'd lost him again.

"Cool, wanna play XBox?"

"Sure, but can't be long, got to pick up the kids shortly."

"Sweet."

The pair climbed upstairs to Sidney's bedroom, as James gave a little OK finger signal to his sister. Sid darted back downstairs and flung his head round the open living room door.

"Oh, by the way, hi Mum. Can I have a cup of tea please?" He winked with effortless charm at Nina. She merely tutted, nodded, then got up to re-boil the kettle.

James sat on Sid's bed and picked up an XBox controller. He flexed it a little and gave a couple of the buttons a thoughtful press. He wished he hadn't been so belligerent with his sister. It wasn't *her* fault their father was so utterly useless, even though she couldn't see it. Sid burst into the room and plonked down on the bed next to James.

"James?"

"Yes Sidney."

"Erm, I lied, I don't really want to play XBox with you."

"Oh?" James puzzled, wondering if he was about to have a meaty teenage heart-to-heart with his nephew. He wasn't ready for that just yet, neither practically nor emotionally.

"Erm, Sidney, you're a teenager with internet access. Surely you know about the birds not having sex with the bees? You don't need to have it explained by your socially uncomfortable uncle, do you? I'm fairly certain that most fifteen-year-olds almost certainly know more about sex stuff that I've never even heard of. Maybe ask them?"

"Oh my god, no. It's about Granddad. You know, yours and Mum's Dad."

James flinched backwards.

"Oh god that's worse! Ask me about rimming, tromboning, golden showers, hard gay stuff. Anything but *him*."

"Christ, Uncle James!"

James squeezed the controller hard. The brittle plastic creaked audibly. Sid eyed him suspiciously.

"Sorry," said James.

"You ok?"

James gritted his teeth hard. "Sure."

Sidney reached under the bed and pulled out a hard A4 box. He paused to take a deep breath, opened the front, and reached inside. He handed his uncle a battered blue exercise book wrapped in an elastic band. The scrappy book curled with overuse; inky scribblings almost tumbled out of the pages. James took the book as Sidney released his grip.

"It's just, I found this in Mum's stuff. She never throws away all that childhood crap. I don't want this to come between you and Mum. But, dunno, thought you should know and maybe not her."

James curled his lip, raised his eyebrow, and removed the rubber band. Almost instantly, something fell from the inside crease and landed in his lap. They were polaroid pictures. Snaps from a bygone era. James thumbed slowly through the slightly dogged, yellowing photographs that belonged to another time. He felt the blood drain from his hands as his heart smashed against his chest and threatened to burst out of his ribcage.

The collection was a primitive, if regrettably memorable, set of selfies.

The photographer was positioned in the foreground, holding the camera at arm's length. He wore the unmistakable lusty smirk of James' father, but unfortunately for James, nothing else. Between his legs stood an almost angry-looking erection. The offending member twitched its way so aggressively into the dead centre of the photo you could almost taste it. Disturbingly for James, it looked like someone was about to do just that. For right next to James' naked father was a female much younger in age. (Her discarded school uniform was the first giveaway.) Reaching for the offending genitalia with an uneasy smile was someone James recognised instantly. It was his childhood babysitter, Sophie Davison. Then, a mere seventeen years of age.

The picture trembled in James' hand. Every negative emotion his brain could conjure swirled in a fog of confusion. He felt his soul might leak from his tear ducts. He tore his eyes away from the image and gave Sidney a silent acknowledgement.

Wordlessly, James scooped up the pictures and diary, then fled the house. Nina knocked over her still warm coffee in shock as her brother slammed the door behind him.

With alarming ferocity, James punched the dashboard and steering wheel repeatedly for the full twenty-minute drive back into Hartnell town.

CHAPTER 6

2019

Worn out from beating the interior of his Ford Fiesta, James Harpman limped his way to the school yard. He'd resolved to put this recent discovery to the very back of his mind, conceding reluctantly that his sister was mostly right; anger wasn't getting him anywhere. Fury had worn him down. Perhaps, he ruminated, to counter the revolting darkness of his dad's deeds he could paint everything in a glossy overcoat of artificial sunshine?

Yeah, that'll show the **bastard**.

The children spilled out of their classrooms in a cluster of coats, bags, and dishevelled hair. James welcomed both of his with an exaggerated handwave, much to their bewilderment.

"Jude! Autumn!" he bellowed, beckoning to his children like a seal gone wrong.

"Hey Dad!" they replied in unison. Both eyeballed the other, suspiciously.

"Dad," began Autumn. "You're not usually this happy unless you've just had an afternoon nap with Mum."

"Erm…"

As they walked home, James engaged animatedly in over-eager chats about every aspect of their day, no matter how inane. His endless jabbering somehow led to a conversation about how long it would take to fill a swimming pool with human spit. As they approached the house, Autumn peered inside her father's car. It was parked terribly, even more so than usual.

"Dad, what's happened to your car?" she enquired, alarmed at the damage to the dashboard.

"Oh, that's just, erm, the garage work we had done."

Jude joined his sister and pressed his face against the windscreen. The glove compartment tray was hanging off, buttons had been dislodged and strewn about, and the speedometer plastic splintered.

"You paid for them to break the car?" he queried.

"Mechanics!" James punchlined, with a desperately unfunny shrug. The children accepted this excuse and escaped into the house, relieved to escape their father's ramblings.

An hour passed and as the children were entertained by the phosphorus glow of their tablets, James had managed to temporarily drown his thoughts concerning useless Nigel. He was concentrating solidly on the other news of the day. He had time travelled. He will time travel again.

Time. Travel.

He stood in his kitchen, absent-mindedly flicking the kettle on and off as his mind drowned in possibilities. The past was being opened up to him like a holiday destination. No longer snatches of hazy recall, he would be able to step back into times gone and experience them like the present. Because they would be! He started listing things he'd like to see: *Sex Pistols'* first gig! No, not the *Sex Pistols* - *The Beatles*! Actually, sod it - *both* of them. He started mentally compiling a legendary gigs of all time wishlist, then realised he could farm out contemporary reviews to magazines and websites. He was deep in thought, wondering how a pasty-faced Englishman might pass off unnoticed in the audience of an early *Niggaz With Attitude* concert when his son burst into the room.

"Jude!" blurted out James, surprised by the mental intrusion.

Jude stood expectant with a puppyish hesitancy. He wore his school uniform much like his cousin: a scruffy, casual indifference whilst his shoulder-length hair flopped over both eyes. Again, rather than take against his son's unkempt manner, James was secretly proud of his offspring's thumbing to uniformity. Or perhaps he was reading too much into it and he was just a lazy scruffbag?

"Can I have some lemonade, Dad?"

"Did you do your homework?"

"Sure," Jude replied, a lilting tremor in his voice.

"If I check your book, you'll definitely have it completed, right?"

"I'll do it whilst I drink my lemonade?" bargained Jude.

"Deal," smiled James. "And have you brushed your hair at all today?"

"Yeah," lied Jude.

"With what - a whisk?"

Jude laughed, then poured himself a soda.

"Well, brush it again, just to be sure. And take your sister a glass too please."

Jude sighed mock-dramatically, and did as he was asked. Then he strolled over to his bag, pulled out a small pile of slightly worn textbooks, and snuck his tablet between the pages of a maths book.

The dimly lit living room suddenly filled with red light as another car reversed into the drive. Moments later the front door opened and Sue stumbled in, clutching bundles of papers and bags of marking.

James bounded over to the door, offering support. She dropped a dozen hardbacks into his arms.

"Thanks," she muttered, distracted.

"Hey gorgeous, how are you?"

Sue frowned. Her face screamed that the day had smelled of arse.

"Did the day smell of arse?" enquired James, gingerly.

Sue smiled wanly.

"Literally," she conceded. "Felicity Shitpants sat on my recorder. Gave a whole new depth to playing Old MacDonald. Honestly, it was worse than your sister's rancid trumps."

"Ew!" retorted James, as he carried the books to the kitchen, trying not to think of his sibling's rotten guts. "Tea?"

"Please." She turned to head into the living room, and her face shed instantly the weary grimace it had been wearing. "And how are my two butterbeans?" she beamed, awaiting a hug from both kids.

"Mum!" the siblings exclaimed with low energy. Both looked up briefly, smiled, waved lazily in her general direction, and turned their attention straight back to their miniature iPads. Underwhelmed, Sue's face returned to its default weary grimace, and she headed to her husband in the kitchen.

"I'm sure they used to be more pleased to see me," she observed, her voice trailing off in disappointment.

"They *adore* you," assured James. "They bang on about you all the time. They're just knackered. Especially this time of year. Well, you know that."

James felt a pang of sympathy for Susan. Just twelve months ago, he'd been the *other* parent, working late and returning home when the kids' enthusiasm for playful hi-jinks had dimmed considerably. Even basic communication had been pared down to exhausted grunts. They were edging towards secondary school. The unfathomable age of the pre-teen was dawning. Tiredness was turning surely to surliness. Sue's work commitments cost her quality time with her kids. Instead of caring for her own two children, she was responsible for twenty excitable school kids, with whom she didn't share quite the same maternal bond. But teaching paid better than being a local news reporter. So, when a full-time opportunity arose for Susan, James had sacrificed his journalism career and she had reluctantly hitched herself to the education bus.

"You know I love Christmas," Susan sighed. "But this has been an absolute dick of a term. We had three angels in tears today."

"What happened?"

"Joseph grabbed Jesus out of Mary's hands and drop kicked him across the manger."

"Holy shit!"

"More like 'little shit'. Do you know how hard it is to comfort and control twenty kids when the son of god's been punted so hard his head came off?"

James stifled a chuckle.

"I'll laugh about it one day," Sue concurred, "but not today."

James hurried about the tea, hoping the bland tonic of a hot cuppa might alleviate his wife's ennui.

"It's just so difficult at times. I love our school, I love all the pupils..."

"Even Callum Agnew?"

"Actually, *especially* Callum Agnew. He's chaotic, but he's a good kid really. It's his Mum that's the problem. She moaned at me about potential terrorism at the zoo."

James stopped stirring the tea, puzzled.

"Do what?"

"Seriously. She said her child might be at threat from explosions or suicide bombers and maybe an escaped lion on the school trip this Friday."

James poured the milk slowly.

"Why are you going to the zoo this close to Christmas?" he enquired.

"Because it's cheap," answered Sue, wearily. "Anyway, how was your day?"

James' brain went instantly to the polaroids but managed to quell his anger to the rear recess of his mind. Instead, he picked up his tea, gave a furtive conspiratorial glance across his wife's shoulder.

"I went back in time," he whispered.

Sue didn't blink.

"Yeah cool, well I bred dodos."

"No, I really did go back in time!" James insisted. Susan shook her head, grabbed the teaspoon and threw it into the sink with considerable ferocity.

"James, do you think I was born yesterday?"

"I hope not, else last night's sex would be *so* illegal."

Sue pulled a disappointed face and decided against pursuing her husband's ridiculous claims. James considered showing her the book, but she didn't seem in the mood for time travel or his stupid sex jokes.

"My car's fixed, by the way. Radiator or some such."

"Did you get the kids' nativity costumes like I asked?"

James cursed, realising he'd completely forgotten to carry out his one measly task. Sue's eyebrows raised in silent judgement.

"Sorry! I didn't manage it! I'll get them online, it's just some clothing!"

"James, we've tried online, and couldn't find anything!"

"I know!" protested James, feebly.

"Please James, just this one thing for me."

"Hey, I took you to see the Northern Lights!"

"That was three years ago! Now all I'm asking is for you to visit real shops where real actual people work and talk to them. Can you do that, or do you need a helper?"

James looked up to the ceiling and took a deep breath.

"Alright, Mrs Harpman, no need to 'teacher' me, I'm not one of your pupils."

"I dunno, getting Max Taylor to colour inside the lines rather than eating the crayons might prove easier than relying on you to get our children the right clothes for a school play."

James wrinkled his nose in objection.

"That's unfair, I went into some vast awful sports warehouse, but it was all logos and arseholes. And everywhere else was just as bad - all cartoon characters and stuff. Honestly, they don't just make plain clothes any more."

"Yeah, guess it was easier to buy straightforward plain clothes in the past," Sue concurred reluctantly. "Remember Boucher's Clothing in town? Antiquated department store that finally closed in the nineties. Place was awash with primary colours, petticoats, and all manner of brown, before it was overtaken by cheap supermarkets and national chains."

"Thank you! Plain clothes were definitely more commonplace in…" James paused, realising what he was saying, "…the past."

"But James, please try a little harder. You've been - how shall I say - absent lately. I know you don't want to hear it, but your Mum's been gone over a year now, and staying angry at your dad isn't helping *you* be a better one. I'm sorry."

James felt his head hang heavy over Susan's advice.

"I've said my piece," she concluded.

Susan poured an entire packet of fusilli into a pan. The clattering pasta ricocheted against her skull, which briefly distracted her from the day's teeth-grinding lunacy.

"*Five* pupils have now opted out of the nativity. All parents citing 'religious reasons'. I've got all the religious conviction of a baked potato, but for Christ's sake, if you're part of a Church of England school, maybe just play along for simplicity's sake?"

"Yeah," agreed James, scared to dispute her.

She thrust a tray full of frozen meat-free sausages into the oven with all the care and attention a prison guard might handle a convicted paedophile. She slammed the door shut, and wondered briefly how her children ever had the energy for anything, given their appallingly limited diet.

"You got enough there for Bill?" James asked, hopefully.

"Bill's coming? What? Since when?"

James' face fell.

"You didn't get the text?"

"Text? I don't get to read texts between finishing school and getting in the car." Susan rattled around frostily in the cutlery drawer. "Where's the wooden fucking spoon?"

James took a small step back.

"You're holding it."

Susan looked down and gave a small, frustrated exhale.

"If I'd known Bill was coming I could have picked up something that isn't this crap."

James grimaced slightly at the oven's contents.

"Takeaway?" he offered, hopefully.

"Definitely," answered Susan. She opened the oven, removed the sausages, then tipped them straight into the bin.

James reached for his phone.

An hour later, the Harpmans and their guest sat around the living room, scoffing cartons of noodles, rice, and a variety of unidentified meats in an immensely salty sauce. Jude busied himself showing Bill a bewildering video game between mouthfuls of prawn crackers, whilst Autumn and Susan took various selfies, adding animal filters and cartoon visages to their smirking fizzogs. James simply sat back, wallowing in a pile of contentment and gluten. He and a mildly drunken Bill swapped the odd story about their shared schooldays to the family, making sure to make themselves sound much less sexless and peculiar than they actually were.

Once finished, James and Bill found themselves tidying away the after-dinner mess in the kitchen. (James hoped optimistically that Bill would take heed of his ordered cutlery and plate storage system. Bill merely fidgeted about, his eyes darting across to the wash basket for some reason.)

James pulled out a bag, hushed his voice, and turned to Bill.

"Well mate, as well as *Car Classics: The 1970s*, I've discovered another document from the past. It's slightly less savoury than the book though."

James opened the diary and removed the photos. He spread them across the kitchen counter like the world's seediest collage. Bill's eyes bulged at the grot on display. He looked away instantly. Then found himself drawn back, like a roadside rubbernecker on the lookout for gore.

"Where did you get this?"

"My nephew, of all people. Dunno where or how he got it. Was too shocked to ask."

Bill inspected the scene a little more closely. Its tawdriness made *him* feel dirty.

"And that's definitely your dad, right?"

"Well, of course it is! Who did you think it was?"

"Well..." Bill looked sheepish and nodded nervously towards his friend.

"Me?!" spluttered James, incredulously. "Why would I show you that if it was?"

"Well, why show me at all?" Bill demanded.

"Finding this now, just when you've made a time machine - it can't be a coincidence, can it? also, you thought I'd show my best friend snaps of me having sex with a sixth former?!"

"Well, clearly not, no, but..." He hesitated slightly.

"What?" demanded James.

"He does look an awful lot like you. You could be twins rather than father and son."

James acknowledged this fact with a pointed look towards his friend. Bill shifted uncomfortably on the spot, then leaned backwards in a contrived display of relaxation.

"James," he asked softly. "Why do you hate your dad so much?"

The question stumped James. Not the answer, but the fact that his friend needed to even ask.

"Exhibit A?" he blurted, pointing to the diary.

"Well, yeah, but you've only just discovered that. You've had, let's say 'Dad issues' for decades now. Was he really all that bad?"

James let out a small sigh and softened slightly.

"What's to hate? He was never there. When he was, he spent no time with me or Nina. He treated Mum terribly, somewhere between housekeeper and prostitute. He would disappear for days, weeks at a time. No idea where he went. He'd come back claiming it was work, though we saw no money from it. Then he upped and left, finally disappearing for good. I was ten years old. He had no interest whatsoever in being a father or husband. Now I'm both, I resent every bit of oxygen that that worthless bastard ever drew."

"Shall I put you down as undecided then?"

James smiled and cracked his knuckles.

Bill lowered his voice to a polite murmur.

"James, ever think about your own relationship with Nina?"

"What do you mean?" James asked and pierced his friend with a squint.

"Well, you're not exactly attentive to your closest living family member, are you?"

James coughed and stared at the kitchen worktop.

"That's different."

"Is it?"

James clenched his teeth and pouted his lips.

"No. There's more Nigel in me than I care to admit."

Bill raised his palm to pat the back of his friend's hand, but immediately had second thoughts and withdrew it instantly. James' eyes followed this movement then cleared his throat.

"So!" exclaimed Bill, at full volume. "I found out something about *Car Classics: the 1970s*," said Bill.

"What was that?"

"It doesn't exist, it's not a real book." Bill air-quoted the last two words. "As far as I can tell, we must have published it."

"Say what? How? That's weird."

Bill told James his theory about the mysterious blurb.

"I'll go to the library tomorrow to find out more. I've still got your ticket."

Bill paced around the room, trying to avoid eye contact with the washing basket, from which Susan's knickers hung out of the lid. He conceded that they were *only* knickers. But seeing something worn so intimately felt like a huge intrusion on his friend's wife's privacy. Also, they were unwittingly distracting him from the matter at hand. Between the underwear and James' Dad's knob, he had very few places left to rest his gaze.

"Also, I think I've worked out how to make the time machine more vehicular."

"Excellent idea," affirmed James. Suddenly, his arms jerked into life. "Hey Bill!"

Bill stopped pacing in shock at his friend's outburst.

"What?"

"The car! The photo in the book!" Think it's our time machine?"

Bill rubbed the back of his neck slowly.

"Could be, but I don't have the page anymore and can't remember what car it was. And where would we have gotten it?"

"Well, in the past." explained James, slightly haughtily.

"Yes, *Father Dowling Investigates*, I get that. But we have to get there in the first place."

"Good point. Wonder if Sue fancies buying me a stupid classic car?"

"Maybe you could find out more about those photos," he suggested, limply pointing to the lurid polaroids.

James wrinkled his nose reluctantly. His father's past wasn't a place he wanted to visit.

"Must I?"

"You said it yourself James," said Bill. "This has to all tie together."

James huffed petulantly.

"So tomorrow," Bill concluded, "you get on those, and I'll find out more about the book. Agreed?"

"Agreed," lied James.

He tidied away the offending photos and poured himself and Bill each a large glass of amber-coloured whisky. Bill accepted it graciously and the two raised their tumblers.

"To the past!" suggested James.

"And the future!" concluded Bill.

Both took a large gulp. Each winced inwardly, neither daring to show the other their distaste for the acidic malt. James smiled, slightly tipsy.

"Hey Bill," he queried. "What if we go to the past and you get off with your Mum? Oh my god - you might finger your Mum!"

Bill blinked back incredulously.

"Is that your go-to sex move - fingering? No one's been fingered for decades."

"Exactly!" James crowed, delighted.

"Oh pancakes, you're right!" feigned Bill. "No wait, you're an idiot. I'm not going to finger my fudging Mum!"

James turned to see Susan had entered the room, clutching several empty takeaway cartons and a near-empty bottle of rosé.

"I won't ask," she deadpanned, and dumped down the items next to the sink. "James, do you think you can get the nativity clothes by next week? Else I'm going to have to do something extreme like sewing. Remember when I last did sewing and that tortoise died?"

James cringed at the memory. Bill's puzzled face demanded an explanation, but James merely waived it away.

"I'll sort it for definite." He smiled encouragingly. Susan raised an eyebrow.

"Last time you said you'd sort something you suggested replacing the cat's leg with a biro."

"Not my best idea, but I've had worse," James concurred.

"Just please, get those clothes. Be the excellent Dad I keep telling everyone that you are." Susan kissed him lightly on the head and headed for the door.

"Oh, and Bill," she added.

"Yes Susan."

"Stop staring at my knickers."

Bill's eyes leapt to the floor immediately.

"Yes Susan."

CHAPTER 7

2019

Martha Sherwin loved to help. Helping was the best. It didn't matter who it was, what they wanted, or the personal cost. Giving someone a leg-up was her thing. Even if it cost her her own legs. Which sadly, it kind of had. One fateful day, she stopped her car at a pelican crossing, despite the green lights still showing. She waved across an elderly gent who appeared simply desperate to get to the other side of the road. Unfortunately, neither her Fiat Punto nor spinal cord were a match for the articulated lorry barrelling behind her, unaware she was stationary.

However, despite that enormous life-changing event, she wasn't going to let it stop her helping. (And how was she to know that the pensioner she'd helped across the road turned out to be a terrible murderer on his way to commit another murder? She was still helping. It just happened to be the wrong person on that occasion.)

But that was who she was: Martha helped. Luckily for her, being a librarian was a fantastic way to help people on a daily basis. Except Sundays, obviously.

Martha would wheel about the large open plan library from shelf to shelf, stacking the books she could manage, and helping out children and the elderly with equal parts enthusiasm. Hartnell Library couldn't have asked for a better ambassador.

Conversely, Verity Foreman didn't like helping. Other people weren't really her thing. Frankly, she didn't need this shit. It was already enough that in the morning, a gaggle of pensioners had somehow crashed the computer system by insisting on using their debit cards in the self-service machines.

"It only takes library cards!" she had warned, scoldingly. Most backed off, sheepishly. One blue rinse wasn't having any of it though.

"It definitely took my card last week," she insisted, with a cantankerous, wonk-eyed hiss.

Verity could have taken a swing at her there and then, but decency and reason took hold. Besides, common assault looks terrible on the CV, even when they deserved it.

She eventually quelled the incident by opening a pack of Martha's biscuits (Martha didn't mind). She dished out the lot until the seniors were suitably sedated by a glucose high.

That done, she felt she deserved the afternoon off. All she wanted to do was alphabetize the thriller section. Really slowly. Then maybe watch an episode of something on her phone whilst pretending to catch up on some admin. Hell, maybe even judge the kids' colouring competition entries. (And by 'judge' she simply picked the one with the least annoying name. Which is why Honeydew Prinkles never won a library prize during her entire childhood, despite sometimes being the only entrant.)

She couldn't do any of that though, because immediately after placating pensioners she found herself arguing with an idiot. A slightly chubby middle-aged idiot with impossibly curly hair and a ticket he wouldn't stop waving at her. (He might as well have been waving his dick around for all the good it would do.)

Bill was struggling with authority. Bill *always* struggled with authority. Rank and file just weren't his thing.

"Sir, as I've explained," reiterated Verity, "That ticket is not valid, because it is not related to *your* membership card."

Bill nodded impatiently, bored of being talked down to.

"I know," he began, through gritted teeth, "But I have the member's card here too, and he gives permission for me to discuss this matter freely." Bill's right eye twitched in frustration.

Give me strength, it's a library book for teacakes' sake, not his medical records!

"And, again," retorted Verity, "You've already said that. But we have no proof of this. For all I know, you've just stolen that card and ticket." Verity smiled, and swiftly corrected herself. "Not that I'm suggesting you have, of course."

Her face was *very much* suggesting that.

"How do you know I'm not James Harpman?" Bill asked.

"You've already told me you're not."

"Oh. Maybe I was lying?" he suggested, his voice raised an entire pitch.

"Well, you were either lying then or now. Which is it?"

Verity tapped her name badge, under which read, "Library Officer". Bill's mind began to flail miserably, utterly hopeless in the face of authority. His body tensed involuntarily, and he adjusted his nervous gaze away from Verity's. Upon presentation of power, the most intelligent, assured man in any room had suddenly given way to a burbling, hesitant quiver.

Come on Bill, get your sugar together; you've defied Father Time for heck's sake!

"Erm…"

"Would you like to speak with the manager?" offered Verity, somehow making it sound more like a threat than an offer of help. Bill hesitated, unsure of how to respond. On the one hand, a manager could sort this out. On the other hand, that's even further up the chain of command! Not waiting for a reply, Verity shouted over to a woman in a wheelchair plucking reading badges from a giant plastic jar. A multicoloured dog lead swaddled around the frame, on the end of which a small gold tag had been attached.

"Martha! One for 'the manager'," Verity called, her voice dripping with disdain.

Martha put down the jar, muttered an inaudible note of encouragement to herself, then wheeled herself over to Bill. She wore a huge smile untouched by cynicism.

Bill raised his eyebrows in relief. She looked much nicer than this woman.

Hell, Hitler's grilled plop would be nicer than this woman.

"Martha," began Verity, presenting Bill. "This is... well, I'm not sure who he thinks he is. I'll let you find out more. It's about some car book or something." With that less than perfunctory introduction, Verity left the pair alone at the desk and headed straight to the Dan Browns to tear out random chapters.

Martha stared at Bill for a fraction too long than was entirely comfortable. He opened his mouth to talk, but his brilliant mind suddenly took the afternoon off. He simply held up the ticket, silently.

"Bill, isn't it?" queried Martha.

Taken aback, Bill merely nodded.

"I'm not actually the manager. That's just Verity's little 'joke'" Martha air-quoted 'joke', then shrugged. "Look, I've got a ten-minute break. Not a lot of *time*, but I'm sure *time's* something you're keen to talk about, yeah?" She winked and nodded knowingly.

"Sorry, have we met?" asked Bill.

Martha raised her eyes in disbelief. For a genius, Bill was astonishingly slow at times.

∽

In his home, James hunched over his laptop, hammering away paragraphs like a man possessed. He had smashed through five hundred words in under an hour: an absolute miracle given his usual lazy work rate. He stopped suddenly, aware that his near violent tapping had almost dislodged his E and A keys. He paused, sipped at his coffee, then re-read the last couple of sentences.

Fear of Beans have all the presence of a severed dick. What they lack in charisma though they lack equally in talent.

James groaned audibly, repulsed by his needlessly vituperative prose. He was being mean simply for the sake of it. More importantly, *Fear of Beans* weren't even *that* awful, just bland. Although he couldn't work out if insipid was worse than actively shit. At least shit was entertaining. Whatever he decided, middling indie band *Fear of Beans* certainly didn't deserve the ire that his father did. He sighed, closed the lid, then wrote himself a reminder to re-write everything he'd typed since he saw those photos of his dad.

It wasn't just learning about his father's infidelities. It was seeing them laid literally bare. The brazen raw lack of shame and animal lustre. Merely hearing about it let his psyche cover up, distracting himself from the truth. Seeing it unfiltered, scorched into his retinas like staring at the sun made it entirely unavoidable.

He stood up, restless. He'd usually treat himself to a quick masturbation break around now but was way too consumed with thoughts of his creepy Dad to even consider cracking one out. A wank firmly off the menu, he decided to pull on his running shoes rather than his plonker. He popped on his headphones to distract him from his own morbid thoughts, then headed out for a head-clearing run.

James pounded the pavement with the same intensity he'd been hitting his keyboard. His feet struck the concrete with an audible smack: the impact reverberated through James' kneecaps with such intensity it was almost certain to cause long-term mobility problems.

He risked a lifetime of bandy legs and hurried on. He leapt over pavements and dodged traffic, sheer bloody-mindedness driving him on. Yet no matter how hard he ran, he couldn't shake the haunting images; his mind threw on a swiftly revolving slideshow of yesterday's grotesque discovery. He slid his phone's volume to max, hoping to drown his consciousness under the distorted guitar feedback. He pushed on uphill, gasping with every step. The pain surged through his legs and out of his lungs. His throat burned as he over-exerted until the very last gasp. His final step ended with a pathetic limp to the grand gates of Hartnell Cemetery.

James lent against the warning notice for dog walkers, as his knees shook and chest burst with fatigue. He tried chewing for saliva, but all he could taste was his own sweat. An elderly gent shuffled out from the gravestones towards the exit. His blotchy red eyes caught James' own as he passed. Exhausted, James tried to smile encouragingly. Unfortunately, it came out so suddenly and unnaturally it just appeared as if someone had rammed a finger up his arse. The old man shuffled on, perplexed.

Still sweating, James wandered over to the graveyard and headed for his mother's headstone. He didn't know exactly what good it might do right now, but he'd spent so much time thinking about his terrible father he reasoned he should devote more brain space to the people who *deserved* his time. Even if they were six feet under and couldn't appreciate it. James approached the plot and clasped his hands together. Self-consciousness gripped him, as he hopped nervously from foot to foot. He almost never visited. What was he supposed to do? Chat to thin air? Have a cry? Dig her up and have a grisly adventure *Weekend at Bernie's* style?

He opted for the former.

"Hey Mum. How's it going?" James paused, then chuckled slightly. "Sorry, daft question."

He looked around the bare grassy patch, and rather plain looking headstone. His Mum had never liked much of a fuss. Though even for her minimal tastes, the laissez faire banality of this resting place felt a little too Eastern Bloc.

"Sorry I've not brought any flowers to tart the place up a bit. But hey, the engraving looks good and that dogshit over there really ties the plot together. And yeah, I know I've not been up much. I just don't know what to say to a corpse." James sniffed hard to straighten his resolve. "I miss you, Mum. *We* miss you. The kids are doing a nativity, Autumn's last before she goes to big school. Jude is good, art's his thing…" James trailed off.

James raised his eyebrows to stop himself welling up. The sweat on his skin had dried to a thin layer of chill and he was suddenly aware of how cold he was. The loss of his Mum had felt like having a limb removed. An absence that upset not just his body, but the entire balance of his life.

He had nothing more to say. He popped his earphones back in and turned to jog lightly back home. He needed to talk with Bill.

~

Meanwhile, in Hartnell Library, Martha Sherwin was also talking to someone from the past. Mercifully, he was more alive than James' Mum. Martha ushered Bill into a small room to the rear of the reception. Windowless and cramped, a single table dominated most of the room, on which sat an old bulky CRT monitor and a computer that had seen better decades. Martha wheeled behind the desk and offered Bill a wonky wooden chair. Bill sat gently, expecting to plummet through. Luckily, yesteryear's engineering was made of sturdy design and he simply eased into its restrictive rests.

"Bill," said Martha, her face breaking out into a smile. "You made it!"

Bill screwed up his face in confusion. Martha raised an eyebrow, slightly annoyed.

"Bill, time travel." She winked for added effect. Bill blinked back a face of dawning realisation.

"Right, time travel! We know each other. Except, don't. You met me in your past, but my future? And this is the first time *I've* met you. Is that right?"

Martha nodded, relieved she didn't have to explain at least that part.

"Who knew time travel could be so complicated?" Martha said with a smirk. Bill melted with ease into his uncomfortable chair. He clapped his hands together and let out an enormous roar of laughter.

"Fantastic!" he bellowed, rubbing his hands together. "So, what can you tell me about the book? About the past - my future? Not much I'm guessing."

Martha slapped the side of the computer monitor and it blinked into life. A dim glow shone from the glass screen and illuminated her face. She tapped hurriedly on the keyboard, much to the hard drive's chagrin, which whirred angrily.

"You were..." Martha stopped to correct herself. "You *will* or I suppose *did* tell me not to tell you a great deal. Something about fate, getting timestreams crossed and whatnot."

"'Something about fate, getting timestreams crossed and whatnot.'?"

"More or less," Martha shrugged. "But I can give you this." She hit return triumphantly and a printer started jittering away.

Very slowly.

Martha smiled uneasily. The printer juddered noisily. Bill moved uncomfortably in his seat, though his room for manoeuvre was limited to say the least. The chair creaked in unison with the clunk of the printer, which fed paper hungrily into its mechanical jaws.

Martha's heart slumped as the excruciating moment trudged on. She had hoped for something much cooler than this. Eventually, the paper crawled out of the printer towards Bill. Martha clasped it and gave the page a small brush with the back of her hand. She loved the cosy warmth of freshly printed paper. She handed it over to Bill, who reached for it cautiously.

"It's a set of instructions you gave to me on a floppy disk," Martha said.

"Thank you," he said, and glanced at the page. The first thing he noticed was the bold all-capital header: "LAMINATE ME!". Bill looked up, concerned.

"Got a laminator?"

Martha smiled reassuringly, took the paper, and headed out of the room into an adjoining office. Bill followed cautiously. As Martha laminated the page, Bill took the small moment to study her. It was a deeply peculiar feeling, knowing that she knew him, but he knew almost next to nothing about her. He felt exposed, his emotional vulnerability bare for her to know without him so much as telling her his surname. He felt cheated, somehow.

"So, can I at least ask how we met?"

Martha turned off the machine and offered the shiny new plastic document to Bill, who merely smiled graciously.

"Well," she replied. "It was chaotic, put it like that."

"Chaotic?"

"I'm really sorry Bill, I can't say. Again, you promised me not to. Or rather, you will."

Bill nodded softly. As much as he understood why he was safeguarding himself in the future, it really clouded his thinking right now. He looked at the page.

LAMINATE ME!
For Bill.
LIGHTBOX INTERIOR IS A TRIUMPH
RAQUEL/100 REVERSES THE POLARITY BY 99.71%.
BORROW THE WORDS TO TAKE THE WHEELS!
DOUBLE YOUR EFFORTS TO DO OVER FATE
PRINCE'S BUG DELIVERS THE MESSAGE
BUNNY HOPS TO THE WARREN

"What the fudge?" asked Bill.

"Sorry," replied Martha. "I'm just the messenger. *Your* messenger."

Bill's shoulders slumped sharply.

"I've literally only just met you; this is so weird. Can't we go for coffee or something? That's a thing that people do, isn't it?"

Martha wheeled herself to the door, and indicated to Bill that he should follow suit.

"We'll go for coffee," she assured him. "But maybe once you're back."

The two locked eyes for the briefest of moments, before Bill looked away.

"I'll be back then?"

Bless him, but Bill was no Terminator.

"I sure hope so Mr Lambert."

"Good stuff!" Bill held up the laminate. "Thanks again, Mrs…"

"Miss," corrected Martha. "Miss Sherwin."

Bill let a broad smile stretch across his face and his face flushed an unsubtle shade of crimson.

"Nice dog lead, by the way. Unusual colouring," complimented Bill, pointing to the rainbow lead wrapped around the arm rests.

"Thanks. He was a very nice dog. Goodbye Bill."

"Until last time, Martha."

Bill strode out and stuffed the page into his satchel. He turned back into the shelving and collided with a strikingly tall man with a jumper over his shoulders. The man dropped a pile of books onto the soft carpet. He stared both intently and incredulously at the sight of Bill.

"Oh, chocolate buttons, I'm sorry old boy!" said Bill, and offered to help scoop up the novels. The man batted away his hands and collected the scattered novels himself. His face had all the warmth of a cancer diagnosis. He stood up straight and pushed a pair of glasses up his long, pointed noise.

"Clumsy," declared the man. He had a voice like a vinegar-filled fountain pen. He sneered down at Bill, who was hardly short himself.

Bill laughed nervously, and looked up to his accuser, Colin Shatterem. The man had been Hartnell Library's Manager since before Bill could remember. A balding beanpole with short black hair in a mushroom sprout from the peak of each ear, he wore black horn-rim glasses connected to a chain around his neck. He tapped a biro against his stack of books impatiently with his velvet glove-clad hands, which he always wore. Bill had never seen him not wearing them, even in the swimming pool.

"Mr Lambert," he began. "If you are going to charge around here like a bull, I may have to reconsider your library membership."

Bill raised an eyebrow at the threat.

"Erm...sorry." He nodded a curt farewell and turned to leave.

"Mr Lambert!" called the man. Bill spun on the spot to face him.

"Yes?" Bill had no idea why Colin appeared to hate him so much. Colin hated everybody, but he did seem to reserve an extra soupcon of loathing for Bill. Ever since Bill joined the library in infancy Colin Shatterem had gone out of his way to make life unpleasant for him. He would state that books weren't available whilst sitting in front of rows of them. He would ban Bill from certain sections for the flimsiest of reasons. He even fined him for bringing books back *early*.

Collin kept his gaze on Bill as he reached down.

"You dropped this." He picked up the laminated document. Bill recoiled slightly. He had dropped it in the kerfuffle. The last thing he wanted was the perma-belligerent Colin prying into his time travel escapades. Colin gazed over the shiny white paper which he grasped firmly in his grip. He was barely able to glance at the printed words however, when Bill snatched the plastic from his long, cadaverous fingers.

"Thanks Colin. Be seeing you!"

Bill sauntered off swiftly, away from Colin Shatterem's toxic gaze. He left the building and stared hard at the laminated piece of A4 with awe. He needed to talk with James.

CHAPTER 8

2019

James pushed the door open to his house and pulled out his headphones. He hadn't been listening to the music anyway. The only sound he could make out was his own heartbeat, bursting against his eardrums. Seeing his Mum's grave under the shadow of his dad's escapades laser-focussed his brain, screaming hatred towards his father.

By god he wanted to punch Nigel in the face.

James showered, dressed, and chugged back a protein shake with a weary grimace. He usually loved the slightly magical feeling of a post-run ache. Less so today. His body was pained but it was his mind that hurt the most, soiled by the unrelenting mental slide show of his dad's cock. Whenever he had managed to suppress it, the offending appendage sprang back into view like a meaty Jack-in-the-Box.

He picked up his phone to call Bill. As he went to call up the number the ringtone blared out. He dropped it in surprise. It was Bill.

"Bill?"

"Who else would it be?" asked his best friend.

"Well, not you."

"It is me," assured Bill. "We need to talk."

"Erm, we're on the phone?" James replied, his voice rising. Bill ignored his friend's frostiness.

"Mate, more stuff has happened. Be better if I discuss it in person."

James looked at his watch anxiously. He only had two hours to go before picking up the kids.

"Harry's?"

"Harry's?" queried Bill, with a little hesitance.

"Yeah, look I'm feeling nihilistic and need a sausage sandwich. K? Be there in fifteen." He threw on his long coat with the floppy collars and left the house.

James pushed open the cafe door with an unusually angry shove. He wished he could shake this ill temper, but it simply wasn't going anywhere. Much like his writing at the moment.

Where the bloody hell was Bill?

"Hey James!" waved a cheery Bill, merely five feet from him.

James cursed his petulant temperament and vowed not to be cross for at least, well, the next ten minutes at any rate. He smiled at his best friend and took a seat facing him. Harry, the miraculously still-alive cadaverous owner took their orders and shuffled back to the coffee machine. Bill had chosen their old 'regular' seats from their teenage years. As he shuffled uncomfortably into the rigid chair, he considered how the cafe hadn't let fashion, good taste, or modernity colour its decor once in the twenty-five years they had been visiting the place. Bolted-down tables, black and white tiled floors, and wipe-down menus. It had worked for generations before and was damned if it was going to change now. James wasn't keen on the seating - too close to the bright yellowing window that baked its patrons on sunny days for his liking. Nevertheless, he conceded to tradition. Beneath the table scratched into the plastic was their initials - JH&BL. It was a mysterious discovery they'd made quite by chance, when Bill once dropped a fistful of change under the table over twenty years ago. Both swore that neither had done it, then wrote it off as an unlikely but pleasant coincidence.

"So, what's up then?" James asked eagerly, in as friendly a manner as he could muster.

"Loads. Complicated and weird and, just loads really."

Bill's stern brow and fidgeting fingers didn't do much for James' confidence. Bill pulled out Martha's laminated document from his satchel and passed it to his friend. James barely looked at it.

"What's this?"

"It was written in the past by me from the future. A set of cryptic instructions. Clues, of sorts."

James raised an eyebrow and cast his eyes over the plastic sheet. With a pessimistic huff, he started reading.

LAMINATE ME!
For Bill.
LIGHTBOX INTERIOR IS A TRIUMPH
RAQUEL/100 REVERSES THE POLARITY BY 99.71%.
BORROW THE WORDS TO TAKE THE WHEELS!
DOUBLE YOUR EFFORTS TO DO OVER FATE
PRINCE'S BUG DELIVERS THE MESSAGE
BUNNY HOPS TO THE WARREN

James finished reading, then stared straight at Bill. Bill thought his friend appeared distinctly unimpressed.

"I'm distinctly unimpressed," confirmed James.

"Well, yes. We don't have a lot to go on."

"Like a hotel with just one toilet. Same result though - lots and lots of unmanageable shit. Really, your guide to the future is bewildering crossword clues?"

Bill nodded. It was hard to disagree when he'd given himself so little information.

"Would you prefer 'Which Way to the Pie?'?"

"At least I'd know where the pie is!"

"Yes," replied Bill. "*Underwater!* Which still makes less sense than 'Prince's bug delivers the message', I might add."

"Does it though?" asked James, his face screwed up tightly. He took another glance at the list. "'Lightbox interior is a triumph'? I mean seriously?"

"Look, I get it, it's annoying, and decoding it is going to be a pain in the spotted dick. But I'm guessing I wrote it like that for, let's say security reasons. Also, I can't correct this when it comes to my turn to write it. I can't simply put more info on and be less oblique."

James was starting to understand.

"Else you'd have already read that better version?"

"Precisely. We need to keep to the same details so we can get into this weird moment we've already established. I want to travel in time, not upset it."

James nodded, annoyed at the sheer logic. Harry brought their drinks and sandwiches to the table. The two thanked him curtly then turned their attention back to the paper. James bolted upright suddenly.

"Hang on, where did you even get this?"

Bill tried not to smile, but the same broad grin that had enveloped his face earlier made a stunning return.

"Oh no one, really," said Bill, as casually as he could (which wasn't very casual at all). "I just met someone who knows us from her past but our future."

"What? Who?"

"She's called Martha. Works at the library. Smiles a lot, drives a wheelchair."

"Drives?"

"Well, I'm not sure what you call it. She's wheelchair-bound?"

James nodded in a limp attempt at reassurance.

"Think that's what you call it. So, Martha?"

"Martha," confirmed Bill with a coy smile.

"She knows us and what we've been up to? Or will get up to. Can't she simply tell us? Would stop us playing stupid detective to your dumb clues."

Bill rubbed his neck in thought then took a bite of a sandwich. James' impatience was wearing down his own reserve supplies.

"You know the answer to that, surely?"

"Knowing the future would affect the future?"

"That sort of thing," affirmed Bill. "At least, that's my understanding of it. We've only time travelled one tiny hour so far and already we're trifle-deep in a world of bewilderment."

"Surely we can get some information? And who is she anyway? Can we trust her? How do we know she's not someone you simply dicked over in the past? Or a stalker?"

Bill conceded that James may have a point. But something deep in his marrow told him that it couldn't be.

"Fair enough, we've every right to be suspicious. I don't know her. But she seems genuine." Bill looked up, glassy-eyed. "There's an indefinable authenticity to her. Clearly, I can't prove that empirically, but I trust my instincts. That's all I've got to offer."

"And all we've got for evidence is this?" queried James, pointing to the instructions and exhaling deeply. He couldn't tell whether to be more excited or frustrated.

Bill took another bite of his sandwich and chewed thoughtfully. His friend chewed the inside of his cheek compulsively and tapped the table in a swift staccato beat.

"Did you find anything out about, er, the photos?" Bill asked, tentatively.

"What, these?" James huffed, then reached inside his long coat and flopped down the worn glossies.

"You bought them here?!" Bill hissed, incredulously.

"I can't leave them at my house, what if someone found them?"

"What, are you expecting to be raided by the police any time soon? Something you're not telling me about your internet search history?"

"Very funny mate. Course not, I just can't let it go, quite literally. Sid hasn't responded so no idea." James thrust the photos back into his inner jacket pocket and sighed. He grabbed a brown sugar cube from the bowl and popped it into his tongue. The slightly bitter tang gave way to a sickly-sweet puddle that pooled slowly to the rear of his throat. It didn't make him feel any better.

Conversely, Bill was grinning like a simpleton. A seed of contentment had blossomed swiftly inside his soul since discovering both time travel *and* now he had met Martha. On the walk from the library to the cafe he found himself smiling randomly, or laughing out loud at things he'd always taken for granted. Mere moments before meeting James he had already enjoyed a delightful giggle fit at the concept of 'shower gel', before going on to sneak a chuckle at the man who lived upstairs with a little dog that was less canine than it was a barking cloud of angry candy floss. His friend's surly manner wasn't going to change that. He leant over to James.

"Come on mate," he corralled to his friend. "Shall we head over to the guitar shop and look at the guitars we can't afford? That normally cheers you up." James relaxed his grimace and smiled thinly at his friend.

"That's a lovely offer, but I really should get back to some actual work. These album reviews and top ten farming tips won't write themselves, sadly." He reached for his mug and drained the contents. "Oh, what the hell, shall we pop in for ten or twenty minutes?"

Bill beamed, and stood to leave.

∾

To the rear of the cafe, unnoticed by James and Bill, sat the hunched body of a middle-aged man, observing keenly the two friends. A tilted stetson pulled down over his beaten face whilst a pair of popped denim collars obscured the rest of his identity. He took a sip of coffee and began rolling a cigarette. His yellowing fingers shook slightly, as he pulled the papers up to his thin lips and darted out a tongue to gum them together. He pocketed the cigarette for later and waited impatiently for the pair to leave.

As James and Bill made their way outside, the stetson-wearer got up and thrust down a crumpled five-pound note. He followed them at a secure distance, discreetly darting in between shop fronts to avoid detection. His sunken eyes scoured every movement they made, careful not to lose them. He was almost distracted several times by passing women but tried desperately to keep focus. He didn't even allow himself the luxury of an ogle, usually very much his thing.

His prey disappeared into a large glass-fronted building, so he took the chance to catch his breath and light a rollie.

Nigel Stanton sucked hard on the cigarette and thought even harder about his next move.

CHAPTER 9

2019

Towards the outskirts of town, James and Bill entered Bobby's Twang Emporium with a light hesitation. Both could play guitar reasonably well - enough at least to impress a toddler or an idiot - but neither felt hugely at home in the seemingly closed-door world of dismissive musos and their spiky approach to outsiders. The shop boasted walls of colourful electric guitars with bank balance-crushing price tags plus a swamp of amplifiers, effects pedals, and accessories designed to confuse the amateur or delight the pro.

Behind the counter sat a pasty-faced twenty-something of indiscriminate gender. The shop assistant hunched over a prohibitively expensive Fender Telecaster. A shiny mop of jet Vantablack hair cloaked a faded grey tee of some faux Satanic band neither Bill nor James had heard of. The employee didn't acknowledge the customers, despite their entrance having clanged the shop's doorbell. Instead, he/she sat glumly and polished the guitar's headstock with an almost obsessive fervour.

"Is Bobby in?" asked Bill with a mischievous smile.

The pasty-faced guitar nerd paused and stared at the pair from behind the fringe.

"He's out the back," replied the automated goth in a deep male growl.

James looked puzzled and pulled Bill to the corner of the shop.

"Why'd you ask him that?"

Bill raised his eyebrows, knowingly.

"You really don't read the local paper, do you?"

"No, course I don't. No one does." James paused. "Well, you do, clearly. What is it?"

"Bobby's 'twang' has been doing the rounds."

James' eyes widened, delighted.

"Blimey, angry husband he's going to have to avoid?"

"Well," countered Bill. "Er, dog owners and pet lovers, actually."

James' face twisted into a revolted grimace. "Ew, down boy! That's just horrible, Mr Twang."

"Understandably, he's keeping a pretty low profile."

From a side room leading to an office, the squat, curly-haired silhouette of Bobby Twang was just visible. Bill nudged James, and the pair darted eyes to him. He disappeared from view.

Clearly fed up with today's innuendo, the assistant shot the pair a withered look.

"Will you be buying anything today?"

James rolled his eyes. Bill looked confidently towards the curmudgeonly clerk.

"I assure you," announced Bill, adjusting his accent a few social classes up, "that I most certainly will be making a purchase in this establishment today."

He didn't need to tell him that it was a 50p guitar plectrum, but still. James threw down his fancy coat with the floppy collars then rolled up his sleeves.

"I'm ready to rock," he snarled at the clerk, as Bill cringed himself inside out.

The pair then spent the next twenty minutes pretending to take interest in all manner of unreasonably costly guitars, pedals, and amps. Taking turns with alternate models, each made a similar feedback-soaked din, regardless of the guitar or effects pedal they played. Whilst Bill favoured a lighter jazz-infused, angular noise, James preferred a choppy, frenetic howl of aural mess. Neither impressed the clerk, who impassively but patiently indulged the pair, wrongly assuming they were just on the precipice of handing over hard cash for something.

Bill handed back a wallet-crushing Gibson Les Paul on which he had been playing *Dead Kennedys*' 'Too Drunk to Fuck'. The assistant clasped the beautiful shiny guitar with delicate reverence.

"One day, James," said Bill, dreamily.

"Why don't you just buy one?"

"On *my* income? I can't afford or justify it, mate." replied Bill, and sighed wistfully.

James picked up a fuzz pedal to enquire about its price.

"How much for the fuzzbox?"

The assistant blinked slowly and raised a pierced eyebrow mockingly.

"It's a Big Muff," he corrected, much to James' delight. "It's £84.99"

"£84.99 for a fuzzbox, eh? Gotta say I love a fuzzbox. God that's fun to say - fuzzbox."

The clerk winced in agreement.

"Fuzzbox, fuzzboz fuzzbox," wittered James, idly. He suddenly shot up in surprise at himself. "Lightbox! Triumph! Could it be? Hang on!" James had a swift mindgasm as realisation rushed through his soul. "Interior lightbox is a triumph! Bill, I know what that means!"

The clerk frowned in confusion.

"What is it?"

"Well, I might be wrong, but lightbox is basically the projector, yeah?"

"OK, so the projector - my time machine - is a triumph?" Bill rolled the words around his head for a couple of seconds as James looked on and smiled encouragingly at his friend. "The triumph is the Triumph car, isn't it?" realised Bill and smiled through gritted teeth. He couldn't work out whether to be happy they got it or annoyed his friend worked it out sooner than him.

James clicked his fingers in excitement.

"Just like I said! It *is* a time machine!"

"Yes, got that. But again, it doesn't explain how we get it."

Bill waved a plectrum at the clerk sulkily.

"Good point," conceded James, who felt slightly aggrieved at his friend's cool manner. Bill was *clearly* annoyed at James for working it out first. "Well, I better be off then. Got writing to crack on with."

The pair made their excuses to the bewildered clerk, before Bill made his paltry purchase of a Bobby's Twang Emporium-inscribed plectrum.

"Would you like a bag for that?" deadpanned the clerk, as he handed over the tiny plastic triangle with gold lettering.

"Very kind, I think I'll be ok," replied Bill condescendingly, and patted his bulging satchel as proof. He raised an eyebrow, then offered the plectrum to James. "You have it, you've earned it. Well done on getting the first clue."

"I will genuinely keep it with me always, thanks." He snatched the pick greedily.

James and Bill left the shop, and the friends walked wordlessly up the path. James felt immensely frustrated. Bill was right, he thought. It was all very well solving the 'clue', but what good was it if they didn't learn anything in the process? Similarly, Bill had more to think about now they knew what it meant. He only had a vague idea and theory on how to harness the power of the time beam and project it safely within a vehicle. It was already fairly unstable in its present form. Finessing it to work in an ugly car from decades prior was going to bleed his IQ dry. He wondered whether his heavy concentration on time travel had left his brain rinsed for inspiration. It would certainly explain how James had got the first clue so far ahead of him. He chuckled inwardly.

"Interior lightbox is a triumph!" Bill said. "Good work, James," congratulated Bill, to James' surprise.

Just as they were about to disappear around a corner a throaty voice sliced through the crisp air.

"Actually boys, the triumph is all mine."

James and Bill stopped immediately and looked at each other in a curious alarm. The friends turned slowly to identify the crooked voice who had beckoned their attention. A tall man with a slight hunch stood just six feet back. The pair could barely make out his face as the fierce winter sun shone from behind him, silhouetting his frame. The light spilled over his stetson and a sharp glare bounced off the metallic object he was holding, which Bill quickly realised was the unmistakable shape of a pistol. He nodded to James, and simply whispered, "gun."

James clocked the firearm. His pulse reacted accordingly, stomach dropped, and the moisture in his mouth evaporated instantly. He squinted at the figure, unsure what to make of this stranger. He looked to Bill, who was simply whimpering slightly. James sucked in a chest full of breath, drawing reserves of boldness he wasn't sure he had.

"Howdy pardner!" James raised an imaginary hat at the man. The gesture fell to unacknowledged silence.

"Get in," ordered the stranger, and motioned to the parking bay opposite the street.

The pair spun on the spot, to face a row of cars. James looked back, annoyed.

"Well, which one, Brokeback?"

The man screwed his face up, puzzled, but nodded towards a slightly beaten up, sludge brown sports model. *That* slightly beaten up, sludge brown sports model from *Car Classics: The 1970s*. The very car James had stood next to in the photo.

James and Bill froze in bafflement. They stared incredulously at the Triumph Dolomite.

"Move!" ordered the man, angrily.

James' pulse raced, as his body caught up with his brain's dawning realisation. The man behind him wasn't any old gun-wielding lunatic. The throaty rasp and jagged hunch should have given it away instantly, only it hadn't seemed possible. But then just last week, time travel hadn't seemed possible. It was him. He looked *awful*. Severely beaten and bruised, but definitely him.

"Nigel," he muttered in a scarcely audible whisper. He tried again. "Nigel." James felt the blood drain from his body, and his knees buckled. His vision blurred as he attempted desperately to keep pace with reality.

"Son," retorted Nigel, confirming James' detection. "Get in the car."

Bill stepped back toward the vehicle. The weapon had all but robbed him of autonomy, but he was damned if he was going to lose his life to his best friend's loser Dad. He shot pleading eyes towards James, but there was no way James was going to capitulate to his father now.

"What do you want, you prick?" spat James.

"For you to get in the car," growled Nigel. "Thought that was obvious."

"Or what? You'll shoot me? You'll murder your son?"

Nigel immediately raised the gun, took aim at the car next to it, and fired a bullet straight into its rear tyre. The deafening explosion knocked all three men back, the pistol's boom a cochlea-shattering wall of noise. James' heart thudded almost as loudly, as Bill trembled with fear. With revulsion to match his reluctance, James took the remaining few steps towards the Triumph.

Nigel opened the passenger door and Bill climbed in. The wood panelled dash and its archaic dials had a new technological neighbour bolted onto the passenger's side, Bill's time machine. It was slightly different, a little more refined here and there, with fewer buttons and the lens a smaller frosted glass, but still unmistakably the same wondrous invention.

James snarled at his father, who simply waved the gun threateningly.

"Do as Daddy says, there's a good boy," Nigel mocked, sneering triumphantly at his offspring. James slowly sat to take his place behind the wheel. He turned to spit at his father, but Nigel slammed shut the door as he did. The flob hit the inside window and made a slow, slimy journey down the glass, obscuring James' view of his dad, who tipped his hat to the pair.

"Now fuck off!" he barked and fired another shot, this time at their wing mirror. It exploded spectacularly, sending shards of reflective glass violently into the air.

"Drive!" hissed Bill. James started the engine, and the car spluttered into life. He revved the accelerator hard and pulled away furiously.

The pair roared down a side street, past the guitar shop, and into a nearby industrial estate. The dashboard started pouring huge wafts of black smoke into the front, which blinded James. He hit the brakes sharply, but the car refused to obey, instead speeding up. James gasped and kicked the pedal. He left his foot off the gas, but still the Triumph rattled on. Bill's contorted face betrayed his terror.

"I can't stop it!" insisted James, and he pumped the brakes harder. Which he instantly realised wouldn't make a bit of difference. He tried to turn off the ignition, he went down the gears, and pulled on the handbrake. Nothing; the controls were all but completely locked out.

Only the steering wheel seemed to still function. The car was climbing up to 50mph. James steered left and right swiftly, hoping to reduce the acceleration even a little. It just made him feel incredibly woozy. Bill wound down his window to clear the smoke, then gasped loudly as he noticed the projector's digital readout. In cruel, bright red numbering, the LED display read '-1,000,000'.

No dates. No months.

Just minus one million *years*.

The year One Million BC.

    Bill's enormous brain tried to combat the pair's immediate problem as his personality panicked out loud to James.

    "Your Dad's rigged the time machine! We're heading back hundreds of thousands of years!"

    "How? Fucker!," shouted back James.

    "Hey, at least my haircut might finally be in fashion."

    "Not really the time, mate," James yelled, as his arms struggled to steer the careening vehicle.

    "Just trying to lighten the mood."

    Bill jabbed at the projector, but the controls had been soldered shut. He fumbled at the unwieldy wooden glove box and popped it open. Nothing but a softcore gay porn mag from the 1970s. He cursed his predicament and punched his satchel in sheer frustration. His fist struck something hard, and he immediately regretted his temper tantrum. Then Bill realised it was his remote control for the time machine. Surely it would work on *this* model? It was undeniably the same machine. Excitedly, Bill reached into his bag and pulled out the device. He twiddled a variety of baffling dials on the unit, then turned a knob. Sweat poured from his hairline as he thumbed a sliding trigger on the side of the slim box. James took his eyes off the road for a microsecond to check on his friend.

    "Think you can stop it?"

A high-pitched squeal emanated from the control, and the box replied in synch. Bill's face lit up.

"Stay on this road and I'll try," assured Bill.

James had no intention of crashing, but he lost a little more confidence with every single graceless nudge of the steering wheel. So fast was he driving, his visibility stretched barely beyond the car's long bonnet. He was guiding the vehicle more through a combination of survival instinct and sheer dumb luck than any intuitive talent he had as a driver. The car raced around factories, narrowly missing workers on a cigarette break, and lorries unloading supplies. Sensing he would run out of road before shortly running out of life, James attempted a frantic U-turn and pushed the horn hard. He overshot the chance to turn back and they entered a large stretch of unused cracked concrete about a mile square, which eventually gave way to rows of untendered bushes, a thin stretch of canal, and nouveau identikit housing estates. James' new number one goal was to stay on the concrete.

"You done yet?" he bellowed to Bill. His friend's brain throbbed with the task at hand. "Or are we going to be dinosaur lunch?"

"Dinosaurs were long dead by then," shouted Bill, with a snarl.

"Sorry Attenborough, just after an update, not a natural history lesson."

"Ssh!" demanded Bill. He squinted hard to muster every bit of matter his skull contained. This was so unfair. He must have set these coordinates, somehow. How the hell was he going to counterprogram against *himself*? "Oh, Christmas pudding!"

The car sped on shakily. Its occupants felt every uneven granule beneath the tyres, their spines reduced to strands of wet ramen. James hit a pothole, and the car took a pitiless crunch. The jolt knocked Bill's satchel over into the passenger footwell, and out spilled its contents. The light bounced off the laminated document and into James' eye, distracting him momentarily. He peeked down to see the offending list of gibberish and cursed the nonsensical plastic page.

"Anything on your girlfriend's bad poetry scroll that can see us out of here?" James shouted.

Bill grunted and grabbed the plastic sheet. He scanned for anything even vaguely helpful. His eye fell on the name Raquel.

'RAQUEL REVERSES THE POLARITY BY 98.1%'

Raquel.

Raquel?

"James, what did you say about dinosaurs?"

James wrestled the steering wheel, his hands already starting to blister.

"Just thought we might see dinosaurs," he replied, straining to keep the vehicle to the concrete. "But obviously not, because we'd, erm, a few thousand years out? No?"

"We'd be sixty-four million years too late. Why do you think they were around only a million years ago?"

"Because…"

"No, I get it!" barked Bill, and excitedly began tapping into the control. "Got it, yes!" he bellowed elatedly, and hit the dial.

The car shook uncontrollably, and the time machine's ear-splitting whir started up. The dashboard emanated a blinding white light that flooded the vehicle. Almost entirely blind, James finally surrendered the vehicle to whatever power was guiding it and covered his face from the searing glean. Bill braced himself and gripped the edge of the seat as the car screamed out of thin air.

The car vanished from 2019.

CHAPTER 10

2019

Nigel Stanton lowered his gun as he watched James and Bill speed off into a nearby street. He allowed himself a small smile, his first proper moment of enjoyment in a week. His eyes narrowed, and he gave a curt wave to the billowing dust cloud the car had left in its wake. He flipped open his son's wallet. He rummaged through the cards and coins, before flipping back to a picture on the inside. Stuck behind a flimsy plastic window was a recent family photo. Nigel pulled it back from his eyes to scrutinise more closely. The image slowly came into focus. James stood proudly with his two smiling children to one side, and a woman beaming with pride on the other. He'd seen her before: Mrs Harpman. Nigel made a low, guttural grunt of approval at the image.

"Now *there's* a good boy," he muttered lasciviously, and safely stowed the wallet back into his coat next to his son's phone.

Today was going very well indeed for Nigel Stanton.

∽

Today was going less well for Susan Harpman.

Sue Harpman smiled through to the end of another exhausting day at Hartnell Primary School. Aside from one minor head injury and a barely noteworthy disagreement involving a swear word, by lunchtime it was on course to be a fairly uneventful 9-5. (Well, 8:00-16:30, plus meetings, safeguarding courses, then marking and planning in the evening, obviously.)

Unfortunately, Callum Agnew's voracious appetite had managed to ruin all that. The young chubber had managed to wolf down his meal then scoff a further two other pupils' lunches. Then threw up into the aquarium. The mostly delighted children had been treated to the sight of usually placid class goldfish Chibbers flap his little fins furiously away from a sudden tsunami of slimy chunks and stomach acid. Sue reasoned it would have been a blessed release for the unassuming orange fish; she often took his constant laps of boredom around the small glass tub as a cry for help. As it was, drowning in a mass of barely digested fruit slices and Dairylea Lunchables probably wasn't what the poor bastard had in mind. Worse still, Sue was then responsible for the entire incident: clearing up the vomit, sourcing extra food from her own lunch, remonstrating Callum, offering sympathy, and providing on-the-spot counselling to the two pupils distraught at the carnage.

Sue reflected on all this after the children had finally left, as she sat not listening to a meeting about the school's need to adhere more strongly to its Christian principles. She longed to be back with her children and thought enviously of James picking them up from school. She then instinctively hoped he *would* pick them up after school, as he had been known to forget now and then. No sooner had this thought entered her head than her phone rang.

Today was about to go even less well for Susan Harpman.

As Nigel Stanton prowled the town's streets wide-eyed and jubilant, the day's apricity beamed through the chill November air onto his immeasurably happy face. Life felt *good*.

He smiled at strangers, tipped his hat to the homeless, and waved cheerily to parking wardens. This fresh release in life felt *amazing*. A new sandbox of infinite possibilities, free from the constraints, consequences, and responsibilities of yesterday. A clean slate he couldn't wait to rub his own filth all over again. He eyed every female within gawping distance. His penis twitched at the sheer potential of it all.

First of all though, he had urgent business to attend to.

Nigel strolled up to a young male busker artlessly strumming out a bland pop tune of the day to the casual indifference of passing shoppers. He folded his arms and waited for the song to end. As the final chord rang out Nigel took off his hat and outstretched his arm, beckoning to the shoppers passing by.

"Ladies and gentlemen, what we have just heard is stardom in the making! Give it up for…" he turned to the bemused busker, prompting a name.

"Darren," replied Darren.

"It's Darren, everyone! Come on people, shake your money makers and dig deep for this cherubic-faced troubadour with his songs of joy and that weird little cake he wears on his head," Nigel brayed, and pointed to Darren's man-bun. A few shoppers had stopped to see what was going on. "We are barrelling along to the festive season, and poor Darren can ill afford to go without turkey. Or more importantly, singing lessons."

The shoppers chuckled their approval. Unsure how to react to this stranger, busker Darren simply raised his eyebrows in thanks and rang out a bright C major in gratitude.

"See," continued Nigel. "The poor lad knows only the one chord. Give generously this afternoon and we'll raise the funds so he can learn a second! Your hard-earned moolah this way please. Who knows? Make enough and I might convince him to give it up!"

Seemingly starved of street entertainment since birth, the small crowd cheered jovially. A few willingly reached for their wallets, and before Darren could start another song, Nigel had whipped up a handy chunk of small change into his hat.

"Thank you, ma'am. Much obliged sir! You're too generous my man," went Nigel, ring mastering the ceremony with a velveteen glee. He turned to the delighted busker and presented him the clattering hat, yet still kept a claw-like grip firmly on the headwear.

"Thank you everyone," declared Darren, weakly. "And thank you, er…" He gestured to Nigel, unsure of how to address him.

"Me?" said Nigel, with mock humility. "Why, I am Mr James Harpman!"

"To James Harpman!" announced Darren, and struck another chord in appreciation.

The small gathering made polite applause and went on their way.

The pair stood in brief silence as Darren fiddled nervously with his guitar's tuning pegs.

"Thanks man," enthused Darren. "That was really good of you. James, yeah?"

"Hey, anytime! Before I go though, genuine question: *has* anyone ever told you you've actually got a really good singing voice? You know, really?"

Darren's face lit up, and his eyes watered over slightly.

"No," he trembled, choking up. "They haven't."

"Good. Because you're *utterly shit*." Nigel roared with laughter at his own cruelty. He turned swiftly to leave, clutching the hat, coins and all. Darren's face crumpled like a bag of wet washing.

He lunged forward and grabbed Nigel's coat. The grip caught him off guard and he jerked back. His cruel eyes glinted with satisfaction, and he flashed his assailant a sneering grin.

"What do you want, Tuneless?"

"You've got my money," protested Darren, his voice trembling.

Nigel raised an eyebrow.

"*Your* money, eh? You think you've earned this, do you? You and your wailing bullshit? Really? You sound like a fucking asthma attack. You've got all the natural charisma of a bladder being kicked down a flight of stairs. And frankly, your guitar looks embarrassed to be with you. So don't for one second think any of this cash is *your* earnings. OK, shitsack?"

Darren's mouth twitched and he felt his knees tremble. God, how he loathed confrontation.

"I just, well... It's my hat!"

"It is your hat, but I am having it," insisted Nigel, and readied his face for the punch he was guaranteed to receive.

But it didn't come. Darren stood motionless, appalled at the man before him behaving so objectionably. Then with a weary and familiar resignation, he limply took his guitar off and started packing away.

"Oi, shitface!," seethed Nigel. "Aren't you going to retaliate?"

"I'm a Buddhist," replied the exhausted busker. "We don't retaliate. This exchange is simply an impermanence."

Nigel scowled at the man. He had to be kidding. Then let out a giggle at his stupid misfortune. The one time he *needed* to get punched in the face and he had picked a fight with a bloody pacifist. He

"Oi Darryl," rasped Nigel, determined to get a rise.

"What?" said Darren, in a withering tone.

"I molested your Mum."

Darren dropped his guitar and launched himself at Nigel. He threw a flurry of puny punches at the glowering arsehole, then grabbed his belongings and fled the scene.

Nigel lay on the concrete defeated, a trickle of blood pouring from his nose. He smiled into the drain as several shoppers ran to help him.

CHAPTER 11

1984

The Triumph screeched into existence. Its exhausted engine roared a perforating howl of apocalyptic rage. A white heat enveloped the tyres which melted them instantly. The car came to a dramatic lurching stop and ploughed through rows of overgrown bushes. An acrid smoke plumed through the interior as its two passengers screamed far beyond the journey's end. Both clutched their heads in dizziness. James slumped forward; his nose crumpled against the unforgiving metal of the steering wheel. A spray of blood had burst onto the dash and his right eye socket sealed over in a purple bulbous clump. James reached for the door and managed to open it just in time to vomit onto the grass below. Bill breathed too deeply for a man in his mid-forties. Both men sat silently, each waiting for the other to speak.

James' remaining open eye stung from retching. He blinked out the pain and finally turned to look at Bill.

"Mate, what just happened?"

Bill exhaled and merely nodded. He grabbed his bag and climbed out of the car. James followed his move, sidestepped his puddle of puke and waded into the unkempt bushes.

"Where are we?" asked James.

Bill surveyed the land's geography.

"We haven't moved," he offered, solemnly.

"We haven't…" James began, but trailed off, realising Bill was right. The canal was exactly where it had been. The power lines overhead had vanished, while trees that weren't there a minute ago had appeared, now metres into the air. The concrete edge of the industrial park had given way to patches of muddy fields and the odd sprouting tuft of grass. James looked back towards town. Some factories had disappeared, but it was thankfully still more or less there. At least they hadn't actually ended up in dinosaur times, he reasoned, trying to stay positive. Bill jabbed at the remote control, but the box merely fizzed in his palm.

"That's town, isn't it?" queried James, pointing to the slightly altered landscape.

"Sure is."

"But…" James hesitated, knowing he would sound like a ninny for saying it. "*When* are we?"

Bill tutted quietly.

"You sound such a ninny saying that."

James nodded in agreement.

"Question still stands though. We've gone back, right? But to when?"

"George Orwell times!" declared Bill, cryptically. James screwed his face up for a second, before the answer sunk in.

"1984, smartarse. I've listened to Bowie, I know who George Orwell is. Why did you bring us here?"

Bill held up the plastic-coated sheet.

"This was the calculation that brought us here."

James removed his coat and patted it down for dust.

"It's certainly a lot warmer than before. What's the exact date?"

Bill grimaced and shook the remote unit a few more times. He climbed into the smoking remnants of the car and tried to awaken the machine, but it remained stubbornly dead.

"Summer."

"Brilliant," replied James, flatly. "An unknown date in a year I know nothing about except what I learned from the album Diamond Dogs."

"Which is?"

"That Bowie's work is better when conceived as a whole, rather than the patchwork quilt of ideas that Dogs ultimately is."

"Thanks NME, but that's not exactly what I was getting at."

"I know, I'm just freaking out to be honest."

"Got to admit, I am too a little," confessed Bill, as fiddled unnecessarily with his coat buttons. "I've been a bachelor my entire life. I have almost near complete autonomy. My time, my goals, my whereabouts. I'm used to doing pretty much whatever I want, unencumbered by the demands of others. Now we're marooned in the mid-80s. Are we going to surrender to chance's fate?"

"Erm," replied James.

"No, fudge that. I don't believe in fate. I believed in determinism, science, and Sugar Puffs making your wee stink."

"Any chance we can get the time machine back on the road?" James asked feebly. The pair looked at the vehicle. It looked like a dragon had tried to fuck it.

Bill tried to look optimistic, but his face was all wrong. Like a murder victim being told to smile as the knife went in.

"Mechanically, that thing is dead. I'll pull what parts I can from the time machine and set about building a new one. And don't forget, that's the first time I've seen the time machine in a car. Now I'll have to reverse engineer something that I'm not entirely sure how I built in the first place."

James' stomach dropped to a new low.

"What are we going to do in the meantime? Where do we sleep? What do we do for money? Clothes? Food? Shitting! Where are we going to shit, Bill?"

Bill felt the embers of enmity and panic emanate from his friend.

"Look, neither am I exactly thrilled, but I'm not going to let the severity of our situation get to my temper. We'll make do, James," he assured, calmly. "This is the 1980s. There's no digital network of checks and balances. We can assume identities, or hell - even use our own. We'll get work easily enough. We'll probably have to sleep in the car to start with, and we can shit in the pub, or something."

James looked like someone had just dipped his cock in hot vinegar.

"Sleep in a burnt-out car and shit in the pub? It's what I've always wanted! So much for Thatcher's Britain."

Bill hesitated slightly, nervous of James' petulance.

"I've still got the clues as to what to do next, don't forget." He raised the laminated document up to face James' disapproval.

"Some use that has been so far. We're stuck - what - thirty-five years in the past. Thanks to a plastic sheet, now I have to kip in a wreck and do my business in a saloon. All praise Blue's Clues! Let's kill our firstborns in deference to the mighty crossword!"

Bill's patience snapped.

"For bread's sake James, get a grip. It was *your* dad who forced us into this situation. We don't even know how he knew about the time machine, how he got it. If it hadn't been for me, we would be thousands of years in the past. Without this, we'd be honey glazed. Eating berries, fending off wolves, and freezing to death come the winter. With nineteen eighties tech, we have more than a fighting chance of getting back to the present. So, calm your bits, mate."

Taken aback by Bill's assertive outburst, James flushed a subtle shade of purple. Part shame, part infuriated, but all panic, he ground his teeth as hard as his jaw would allow. Whilst barely opening his mouth, he seethed back at his pal.

"But it was your stupid time machine that stupid Nigel took. Without that invention, my old man wouldn't have followed the fucking van and dilly-dallied us back to this bullshit decade!"

"Yes James," concurred Bill, exasperated. "I agree. Which is why we need to work out a solution to this problem, instead of bitching about it like a pathetic baby."

"Oh, get fucked Professor Yaffle! I was doing fine until you parked your Turdis into my life. What have we got from it? Stranded in time and my dickhead sperm donor resurrected to cause havoc in my present. Nice going."

Bill's blood tingled with anger and resentment.

"Not everything is either mine or your dad's fault, James. Take some responsibility."

"Oh, I'm taking responsibility all right. Know what I'm going to do?" asked James with a menacing growl. "I'm going to find my dad. Perhaps he's still here in this shithole town? Maybe I'll follow him to the future. Wherever he is Bill, know what I'm going to do? I'm going to murder him. Does that fit into your little list of riddles?"

"You can't...*what?*"

"I'm going to kill my dad."

James appeared deadly serious. Bill snorted derisively.

"Mate, look it's been a helluva long, weird day and..."

"I mean it Bill. The guy's literally dead to me already. He's screwing up my future from his past. I have no hesitation whatsoever in ending his life. It's just twatricide at this point."

Bill blinked back a weak smile.

"Really though James," he replied, softly. "Could you honestly murder another human, no matter how much you hate them? Could you look someone in the eyes and be responsible for ending their life?"

Bill cowered a little. A passionate fire had enveloped James that Bill had rarely witnessed. James blinked back at his pal. He bellowed a frustrated yell, then kicked the car's passenger door several times. The potency of his fury ploughed through the flimsy panel, and the door hung loose from its hinges. James stopped and exhaled, exhausted.

The two friends stood in awkward silence. Bill finally spoke.

"Good *Street Fighter II* impression. Which one were you - the green monster fella or the fat lad with the slappy hands?"

James smiled weakly.

"Fat lad, every time."

"Feel better?"

"No."

"Fair enough." Bill searched through his rucksack and pulled out a large chocolate bar. "Fruit 'n' Nut?" He offered a chunk to James. "It's past its sell by date, but, well, I suppose it sort of isn't now."

James took the snack and wolfed it down hungrily. He leant against the Triumph and sucked the melted chocolate from his teeth thoughtfully. Bill tended to the time machine's remote control tenderly and took out a small screwdriver to start tinkering.

"We should hide the car."

"Why?" asked James.

"We really don't want the locals discovering it. It might be a wreck, but it really is our only ticket out of here." Bill pointed to the shrubbery. "Shouldn't be too hard with all this foliage. As I said, I'll salvage what I can from the time machine, then we can roll her under one of these bushes. Hopefully the only thing that'll notice it is the odd starling or robin. Then head into town. See for ourselves what the 1980s has to offer?"

"All I remember is the AIDS crisis and the Police Academy movies," replied James, grumpily.

"Well, if you happen to shag Steve Guttenberg, wear a condom."

James laughed.

"Knob." He tried to imagine a worse scenario. At least he wasn't listening to *Fear of Beans*.

The friends pushed the car into a bush and started the long walk back into their past.

CHAPTER 12

2019

Sue Harpman tapped furiously onto her phone screen. Where was her husband? And what was he playing at? It was embarrassing enough as a mother fending off a smarmy school administrator, but now had the added shame of being in the profession currently accusing her of negligence. And to be fair, they had a point. Sort of. Because this was James' fault, not hers.

"Pick up you dozy git" she hissed as the phone rang. The dial tone eventually gave way to James' recorded voicemail greeting. She prepared to be enraged even further by James' cheery welcome. But the friendly greeting made her heart thud and stomach churn. She'd spent so long being cross she hadn't considered he might actually be in trouble. Injured? Arrested? Trapped?

"Oh, shit James, what's happened to you?"

Three hours, one police search, and many tears later, Susan and her children met 'James' at their front door. Accompanied by two kindly-faced police officers, Nigel could barely stand, withered by the day's as yet mysterious events. With torn, blood-splattered clothes, and a face that looked as if he had peered into an open blender, Nigel less resembled his son James than he did a crash test dummy one day from retirement.

"Mrs Harpman?" asked PC Paxton.

Shellshocked and bewildered, Susan simply nodded and ushered the trio into their home.

Nigel hoped his face was smashed up enough for the ruse to work. It was a big gamble, but with enough confidence and two fat fistfuls of luck, he might just be able to pull this off. The police officers led him through the Harpman's hall into the living room and settled him down onto a sofa. He winced as his exposed skin pressed against the cold leather.

Susan clutched her children tightly, as they took in their sight of their injured father. Autumn smiled through tears of relief, as Jude remained rigidly suspicious of the man in their house. The small child inspected his father closely. He was certainly James-shaped, of sorts. But the state and condition of him felt off. Nigel cocked his head at the two, almost quizzically. He opened his gangly arms and beckoned the children in.

"Cuddle for your Daddy?" he burbled through bruised, swollen lips.

Reluctantly, Autumn embraced him, but pulled back mere seconds into the hug.

"You smell weird," she stated, with a fearful honesty.

Nigel smiled. "None taken."

"Could we have a word Mrs Harpman?" asked PC Paxton.

"Sure." She led the officer into the kitchen, then closed the door softly behind her. Instinctively boiling the kettle, she mimed offering a drink to the officer, who politely declined. Also, oddly, in mime. Words weren't exactly high on either's agenda.

"Mrs Harpman, when did you last see your husband?"

"Just this morning as I was leaving for work. What's happened to him?"

"Well," answered Paxton, tapping their hat, "He was attacked."

"Attacked? Who would attack James?" Almost as soon as Sue had asked the question, she remembered her husband's big trouble-starting mouth.

"A busker."

"A busker? What? Who? Where?"

"We don't have the suspect, but he was seen running from the scene. Your husband hasn't been able to provide us with much information. Understandable, given his condition. We're scanning CCTV footage, and we've got a few witness statements, but nothing concrete sadly. We'll keep an eye out and log the crime officially."

Susan thought that final sentence sounded suspiciously like police code for, 'we haven't a hope in hell of solving this. It'd be easier if we pretend it never happened.'

"Could any of his daily activities lead him to be the victim of assault?" asked Paxton.

"He works from home writing, and almost certainly masturbates too much."

PC Paxton blushed a little but smirked knowingly.

Susan continued. "Not sure either of those warrant a beating." She pulled two mugs from the cupboard and wearily threw a teabag into each. PC Paxton scribbled onto a small notepad and pocketed it immediately.

"We strongly recommend he go to the hospital."

"He hasn't seen anyone?" Susan shot Paxton an accusatory look. "He looks concussed at the very least."

"We can't force someone to undergo hospital treatment. When we picked him up he was absolutely insistent on coming straight here. Plus, *he* hasn't broken any laws," explained the officer.

Susan softened her stance a little and pulled the milk from the fridge.

"I suppose. I'll march him up there myself if I have to. Hell, I've got the zoo trip tomorrow!"

PC Paxton responded by simply staring at the floor in silence.

The kettle's boil made for a welcome distraction, and Sue poured the bubbling water into the mugs.

"Sorry, I'm very grateful for you bringing home my husband, so thank you. There's nothing left for you to do, is there?"

"You're welcome, and no, our work here is done. If your husband does remember or mention anything else, just give us a call. But for now, we'll see ourselves out."

The officer turned, grabbed their partner, and both left promptly. Susan finished the teas and brought them into the living room. Autumn and Jude sat on the floor, staring at their 'Dad', eyeballing his every move cautiously.

"Bet you need this," said Sue, and placed the mug on a coaster next to Nigel. "Two sugars, just as you like, yeah?"

"Ooh lovely, ta Just what the doctor ordered." He made a theatrical display of self-pity, then took a huge gulp of the beverage. The piping hot liquid tore into his throat like lava through a plastic carrier bag. He merely beamed a grateful smile back at Susan, his eyes dancing in agony.

Susan took the armchair opposite and peered at him over her mug. The steam curled up around his bloodied face, obscuring his features even further.

"What happened, James?" queried Sue.

Nigel recounted the story with the busker, embellishing parts, and without mentioning his cruelty.

Sue sipped her tea tightly and tried to take in the beggar's breadcrumbs of her husband's skeletal story. He looked *pathetic*. She had no idea what to believe, but whatever was going on, this man was clearly in pain right now.

"You finish your tea. I'm going to take mine upstairs and put these two to bed."

"Aw Mum!" both children cried in unison.

"Think an early night will help us all," she insisted, then very deliberately winked towards Nigel and raised an eyebrow.

With this single gesture Nigel's synapses fizzled into life in an instant. His fingers, hairline, and balls all tingled simultaneously, and his penis felt the urgent call of his owner's Bat signal.

"You could do with a shower," suggested Susan. Nigel merely nodded attentively. The children clambered upstairs behind the watchful eye of their mother, who followed carefully.

"Mum, Dad doesn't smell right," whispered Autumn, as they reached the top of the stairs.

"Well, all the more reason he has that shower then."

Finally left alone, Nigel took a moment to survey his surroundings. Get a peek around his son's life. Drink in the life of James Harpman. He stood up and pulled his sweaty balls free from his leg. As he nosed around the room he left his hand inside his trousers, resting on his member.

The large wall facing the television was a virtual tapestry of family portraits and happy moments. The kids flying a kite on the beach. Autumn pulling a face in a forest. Jude being flung into the air by James. Susan clutching both children on a railway platform. All four of them posing with ice creams. Nigel found the sincerity nauseating. As if *any* family is this happy! He cast his eye over a jumble of instruments tidied hastily into a corner. Two electric guitars balanced precariously on a violin case. A banjo neighboured a xylophone which sat on a stack of cymbals and a dozen or so recorders. At the foot of this small acoustic mountain was a mess of mouth organs, clarinet reeds, and spare guitar strings. Beyond this stretched into the dining room in which an electric piano, drum kit, and cello left very little room left for actual dining. Nigel approved of this dedication to melody over the stupid family snaps.

He peered with disdain at the large flat screen that passed for a TV. How were rock stars supposed to hurl that thing out of a hotel window? He stared at a wi-fi router dismissively, unsure of its purpose but mistrustful nonetheless.

Nigel wandered into the kitchen, opened the fridge and gazed inside. His stomach surged in despair. Hummus and olives and tomatoes and pots of organic yoghurt took vital space where meats and beer should be. He frowned hard, then finally helped himself to a vegan sausage, which he spat out immediately. He grabbed a small plastic tray with brightly coloured packaging and tore off the lid. So new to 2019 was he, he had no idea what a Dairylea Dunker was, but at least it wasn't pretending to be healthy.

His first true disappointment of the day, he shut the fridge door and scanned the shitty children's art held up by magnets on the front. He hoped these were very old pictures. If not, he mused, his grandchildren might well be spastics.

Susan called from above.

"Kids have brushed their teeth. Bathroom's free if you want your shower now, James."

"Thanks flower!" he shouted back, and knocked back a final swig of tea.

He climbed the stairs slowly, trying to scope out which room was which on his short journey. Luckily, the bathroom door was ajar. This eliminated one of his options, greatly reducing his chances of messing up. Another four mystery doors remained. With feigned confidence he pulled one open. A small wall of towels and a water tank greeted him. He smirked, grabbed the biggest towel he could find then disappeared into the bathroom.

Once inside he flicked the slide on the vanity lock and peeled off his ragged clothes. Swilling a gobful of mouthwash around his false teeth, he reached to turn on the shower, and set the water's temperature to scorching.

Nigel Stanton was about to pressure wash away any lingering sense of guilt about what he was planning to do with his son's wife.

CHAPTER 13

1984

James scampered hurriedly along the grassy verge towards town. Bill kept up as fast as he could, but his pace was no match for James' athletic strides. Besides, he had managed to wallop his left leg hard against the car door, leaving him with a rather pathetic limp. And he was carrying lumps of electronics and machinery. James had inconveniently not offered to help, Bill noticed ruefully.

James followed his instincts, desperate to find anything that might get the pair out of this predicament and back to his wife and children. Powered by urgency, he needed Bill to rebuild the time machine now. He needed to burst back to the future and confront stupid bloody Nigel with a vengeance.

The pair eventually cleared the overgrown grass to where the town's industrial edge had stretched. The same streets they had been racing through just minutes before, yet now largely untouched by development. The vast warehouses and storage units had disappeared, leaving a small spattering of abandoned factories. In fact, James noticed, it appeared as if the 1980s had yet to leave any mark whatsoever on the somewhat sparse street fixtures. Once former grand street signage from a decade or two prior sat awkwardly on crumbling low level brick walls that betrayed a lack of care and investment.

"You sure this is 1984? It doesn't look like 1984."

"What? Not enough Rubik's Cubes lying on the streets?"

"Alright, I wasn't exactly expecting Eddie Murphy to come body popping along in a Sinclair C5 but thought someone might at least have had Cyndi Lauper on a nearby radio or something."

The two stood silent for a moment and waited for the song to drift over the airwaves. It didn't. Bill prodded his remote control and affirmed the readout.

"It's still 1984, no matter how few contemporary hits we hear."

"Let's get lunch, I'm famished," suggested James.

"How? We've got no money."

"Well, you're not going to like this, but hear me out…"

                    ∽

Thirty minutes later, having robbed a milk float of the milkman's entire week's takings, the pair sat in Harry's greasy spoon cafe, yumming down a hearty English breakfast of congealed fat, paracetamol, and guilt.

"Did you *have* to smash his bottles onto the road?" whispered Bill.

"I got a bit carried away I admit," lamented James. "But it was your idea."

"No, it wasn't. I advocated for covert stealth. Not leaping at the poor sod and taking out several pints of delicious creamy milk."

"Great diversionary tactic though, wasn't it? Besides, screw him, I only did that after I noticed a National Front sticker on his dashboard and an SS tattoo on his massive neck."

"A racist milkman? Well I never. You're right then, fudge him."

"Mind you," said James with a hesitant concern, "this does seem like *a lot* of money for a milk round. *Especially* in the eighties."

"Yeah, nearly four grand in cash for a few bottles of gold top seems a bit jolly unlikely. Oh, buttery puddings, we've stolen a huge amount of money." Bill pored over this information for a few seconds, chewing the inside of his cheek as he did. He then decided that he had enough to worry about without adding a vengeful milky to the mix.

James leant back in his formica chair. He surveyed the cafeteria with a suspicious eye, still not convinced he was residing back in the past.

"This place is *exactly* the same," he observed. "Same shitty furniture, same terrible food. Harry looks like he's *always* looked. Bloke must have been born in his late fifties." James motioned to the solemn-faced owner in a pale green cardigan. The lines etched onto his face told of a life lived hard already. Breathing heavily, his moustache bristled with every exhalation.

"Yeah," concurred Bill. "He's either really old looking for his age here or relatively young looking for his age in the future."

The front door opened and a curmudgeonly man in a black peaked cap with a yellow band strolled into the cafe. Bill ducked down onto the surface of the table and hid himself with a wipe-clean menu.

"Holy mackerel James!" he hissed at his friend. "We're done for!"

James rolled his eyes and shook his head.

"He's a traffic warden, not a copper."

"Coffee please, Harry," ordered the traffic warden, and he turned to nod at James and Bill. James gave him a courteous thumbs-up whilst Bill flashed him a petrified rictus grin. The public servant spinal took a step back, perturbed by Bill's deranged looks.

"Mate, just chill," advised James.

"I can't 'just chill'," argued Bill. "You know what I'm like with authority! A toddler in a uniform could command me to eat my own kneecaps and I'd be asking for extra sauce. Hell, a muon could order me around if it was wearing a lanyard."

"What's a muon?"

"If I started explaining now, we might make it back to 2019 in real time."

"Fair enough. Hey! Wonder if our initials have been carved yet?" James ducked under the table to check for the distinctive JH&BL that he'd first stared back at all those years ago. There was no marking. He climbed out from under the table disappointed. "Got a penknife?"

"No, I'm not a Cub Scout," replied Bill, uncharacteristically grumpily.

James frowned. He snatched a butter knife from his plate then crouched down surreptitiously and set to work on the underside of the formica.

"What in the name of streaky bacon are you doing?" seethed Bill.

"One mystery solved! *I* did it. It's the only possible explanation."

James etched deep into the plastic, cutting a curled groove that began the J's tail. Bill grimaced, and hoped Harry wouldn't notice from behind his counter that a middle-aged patron was vandalising one of his precious pieces of furniture. Harry stared blankly at a row of china mugs, oblivious to the damage being meted out. Having finished the J, James was about to start on the ampersand, when suddenly he leapt up from beneath the table, and cracked his head as he did.

"Wait a minute - I don't need to do this! Also, ow."

"What is it?"

"I'm not going to do it. Ever. Why should I? Just because we know it's there in the future doesn't mean we have to slavishly follow some stupid predetermined path."

"So, what? What does that prove?"

"That we're not bound by pre-written nonsense. There's no such thing as 'destiny.' I don't finish that graffiti, and it frees us from having to follow those rules of yours. Just because you've met someone in the present doesn't mean we have to aspire to that particular journey. We're here now, we can do what we like."

"We've been through this," countered Bill. "We already know how it ends."

"Do we Bill? Because I really don't think we do. We're here now literally carving out our own path - well, our own graffiti - and I'm going to change it right now."

James petulantly sat back down under the table and started boring into the plastic again. Only instead of completing the original JH&BL, he carved a crude cock and balls complete with spunk lines and a crescent of hairs. Content with his juvenile thumbing at destiny, he climbed back to his seat and swigged back the remnants of his rancid coffee mug and beamed smugly at Bill. Bill sighed deeply.

"Happy now?" he queried, mockingly.

"Not really, I'm still stuck thirty-five years in the past with only a suspiciously wealthy milkman's wages and no way of returning to my family. But it doesn't mean we have to follow your instruction manual."

"Can we at least use it as rough guidance?"

"If I don't like it, I'm out." bargained James.

"Fine," acquiesced Bill.

Bill retrieved the laminate from his bag, and dusted it off. James eyed the page suspiciously, already distrusting the next clue. Bill acknowledged his friend's protestation with a curt nod but read on.

"BORROW THE WORDS TO TAKE THE WHEELS!"

James sneered at the clue and cracked his knuckles.

"Why the exclamation marks? Just looks obnoxious."

Bill ignored James' antagonistic tone.

"Borrow the words…" Bill ran the clue around his mouth several times. "Borrow words!" he said with a sudden jolt. "Where do you borrow words, James?"

"A library?" replied James, with withering disdain.

"A library, yes!" Bill enthused.

"So, we go to the library to get the car. I get it, great. Where? What car? How?"

"We'll figure that out when we get there."

James motioned to get up. He tenderly brushed his facial injuries and whimpered lightly. Then wondered again where on earth they were going to sleep and shit that night.

Just twenty minutes later, Mandip stood in the Hartnell Library staff quarters, giving employee Simon Colenutt a remarkably brief training brief.

"Our esteemed library manager, and your new boss, Colin Shatterem loves to hate. For him, hating is the best. It doesn't matter who it is, what it is, or the personal cost to him. Hating is his lifeblood, hard-wired into his DNA. Driven by an impulse to loathe, every moment in his life is dedicated to detestation."

Mandip paused, clicked her pen, and allowed herself a small smile. Simon squirmed in his seat. He bit his upper lip, darted his eyes around the small, cramped windowless office, and reached for a non-existent glass of water. Realising no one had poured him one, he simply licked his mouth and cleared his throat. He removed his glasses, wiped the lenses with his tie, popped them back on then nodded for her to carry on.

"As a default setting, some may argue, loathing is easier to deal with. At least you know where you are with an arsehole. It'll shit on you regardless, so be prepared." Simon frowned. He wasn't sure where she was with the similes anymore, but nodded nonetheless.

Mandip carried on.

"Colin is one hundred percent arsehole. Shits constantly and doesn't have a good side. He knows no joy."

"But you just said he loves to hate…"

"Don't interrupt, Simon."

"Sorry."

Mandip huffed at Simon and adjusted her name badge. She wasn't sure her replacement had it in him to take on this role. "An arsehole constantly pouring out shit means you'll need your umbrella up permanently."

"A beautiful analogy. Can see why you work in a library."

"*Worked*, Simon," Mandip corrected. "Also, no one works in a library because they like literature."

"I do."

"And I *did*. But then I worked here. That's why I'm worried about you Simon. This job is not about sorting your *Sophie's Choice* from your Stephen Kings."

Simon pulled at his fingers anxiously.

"Then what *is* this job about?"

Mandip stood up, straightened her skirt, clicked her pen for the final time, and threw it into the wastepaper basket next to Simon.

"It's about pleasing Colin Shatterem. And *that* is it. Welcome to Hartnell Library, Simon. I wish you all the best."

With that, Mandip left the cramped staff room and strode confidently past the front desk. She pushed open the metallic framed door, saw herself out for the final time, and tasted the refreshing air of freedom.

Before the slow-closing door finished its glacial journey back to being shut, Bill & James grabbed the handle and sauntered into the building. Wide-eyed with delight, James surveyed his surroundings and let out a small, excited chuckle. Now *this* was a library! No computers, no automated self-service machines, barely a bright colour in sight, and certainly no posters advertising diversity mornings, baby weighings, or exhibitions featuring local talent vacuums. Just uniformed rows of impractically tall metallic shelving and a damp odour of dead Nans and bibles. Reading reduced to a regimented structure of conformity and joylessness. Even the children's section looked like it had been knocked up by a retired colonel. Walls of dreary storybooks in neat rows sat untouched and unloved by a generation of readers. Laid on the floor was a cartoon elephant rug that smiled wistfully back at a pair of rigid red plastic chairs. A solitary alphabet poster adorned the wall, rounding off the fun-deficient atmosphere of the area.

Bill instinctively wandered over to the children's section. He reflected fondly on his childhood years spent hiding out there, voraciously devouring everything the shelves had to offer. He leafed through a series of educational books emblazoned with the logo 'Young Discovery!' across the cover. The memories of absorbing information *for free* still excited him today.

"I don't remember it like this," said James. "Must have been refurbished, no?"

Bill nodded, annoyed that James could forget his past so easily.

"Libraries gave us power," he whispered to James.

"Didn't have you down as a *Manic Street Preachers* fan," James whispered back, surprised.

"It's a better line than, 'we only want to get drunk'."

"That's the same song. Anyway, we're not here for power, we're here for..."

"SSHHH!"

James and Bill turned swiftly to see their enraged shusher. A tall gentleman with a face of thunder, lightning, and flash floods stood with an indignant gait and long, bony finger to his lips. Bill let out a small tut and sighed.

"Of course, Colin Shatterem," mouthed Bill.

Colin arched his eyebrow in surprise.

"You know me?" he queried with a curious incredulity. Bill found Colin's ability to speak in a barely audible whisper faintly unnerving.

"Who doesn't? You're one of Hartnell's most trusted public servants," Bill bluffed.

Colin showed not a slither of reaction to this flattery. James reasoned that he might make a good poker player, if poker players were supposed to look permanently incensed.

"This is the children's area. Please remove yourselves. You are not children."

Bill and James obeyed sheepishly under Colin's distrustful eyes.

"Simon," he called softly back to the adjacent staff room. Startled, his new employee appeared with an eager fervour bordering on obsequity.

"Yes, Mr Shatterem?"

"Please," hissed Colin. "Call me sir."

"Sorry sir. What can I do for you?"

"Keep your eyes on those two. They are up to something. Do not let them see you."

"Sir," obeyed Simon, and scurried off out of sight.

Bill and James sat at the optimistically labelled 'study desks' - four large chipboard ex-school tables on which yesterday's papers had been discarded. James shrugged at Bill, aware they were still being watched. He motioned to Colin, whose fearsome eyes were still fixed on the pair.

Bill glanced over discreetly and delved into his bag. He brought out a pad and pen and scribbled quickly onto the page. He turned the pad towards James.

'Motoring section?'

James shrugged then drew a giant question mark back.

Bill glared through his friend, removed the document from his bag and pointed at the clue, 'BORROW THE WORDS TO TAKE THE WHEELS!'

'Oh!' wrote James.

Bill tapped 'Motoring section?' again.

'Where?' replied James on the page.

Bill stood, so James followed him to the rear of the building. They walked past biographies, encyclopaedias, and politics, until they hit the incredibly limited 'hobbies & interests' section. With just a dozen knitting pattern annuals and a guide to wood planing, it looked like Hartnell's spare time might still be going spare for quite a while yet. Convinced they had briefly escaped the loathsome glare of Colin Shatterem, James risked a whisper.

"Who is that?"

"Colin. Library manager. Still is in our time. Less hair now, but just as waspish."

"Not very friendly, is he?"

"His customer service skills *are* somewhat lacking, plus he hates me. Weird to see his bare hands, mind. Never seen without his paedo-gloves in the future. Must be some affectation he picked up."

James, not really listening, looked for the car books, eager to find a pointer to the promised 'wheels'.

"You said this is the motoring section!"

"I thought there'd be something here. Some clue." replied Bill, as he furtively inspected every inch of the building's contents. A gleam of sunshine glared from a reflective surface through the window straight into his eye. He squinted at the bright light and adjusted his gaze. Bill smiled and pointed to the rear window. "Oh James, this *is* the motoring section."

James turned on his heels and looked outside the smoky glazed pane. Immediately behind the building was the staff car park, a small square of concrete just large enough to accommodate six family saloons. Parked in a space marked with 'Manager' with the easiest access in and out was the Triumph in glorious sludge brown.

James gasped at the sight. Bill raised his eyebrows and smirked.

"Holy shit," whispered James.

"That's our car," replied Bill. "Well, it's *someone else's* car, specifically Colin's. But that's the one in the book. The same car currently burned out and nestled under a bush a mile out of town."

James' forehead wrinkled as his brain tried to follow the timeline.

"How are we going to take it? Outside of *Grand Theft Auto* on the PlayStation, I've never stolen a car."

"Easy," answered Bill, and pulled a key from his pocket. James' jaw fell. "Same key, same car."

"How does that work?"

"For once I'm not interested in the how, let's just grab it and go."

"Doing quite a lot of stealing today, aren't we?"

The friends made their way back to the library's front desk. Both tried to walk casually out of the front door, but realised that their legs had started to wobble under the pressure. Bill's limp already looked suspicious, but now jelly mode had been activated, he looked like a giraffe still learning to walk. Adrenalin powered through his veins and limbs. Robbing a racist milkman was one thing, but taking a car seemed a whole new level of jail time. He looked over at James for comfort but could tell he was no better. Both trembling with anxiety, they made a clumsy exit, fumbling through the door with hands that wouldn't stop shaking. Both were so preoccupied with terror, neither noticed Simon Colenutt tailing them just a few feet behind.

"Where's the car park?" James stammered.

"Ssh, just keep walking, follow me, we'll get in and go."

"Who's nervous?" James queried, unconvincingly. He farted. "Alright, I am *a bit* nervous."

The pair reached the car park and immediately saw the Triumph. James felt a little sorry for the car, almost as if it was waiting nonchalantly to be stolen. Bill didn't have the time to admire the glossy paintwork or twin headlamps. He groped about sweatily in his pocket for the key and retrieved it.

"You ready?" he gulped.

"Let's do it."

Bill unlocked the driver's side and got in. As he reached across to let in James, a fey voice entirely lacking in authority rang across the car park.

"Stop!" it commanded, pathetically.

James didn't even turn to see who it was. He leapt into the vehicle and bellowed. "Bill, drive!"

Bill froze solid. He cast his eyes into the rear-view mirror and caught sight of a lanky, balding pool cue of a man galloping up the parking bay, a fist raised high.

"Stop!" His reptilian voice scythed through the still summer air. Simon Colenutt appeared to be crying. Bill's heart crashed through his chest cavity.

"Bill, *drive*!" repeated James.

Bill didn't wait to be told again. He twisted the ignition and slammed his foot on the accelerator. The car roared into life and sped off away. Away from the dead-eyed library, the belligerent Colin, and poor, impotent Simon. Neither of the car's occupants dared look back, as they hurtled through the streets until they reached the field where they first arrived. They hid the car pretty much nose-to-bumper exactly as they had its burnt out doppelganger; under a bed of shrubbery and tree branches.

"So, we've followed the clue, and we have a new car," summed up James.

"Yup. So, we do this car up as closely as that car," said Bill, pointing to the wrecked Triumph.

"Then we get the fuck out of 1984?"

Bill nodded.

"Then we get the fudge out of 1984. Right, let's find a B&B," he suggested.

"Sure," replied James, not really listening.

He stared at the shiny new Triumph, itself literally facing its grim near future. He was beginning to know how it felt.

CHAPTER 14

2019

Nigel Stanton was having a considerably better time of it than his son was three and half decades prior. A piping hot shower with generous handfuls of shampoo had seen him transform from withered and beaten to the same sprightly zest he felt just earlier that day. He applied a cloud of baby powder to his pampered balls and reflected on his new family's reaction to his arrival. Engineering getting his face pummelled to a paste had been painful, but essential. They were all still confused, sure, but Susan's sexy wink had confirmed that he had pretty much got away with it. And who gives a fuck about kids anyway? Not him!

The next chapter of his deception was the harder part. One that, he noted with thrill in his veins, would require his harder part. It was all very well convincing someone suffering from shock that the bloodied-up mess was their long-term partner, especially given he had police backup on that one. Trying to get a leg over might take more than a bruised face and confusion. As he patted down his scrawny legs, he realised he might need the cover of dark for a bit longer. At least, just long enough for Susan to fully embrace him for good.

He wrapped the towel around his body, turned off the bathroom light, and headed for the bedroom. Sat on the bed was Susan. Holding a wide chalice of red wine, she slowly swirled the liquid around against the bulbous glass. Nigel stopped to lock eyes with her. He felt his prick press against the towel.

"OK?" he enquired.

"No James, I'm not," began Susan. "I had a really hard day at work, then my husband goes missing, he turns up later looking like he spent the last decade trapped in a tumble dryer, our kids are confused and frightened, and…" She paused to lower her voice. "I'm absolutely gagging for some."

Nigel's erection started to push the cloth apart. Susan turned away and quaffed back her wine. Nigel reached to hold her head for a kiss, but she backed off, startled.

"But," he protested.

"James," she resisted. "Let's not rush."

Nigel gurned in desperation.

"You're right, no rushing," he lied.

"I'll go downstairs for another one of these," she said, waving the now empty glass. "You put some clothes on, and we'll make a night of it. If you're up for it, that is, given your injuries. Are you ok with that?"

"Susan, you could cut my foot off and punch me in the cock and it'd still be a yes."

"How about we let the dice decide what we do?"

Nigel's face froze in bewilderment. *What was she on about?*

"Dice?"

"Has it really been that long since we rolled the dice?"

Nigel's rictus bafflement confirmed it had been.

"You know, you write your fave sex things down numbered one to six, and I'll write mine. Then we roll and take it in turns. James, I'm worried you're not right, perhaps we shouldn't do this?"

"Oh! The dice! Of course!" exclaimed Nigel in ersatz triumph. "No, we should definitely do the dice thing, certainly."

"OK, I'll be downstairs. Give me a few minutes," she purred. Nigel nodded obediently and watched her leave. As soon as the door shut, he punched the air in celebration and danced a small jig. His boner popped through his towel, and he fell over trying to unwrap himself.

Five agonising minutes later, Nigel headed downstairs as casually as his libido would allow. He'd found some pyjama style trousers in a drawer plus a loose flannel shirt. No need for pants, he thought. He had scrawled his six things on a pad he found in James' bedside cabinet. Handy to have a writer for a son. He crept into the living room and opened the door gingerly. The lights were dimmed (yes!) and Susan perched on the end of the sofa, two wine glasses in hand. One very much nearly drained, the other almost overflowing.

"Might take the edge off your injuries," she suggested, and offered the full glass to Nigel.

"Cheers." Nigel swigged the entire glass back in one mouthful. His Adam's apple vibrated as the alcohol glided down his throat.

Susan fiddled with her phone and the room suddenly filled with the low thrum of music. *The Police*'s 'Walking on the Moon' struck up its familiar bass riff and Nigel smiled lasciviously.

"Nice, good choice," said Nigel. "Love a bit of these boys."

Susan produced her piece of paper. "Have you done your list?" she asked in a low whisper.

Nigel nodded and raised his eyebrows as if he was Robin Askwith who'd just won the sex lottery. He reached into his pocket and pulled out a tatty folded note.

"And we'll do it all here, yeah?" he confirmed.

Susan waved a little red die at Nigel and shot him a lustful gaze.

"As long as it lands on the dice."

Nigel winked at his "wife" and the two swapped notes.

Nigel leant back into the sofa and opened Susan's list of numbered sexual requests. He took a short look down the page and his blood went cold. In neat handwriting Susan had written:

1. Back tickles
2. Sensual massage
3. Long slow kisses
4. Hair strokes
5. Neck nibbles
6. Staring into each other's eyes

Nigel felt faint and re-read the list twice. A hot drench washed over his palms as he bit into his fingernails.

Susan opened Nigel's list.

1. Up the arse
2. Up the arse
3. Up the arse
4. Up the arse
5. Up the arse
6. Up the arse

Nigel didn't dare look across to her. She exhaled deeply, then rolled her eyes over to the man responsible for this delightful gesture. Nigel cleared his throat.

"So, you've gone very much for the romantic angle I see." he said.

"Yes," agreed Susan. "Whereas you've very much centred on…"

"The arse, yes," agreed Nigel. He hung his head a little puppyish in an attempt at contrition.

"I mean," began Susan "I don't know where to start."

"Well, you have to be pretty relaxed and lubed up at first…"

"Not the sex, James! I meant with your list."

Nigel cursed his stupidity and went to say something else, but he knew he'd only make matters worse. He was certain he'd ballsed up sex with Susan now. He wanted to punch himself in the cock, but felt that he'd let that organ down enough already. Besides, he was feeling bloody woozy anyway. That wine had gone straight to his head. The horizon became unbalanced as he moved his limbs sluggishly to pinch at his own face. He looked up at Susan, who was now somehow towering right in front of him, looking nervous.

"Bloody hell, how long does this take?" she scowled, to Nigel's confusion.

Nigel blinked a few times. He felt alarmingly sleepy. The walls drifted into the floor, and he thought his head might float away. Small clusters of bright sparkling lights exploded into his vision and he struggled to keep his eyes open. Had he been...drugged? Without warning, Susan leapt on top of him. Which would be the result he was after if she wasn't strangling him with a belt.

"Sue!" he spluttered through gasps of air.

"Where's my husband, you motherfucker!" she hissed as she pulled the leather strap around his neck. Nigel stumbled to his feet, but the combination of intoxicant and oxygen deficiency meant he was barely able to shake off his attacker. Susan landed some minor punches to his head, but her small fists were more annoying than effective. He struck out like an angry, confused bear and hit Susan on the back, winding her. Startled, she dropped the belt and fell back to the floor. More determined than ever, she reached angrily for anything to hand to subdue her faux husband. She grasped the empty wine glass and pushed it into Nigel's chest. The glass shattered upon impact, pressing hundreds of razor-sharp shards into his skin. He screamed as he recoiled back into the Christmas tree, taking family photos with him. Sue grabbed the bottle and thumped it into his head. It made a terrific smack against his skull but didn't break. Nigel's eyes rolled back a little, and he vomited onto the carpet.

Breathing heavily as her heart pounded through her ribcage, Susan wasted no time and double-tapped the stranger. The bottle shattered this time. She tied his hands with the belt then produced another from her dress, and secured his feet together. It was somewhat sloppy, but she was hopeful his anaesthetised state would take care of the rest. Nigel burbled through the procedure, barely conscious, but still not out cold.

Confident he was sedate and secure enough, she grabbed Nigel's shoulders and with an ungodly summoning of strength, pulled his limp body from the floor to the sofa. She quickly tidied up the carnage of their brief scuffle before returning to the prisoner.

Susan sat up Nigel and threw a small cupful of cold water into his face.

"Who are you? And where is my husband?"

Nigel convulsed then spat on the floor.

"Shit," seethed Susan.

Nigel's bruised eyes opened a little, and he glared at Susan. Only minutes had passed yet they seemed so different now. Every last vestige of charm had drained from his visage; just a thin, angry mouth and angry, pitiless eyes peering out from the bloodied mess of a face. His lips curled into a snarl as he stared through her pupils and straight to her soul.

"How did you know?" he asked in a low, disappointed growl.

"Are you kidding me? I know my husband innately. Ridiculous to think you could have got away with it. But whilst you're here, just off the top of my head - my husband doesn't take sugar in tea, doesn't drink wine, and most importantly, he hates *The Police*."

"Bet he loves it up the arse though," sneered Nigel.

"Who the fuck are you?"

Nigel tutted mockingly. "Oh, Susan darling. Such bad language for a lady."

"Don't try me you creepy bastard, I'll mash your balls to a fine paté. Now where's James?"

Nigel bristled with frustration, and curled his hands into tight, bony fists.

"I can't believe I've let myself get into this position. Especially given the position I was thinking of just a moment ago. Much more agreeable. Well, not so much for you. Suppose that's all academic now." Susan glared at Nigel for an answer. "Look, your husband is safe and well. He just can't get to the phone right now."

"Tell me where he is."

"He's safe, I just told you."

Susan had had enough of this interloper. She jabbed a thumb into Nigel's bruise just beneath his eye. He yelped in agony and instinctively tried to bite her in retaliation.

"I'll scream!" he threatened. "I'll wake up your kids and the whole street and you'll be locked up as a feminist nutter you mad bitch!"

Susan sighed, leant right into Nigel's face, and whispered. "I've dealt with bastard governors, bastard parents, and bastard OFSTED inspectors. One extra bastard is just playtime for me."

Nigel saw his opportunity and swung his head at Susan. He cracked his skull hard against the bridge of her nose. She flew back as the pain burst through her face and spread instantly across her whole head. Her eyes began to stream uncontrollably. Dazed and confused, and before she could take stock of the situation, Nigel had leapt from the sofa and thrown himself at her. His hands wriggled free of the poorly tied belt and pushed Susan's head onto the floor. She grabbed his arm, but his other had reached under the sofa and removed out something heavy and metallic. He pressed it against her forehead and pulled her hair back. Susan froze as she realised what she was staring down. Nigel pulled back the hammer on the pistol. Susan shuddered as it clicked.

"No more silly bollocks," insisted Nigel. "You will do as I say from here on in. Or I will make orphans out of my grandkids up there."

Susan heard the words, but they didn't quite sink in. Nothing about them made any kind of sense.

"What did you just say? Grandkids?"

"Let's start again then, shall we? I'm Nigel Stanton. Your other half's old man. Your father-in-law. Delighted to make your acquaintance."

CHAPTER 15

1984

Bill woke with a shudder. His limbs ached, eyes had crusted over, and there was a faint smell of sulphur in the room. He wiped the gunk from his tear ducts and hoped yesterday had been an awful nightmare. He took in his surroundings, which included a tatty bureau, a musky wardrobe, and a coin-operated black and white television on a rickety chair. Nope, not a nightmare. Reality. Stupid reality.

A tuppenny bed and breakfast with a no-questions-asked policy and net curtains that were more hole than thread, the dilapidated Victorian town house's only benefit was that it suited Bill and James' immediate needs.

Bill turned to look at James occupying the bed next to him. His friend lay glumly on the mattress, already wide awake.

"Morning," he said drily.

"Sleep well?" enquired Bill.

"Not really," answered James. "Too worried, too uncomfortable, too much snoring."

"Sorry, I'm a bit sinus-ey" apologised Bill.

"No worries, mate. What's the plan?"

"We need to get back to 2019, agreed?

"Agreed."

Bill leapt out of bed, his testicles flapping in his boxer shorts. James looked away and covered his mouth.

"To recap then, we discovered a book in 2019 that was written presumably in this very year, 1984. It contains a photo of a car we've just stolen."

"In the absence of any better explanation, I guess."

Bill paced the small gap between the beds, clutching his collar with one hand and pointing the air decisively with the other.

"So, we need to get a photo of you for the book."

James brushed back his buoyant quiff, and beamed broadly for an imaginary camera, together with a coquettish game show host wink. His smile dropped suddenly. "Hang on, I'll have to write the fucking thing, won't I?"

Bill pointed at his friend.

"You're the writer, I'm the scientist."

"But I don't know anything about cars!"

"Surely you don't know anything about half the stuff you write about?"

"In 2019, yes, but that's where I've got the internet. It basically does all the work for me."

Bill netted his fingers together delicately.

"I'm sorry James, but I've got to - you know - build a time machine! You need to write a few pages on old cars. Think you can manage that? Meanwhile I'll fix up the Triumph as swiftly as possible to get us back to the present."

"OK," James responded unenthusiastically. He reached across to his bedside table, grabbed a short glass of clouded room temperature water and knocked it back with a weary glower.

"Meanwhile," cajoled Bill. "Why don't you try to enjoy yourself a little in this decade, eh?"

"Take in a miner's strike, write to Jimmy Savile?"

"That sort of thing, sure! But why not? The time machine will take a few days, given I'm building from scratch. Treat it as a holiday."

James grunted non-commitally, stretched, then got up. He was still in yesterday's clothes and had started to smell like bad ham.

Each took turns in the B&B's sorry excuse for a shower, which was more a pipe with a leak than your average Mira. They then headed down for a disappointing breakfast of dry hard-boiled eggs and warm pineapple juice. The monotonous drone of Radio 1 buzzed over the small radio from the kitchen, much to Bill's annoyance.

"Urgh, Mike Read. This silly teacake will end up writing a racist song promoting UKIP. Remember?"

"I try not to," murmured James, attempting to keep his egg down.

Their host, a wiry lady with her hair tied sharply into a bun, busied around the pair, and collected their plates.

"Will you gentlemen be staying another night?" she queried, with just a hint of impatience.

"Alas, I will not," confirmed Bill. "But my friend here shall be. I'll square up shortly, then leave James here to settle the remainder of his stay."

James simply stared at Bill, incredulous. He waited until the host had left the dining room before confronting his friend.

"Mate, what the shit? Where are you going? Why am *I* staying at the guest house of doom?"

Bill wiped toast crumbs from his face, then using the serviette, waved away his pal's worries.

"James, I think we should spend a bit of time apart."

"Sorry, this sounds like you're breaking up with me. Just to be clear, we're not dating, Bill."

"Very funny James. I just need to work alone to get the time machine up and running. I can't do that with you there. Besides, a bit of time to explore might do you good. I'll be done in four days. Five tops."

"Right. It definitely sounds like you're breaking up with me."

"Well, in that case I promise you the make-up sex will be dynamite."

James smiled begrudgingly and got up to leave.

"Where are you going to sleep then?"

"Wherever I can get the machine up and running," said Bill. "I'm not planning on sleeping much."

"Can we just spend today together? Please?" begged James.

Bill sucked hard on his teeth and folded his napkin slowly.

"I suppose we do need to get the clothes for the shoot, and I'll have to take the photo."

"Attaboy Bill!"

James and Bill spent the rest of the morning in and out of shops together, marvelling at the new of the old. They headed first to a toy store, and took their time perusing shelves, tangibly exploring their own childhoods. James picked up a Care Bear and gently caressed the heart-shaped logo on its bottom. His fingers had managed to grasp an emotion he hadn't felt since he was in infant school: the assuring safety net of parents plus the joyful bliss of zero responsibility. He hoped all children experienced this comfort blanket of childhood. Though he knew that wasn't even possible in his hometown, let alone around the world. He put the Care Bear down gently and felt his eyes sting a little.

Bill inspected a row of immensely ugly felt baby-faced dolls encased in banana yellow boxes wrapped in thick, clear plastic.

"These little wankers started riots," James bemoaned, shoving a Cabbage Patch Kid into Bill's horrified face.

"I'd start a riot if I got one for Christmas."

The pair moved on, oddly dispirited by the experience. They strolled down the high street and took in Britain's mid-nineteen eighties shop facades. Colourful yet sterile, the charmless rows of aggressive corporate retail had sucked dry any unique character the town centre once had.

"Dunno, is stepping back into the past all that?" asked James, a wilting tremor to his voice.

"How do you mean?" questioned Bill as they walked into Boucher's Clothing, Hartnell's large family-run department store.

"Nostalgia's one thing, sure. But actually visiting, being part of it…"

James left the thought hanging without resolution, and merely pointed to their environment. The store screamed at them in beige. Rows of drab floral pinny dresses and starched petticoats had been arranged neatly beside price signs in washed-out magnolia.

"Time travelling isn't like some nostalgic clip show or themed nightclub. Did you spend every day of the nineteen eighties watching *Transformers* and drinking New Coke?"

James shook his head.

"Exactly," said Bill. "This is real life, not a thumbnail."

"Boucher's Clothing" said James, his voice barely a whisper. "The Venn diagram of middle class and middle aged that's just a perfect circle."

Bill nodded his head in agreement.

They headed hopefully to the men's section and pulled out various outfits roughly analogous to the one James had worn in the photo. They didn't have the remainder of *Car Classic: the 1970s* on them, and neither could remember the image exactly. It was all academic anyway, as the picture they needed had been scorched from the planet by the time machine's beam. Bill grabbed fistfuls of woollen jumpers, functional shirts, and impossibly straight trousers. James took the lot and grabbed armfuls of socks and pants too.

"Shoes?" offered Bill and waved a pair of pointed brown brogues at James.

"Hmm, I'll try them on," deliberated James. "But I'm not convinced I'll need them." He noticed the size - nine and a half. "Mate, I'm a ten," he complained. "It was the one thing Nigel always boasted. 'You'll inherit my size tens', he'd say, as if a foot length was the only thing he could bestow on me."

"You look more like a nine and a half," said Bill.

James scowled at his friend as his foot slipped perfectly into the open shoe.

"Well, that's disappointing. Was convinced I had bigger feet. I feel vaguely offended by that. Like having your dick downgraded to 'fun size'."

"Fun for who exactly?"

"Well, not her, clearly."

James stood up in his outfit. Slimline brown trousers, navy blue shirt, and a green pullover with cream piping completed the look.

"How do I look?"

"Like a rubbish Doctor Who."

"Peter Cushing? I wish!"

"He's not canon. Let's just grab this lot and head on," insisted Bill, who had simply pulled three identical grey suits from a rack.

"Shopping Isn't really your thing, is it?" observed James.

"No. I like science, reading, and reading about science. Retail is simply a means to an end."

"Also, shopping means store detectives! Bet you shit yourself whenever you see one."

"I'm not keen, I'll give you that. But whilst we're on the long arm of the law, I'm not convinced we should stay in any one place for too long. Our misdemeanours may get us noticed."

"Hadn't thought of that. You're right, let's go." James grabbed some children's clothes, then pulled a pair of drainpipe jeans from a neighbouring shelf and headed to the till, still wearing his purchases.

Following a good rummage around town and plenty more shopping, James and Bill settled on a park bench next to the town's parish church. They chugged back cans of Quatro, ploughed their way through packets of Puffs crisps, and munched various small, perfumed sweets that tasted like caramelised air freshener.

The pair then headed to their stolen car for a Polaroid photoshoot both would rather forget in a hurry. (They spent the best part of an hour arguing whether James was giving a thumbs-up with his right or left thumb. It was such a protracted and pointless bickering session neither could remember which side they were on by the time it ended.)

The friends finally staggered back to the B&B as the late afternoon sun blazed across their backs. Bill helped James into the room with his belongings, then split the remaining money. He turned to leave almost immediately.

"Hang on," protested James. "You can't just go! That's ridiculous."

"I'm off to the Triumph. I've got to get started now. We've both got plenty of money and then some for a week. Oh, and turn your phone off."

"I haven't got my phone on!" lied James.

"You were taking photos of the He-Man figures! Look, you might need it, and we've got no way of charging it. It's not like there's 5G coverage in 1984 anyway."

James dug his phone out of his pocket and checked the battery. 59% wasn't bad, but Bill was right, dammit. He had no idea how long he might be here. He reluctantly turned it off, slumped down onto the bed, and flicked the kettle's switch to make a Pot Noodle.

"It's fine," he sighed. "I'll see if *Top of the Pops* is on. Might see Dexy's, Madness, or if I'm lucky, a sex offender."

Sensing his pal's ennui, Bill tried a little reassurance.

"My friend, we *will* get home. It'll be like we never left."

James gave Bill the most insincere thumbs-up in history, and peeled the lid wearily from his dehydrated snack.

"And one last thing, James," Bill softened his voice. "I can't imagine how strong the urge is, but please, please don't…"

"…attempt to meet up with my Mum?" interrupted James, guessing correctly.

Bill nodded solemnly.

"Bill, if the thought occurred to you then you can bet your enormous brain and tiny wang I've thought it too." He looked away from Bill's gaze.

"You won't though, will you?"

James said nothing.

"Because no good can come of it," insisted Bill. "We're not supposed to be here. We can't interfere with our own family's timelines. One wrong move, one tiny rupture to the fabric of time, and we could disappear from existence."

The room stayed silent save for the kettle's struggle to heat its contents.

James cleared his throat pointedly.

"Don't worry, I'll get this book together, somehow."

"Somehow?" queried Bill.

"Well, I'm going to need to write it properly, if it's going to sit on the shelves for the next thirty-five years. No chance of a quick Google, and I can't exactly go waltzing into the library for research. That mad bastard might just want a word about his car we stole. No worries, I'll just have to go old school."

"Old school?"

"Yeah, just copy someone else's work."

"Like you used to do to me?"

"Exactly!" beamed James, and he gave his friend a little salute and turned back to preparing his snack.

"Remember old boy, keep your family distant!" reminded Bill.

"You have my word, 'old boy'!" shouted back James, as he dug both hands hard into his pockets and crossed his fingers.

Bill left his friend with his Pot Noodle and headed back to the Triumph.

Once James had downed his plastic cup of heart-troublingly salty hot rubber bands he immediately took the next bus to Alfred's Valley with the express intention of seeing his Mum, the massive liar.

CHAPTER 16

2019

Susan laid rigid on the bed, a confusing and unwelcome mix of fear and fury. Tension clouded her body as her fists clenched defensively. She felt the raw pain surge through the bridge of her nose. Despite this, she didn't think it was broken; it was more likely the surprise of the attack rather than the power. Her veins ached with the rush of adrenalin. Every nerve ending throbbed with discomfort. The pure shock of what this intruder had just confessed clattered about her brain. She tried to make sense of any of it.

Nigel paced the bedroom as much as his injuries would allow. He clutched the gun tightly and bit his yellowing fingernails. Looking for a hanky to mop up his bloodied chest, he pulled open a drawer. Faced with Susan's underwear, he leered at the lingerie momentarily then slammed it shut.

"I'm going to the bathroom to get cleaned up," said Nigel. "You try anything, you know what happens."

He returned just minutes later to find Susan in exactly the same position; utterly immobile, but for her breathing. Nigel had wiped himself down and tended to his wounds. He still looked like a peach that had been kicked across a mile of sandpaper, but at least he was no longer dripping blood everywhere. He offered Susan a damp flannel. She flinched as the cloth went near her. Sensing her nervousness, Nigel laid it gently next to her then stepped back.

"It's alright," he said softly. "As long as you behave, no harm will come to any of you."

Susan trembled slightly, then arched her back in venomous defiance.

"No man has ever attacked me," she said, plainly.

"Self-defence," disagreed Nigel.

"*No man has ever attacked me,*" she repeated, with a little more confidence.

"Self-defence," insisted Nigel.

"'Self-defence?'" Susan repeated, disgusted. "Look, are you going to…" Susan looked down, terrified to say any more.

Nigel protested in mock indignation. "Woah there! You think I would force myself on you? Trust me, I would never do that."

"You tried to have sex with me by pretending to be someone else. How can I trust you?" Susan had shaken off the fear and instead opted for outrage.

"But you would have done it willingly!" chuckled Nigel.

Susan gasped in disbelief. Perhaps this guy really was from thirty years ago? Given his attitude, it was the only thing that made sense. This guy didn't consider sex by deception as deviant in the same way that, say, Henry VIII never considered marriage counselling.

"Well, what do you want with me? And who really are you?"

"I just want to get to know you, Susan. And I've told you, I'm Nigel Stanton, James' Dad."

Susan rolled her eyes then stared deep into Nigel's.

"You've entered our home under false pretences, tried to delude me into bed, assaulted me, have my husband kidnapped christ-knows-where, and now you expect me to believe you're my long-lost father-in-law?

You're not even old enough! How stupid do you think I am? How little must you think of women in general? Jesus!"

Nigel relaxed his stance a little, then rubbed the back of his neck thoughtfully.

"I didn't ask for any of this. Your fuckhead husband - my only son, that I know of - turns up in 1984 with his curly-haired mate spouting shit about time travel. And now I'm here and he…" Nigel paused to choose his next words carefully. "He is elsewhere."

Susan pondered Nigel's explanation with a pinch less cynicism.

"Curly-haired mate? Bill? Bill was with him?"

Nigel grinned.

"You believe me?"

"I'm not saying that, just trying to establish facts."

"Yes, Bill. He's the sciencey one. James couldn't wire a plug, let alone work a time machine."

Susan felt her blood chill and eyesight blur as the realisation embedded itself into her consciousness. James had casually mentioned time travel in the kitchen a couple of days ago, but she assumed he was talking nonsense, as usual. She remembered Bill and James' strange sexual conversation in the kitchen about Bill's Mum. She had dismissed it as their usual adolescent ramblings, but their clandestine clamming up now made horrid sense.

"James *can* wire a plug actually," was all she could think of retorting. "As long as he watches it on YouTube first. Then I often get a little man to check it over, you know." Susan surprised herself with how easily she was suddenly conversing with this ugly newcomer. If he was who he said he was, perhaps the familial link made her naturally connect with him more organically than a total stranger. Perhaps.

"Why pick a fight with a busker?"

"I had to get my face smashed in to pretend to be my son, plus get picked up by the police, I didn't know where you lived."

"So, what now? And where's James?"

"All in good time, flower!" Nigel perked up immediately. "Let's see what tomorrow brings, eh?"

"Tomorrow brings a nightmarish school trip to a zoo."

"Well, don't go. Call in sick."

"I can't just call in sick. That's not how teaching works."

"Tell them you're a paedophile. They'll gladly let you have the day off then."

"What?"

Nigel smiled thinly.

"Joke."

"No jokes," begged Susan, thinking that was exactly the sort of tasteless crack James might make.

Nigel hovered with unease.

"Well, I'll come along. Just say James has a day off and wants to help."

"No, you can't just come along on a school trip. It's not Bring-Your-Pretend-Husband to Work Day. You've not been security cleared, you'll get in the way, it's weird, and no. Besides, James picks up the kids from school. There's no way I'm letting you near the children."

"They can come too!"

"No, that won't be happening."

"Well, I'm definitely coming," Nigel ordered. Sue noticed a flicker of irritability flash across his eyes and remembered the gun.

"Right. Well, I'll have to see about someone else picking up the kids then."

"Excellent!" declared Nigel in triumph. "Right, let's get some much-needed shut-eye, eh?"

She lay on top of the covers, still fully clothed, seething at the man in her bedroom. Oblivious, Nigel climbed into James' side and laid the gun down next to his head. With any luck, thought Susan, he might accidentally blow his brains out in the middle of the night. And then what? Traumatised children, a lifetime of explanations, and never getting to know where James is and losing any hope of getting him back. No, she would have to ride this out. Tease out some more information then pick her moment carefully.

And by 'picking her moment', she meant kicking him so hard in the nuts they evaporate on contact.

CHAPTER 17

1984

James sat on the front seat at the top of the bus and peered into the glass window periscope at the driver's head below. Every once in a while, the thinning pate would change into a pair of bloodshot eyes and stare back. Generally though, the guy with the steering wheel was unbothered by his passengers on the top deck.

James fumbled with his coat buttons, unsure of himself. Balding driver notwithstanding, he knew what was driving him and why. James' Herculean urge to see his childhood home in its raw 1984 state was a feverish compulsion that outstripped any semblance of common sense he'd been holding onto since they arrived in this year. He wanted to see the avenues, smell the dinners, and dive into that life of a carefree child with no responsibilities.

As the bus made its familiar journey James took a glance for any major changes that may have un-occurred over the past three decades. Since demolished buildings stood tall, modern housing estates had been replaced by bramble-strewn fields, and a total absence of speed cameras gave the landscape an almost frontier-like feeling. The bus made a perilous bend around a quarry whose precious commodity - whatever it was -

hadn't been mined in either decade. Only the steel gates and CCTV were missing.

The vehicle finally made the steep descent down into Alfred's Valley. James' stomach lurched along with the geography. If he felt anachronistic being there in the modern day, what would actual 1984 do to his temperament? He'd find out soon enough as the bus wound its way down past the town's outer edge woodland, the retirement complex, and the children's playpark where classmate Steve O'Brien once claimed to have fingered his own sister.

James couldn't tell if it was nerves, the journey, or the memory of Steve trying to push his stinky fish digit under his nose, but the queasiness reached intolerable levels as his stop came into view. He pushed the bell and made his way down the steps and to the front of the bus and thanked the driver for his services.

Out on the street, the warm summer evening greeted his neuroses with a welcoming calm. He trembled with every emotion his senses could muster. A jitter of fear, a pang of melancholy, and the thrill of anticipation all gripped his mind at once. He glanced down his road and drank in the view. These were the streets where he rode his first bike, had his first beer, cried sometimes, and laughed a lot. He also lost Nina's skateboard to an oncoming lorry when he lost control of it. She never let him forget that.

A couple walking up the road caught James' attention, and he instinctively shrank back behind a lamppost. He recognised them instantly: it was Bill's parents. The man wore an ill-fitting cream suit, the trousers of which bothered his ankles. A heist's worth of jewellery adorned his neck and fingers. Alongside him a lady dressed in a patchwork frock of violent, clashing colours. Her teased bouffant of rusted orange hair remained utterly unmoved by a sudden gust of wind, even though it blew a lit cigarette clean from her overpainted lips.

"Oh, fuckin' teacakes, Cecil!" spat the woman.

Cecil looked across, and drew a large gummy guffaw, his bushy moustache trembling as he chuckled.

"How many times have I told you to keep in your fucking mouth, Bunny?!"

"Gis' another!" asked Bunny. Cecil obliged, and drew a Benson & Hedges from a carton in his jacket pocket. The two ambled on into the evening.

James could feel the sweat inch down his back. This wasn't mere nostalgia, he reasoned. He had idly watched old television adverts and played classic video games for that simple slice of sense memory. That was a repackaged snapshot of the past, nothing more. This tangible third dimension in crawling actively through the years gone by was an eerie mess. He wasn't sure he'd necessarily recommend it.

James shuffled slowly to his childhood home; number 24, or as his Mum had affectionately christened it, The Christmas Eve house. A plain, utterly nondescript terraced three-bedroom house to anyone else, but to him, the entire building blocks of his childhood. He stood by the edge on the neighbours' drive so as not to be detected and stared at the front room window. The television's soft amber glow filtered through the cheap net curtains. James could picture his younger self inside sitting cross-legged, scoffing Bombay mix and petting the family dog, Ace. Memories of his Mum, Christmases past and future, and family get-togethers swam through his mind. His spine stiffened up, yet arms loosened. He screwed his eyes up as a debilitating fog charged through his skull and screamed at him to let this go.

Just as he was thinking better of this maudlin detour, the front door opened. James leapt back behind the neighbour's wall and crouched down out of sight. His jaw dropped as he spied the very last person he wanted to see: Nigel Stanton. Decked in double denim, the tall figure swaggered out of the house clutching a packet of tobacco and a set of keys. James felt a whirlwind of resentment whip up inside his heart. It stopped immediately then broke a little instead. For directly behind his dad, was the unmistakable figure of his Mum.

Time stood still for James. His Mum. His real, living, breathing Mum: Rose Stanton. He hadn't seen her alive for the past agonising year. In his present she was nothing more than memories, stories, photos, and one short, treasured video clip of her reading The Guardian and idly sipping tea. But here she was! Honouring the earth with her presence again, not ravaged by cancer and removed cruelly from existence. And young! So incredibly, improbably young. Her almond eyes sparked with a verve, and shoulder length brunette perm bobbed with every bird-like twitch of her head.

James tried some spontaneous mental arithmetic. Given his terrible maths, he might as well have tried to pull the Shroud of Turin from beneath his foreskin for all the good it would do. All he knew was that she was born in 1948 and it was 1984. The fact that the last two numbers were an inversion of each other only confused things further. But at the very least, he surmised she was younger than him now. That felt *immensely* peculiar.

She trotted out after Nigel, waddling slightly. James had forgotten her funny little walk. James cursed his memory for erasing this delightful detail.

"Nigel, where are you going now?"

"Work, I've got a gig, I told you Rose!" blared back Nigel, irritably.

"You didn't mention that?"

"Well, I'm mentioning it now, aren't I?" Nigel lit a cigarette and exhaled angrily.

"How long are you going to be? Where is it? You've not even got your guitar."

"Bloody hell woman, it's in Hartnell. Guitar's already there. It'll probably be all night so don't wait up."

"How are you going to get...hang on, where's the car?"

"In for a service, I told you."

"No Nigel, you didn't," Rose argued back. She lowered her voice, suddenly aware that the neighbourhood was privy to this public spat. "You didn't bloody well tell me."

"Yeah, well," struggled Nigel in retaliation. "You didn't put the bins out again! Do you even know where the bins are?"

"Do you know where my clitoris is?" screamed Rose, and stormed back into the house.

Both Nigel and James gasped incredulously. Nigel headed off down the street to the bus stop. James tried to process what he'd just witnessed, but noticed the bright lights of the bus on its return journey. He wanted nothing more than to run into his childhood home to spend rhodium-level precious extra time with his Mum. He felt his legs almost start walking towards the door for him. But Bill's advice to leave well alone burned through his impulses and started a fire in his conscience.

It pained him to the very tips of his essence to do so, but he figured he'd best keep tabs on his dad, rather than complicate things with his Mum. Where was the slippery sod off to? Where had been all those times that James had sat alone, watching telly, yearning for his father? Time to find out. He followed his father to the shelter, but kept his distance.

Nigel got on and James followed, much to the surprise of the driver, who had not long dropped him off.

"Your date went badly then?" he chuckled.

"Yeah, your Mum was worn out from the postman," James snapped back, and winked. The driver roared with laughter and shut the doors. James kept his head low and took a seat a few rows behind his dad. He stared after him the entire journey, as he re-lived the past few minutes over and over in his head.

James nearly ground his teeth to a fine powder, and his fingernails dug into the seat fabric, so infuriated was he by the way his dad had dismissed his Mum's concerns. He was, however, impressed that she was clearly no pushover. His Mum had rarely discussed their father after he left. James had never worked out if that meant it was too much to bear or if simply, she wasn't that arsed about him. Tonight's small performance had pointed heavily towards the latter. A droplet of relief poured over his rage and sizzled ever so slightly.

James found himself at the end of another small performance later that evening, as he sat in the almost entirely deserted pub, The Cloven Hoof. With just an acoustic guitar and an overabundance of confidence, his dad belted out bullshit folk covers. Sat as far out of view as possible, James supped a small glass of something brown, warm, and foamy. He clapped limply between each tune. Although enthusiasm far outweighed his ability, Nigel could still play, and the small crowd of barflies and people with nothing better to do were at least receptive to his output. Nigel smoked, winked, and grinned at the audience between songs, his roving eyes paying particular attention to a woman near the front throughout. The set finally finished, Nigel thanked the audience again for their generosity then made a hasty beeline towards the lone woman on the table at the front.

"Nigel," greeted Nigel, in an enviously self-assured manner.

"Ruth", answered Ruth, several shades lighter in certainty. She had no idea how much she would come to regret this meeting the next morning.

James ordered a Coke then coughed through the smoke-filled haze of the bar. Over the next hour he watched his wretched father somehow charm a woman away from her own sense of self-worth. As soon as James couldn't bear to watch any more naked flirting and disingenuous giggling, his father stood up and offered a hand to Ruth. She gripped it uneasily, but followed Nigel nonetheless. Both necked their last drinks and headed for the door.

"Twang," shouted Nigel to the bar. "Can I leave all this?"

"Wossat Nige'?" came a reply.

James kept low but spun round to see who his dad was talking to. James stifled a gasp as he recognised Bobby Twang, future owner of Hartnell's guitar store. His pot belly was a little less pronounced, and huge mop of black hair certainly more prominent, but it was absolutely him. Same sad hangdog eyes he'd always had, although his skin had less the texture of sandpapered leather as it would do in the future.

"Can I leave this stuff here?" asked Nigel again, and pointed to the audio equipment littering the low-level stage.

"Oh, er yeah, sure," said Twang, with all the conviction of a man risking a fart that could be a shit.

Nigel muttered something under his breath, grabbed his guitar and date, then hurried out of the pub. James made tracks after the pair through the Hartnell back alleys. Nigel and his lady friend drunkenly lurched towards their destination in near darkness, as the streetlamps' feeble radiance barely illuminated the pavement. Careful to keep his distance, James almost lost them a couple of times. Luckily, the orange smoulder of Nigel's perennial cigarette made a handy 'twat beacon' for James to follow.

The pair eventually stopped at a building James didn't recognise. They were in the Pemberton district. It was a part of town that had seen huge regeneration in the 1990s, the majority of its dilapidated properties since having met the wrecking ball. This place, James guessed, must have been a deserved victim of that overhaul. A jutting, ugly brick fist of post-war architecture containing a dozen rushed-together flats. Its entire lifespan was barely fifty years, and even that seemed two decades too many. Nigel fumbled for his keys as he made Ruth hold his guitar and lit ciggy. He opened the door and reached for the cigarette from her lips, then brought her close for a long, ugly, and aggressive smooch. James' could feel his fists clench tightly in his pockets. He squeezed so hard he thought his fingers might actually burst. How the fuck was his dad funding a second home?

"Ladies first!" Nigel declared, then smacked her on the backside as she went into the hallway. His hollow, smoker's laugh echoed into the street as he shut the door behind him.

From his vantage point on the street opposite, James learnt against a wall and sucked in the night's unusually dry air. He exhaled deeply, took his hands out of his pockets and straightened the floppy collars on his coat.

Seven hours later, once Ruth had left, he rang on his father's doorbell, then punched him in the face.

CHAPTER 18

2019

The Harpman residence was unusually quiet for a Friday morning. Dawn tended to be a noisy, alarming affair; bodies rushing towards food, showers, and piles of clothes in a mad panic to make the day happen. James would head down first to prepare everyone's daytime meals. He'd sometimes write encouraging little notes to Autumn and Jude, wishing them well on their day, then sneak them into the lunchboxes. For Susan he'd just doodle a penis on her sandwich bag, no matter how many times she asked him not to.

Autumn would follow next with a needlessly long shower, already sliding comfortably into her life's next chapter - adolescence. James would make sure to take Susan a tea: stage one of the Herculean task of rousing his wife. Her devotion to the duvet was legendary. Once she hit the mattress fatigue engulfed her. Waking was a monumental effort; just the simple act of opening her eyes felt like some fiendish biblical punishment. James would take multiple mugs of tea until she acknowledged and sipped one. He could sometimes deliver at least *four* until she stirred. This would be paired with a despairing moan of realisation that the day had begun. Son Jude was much the same, but at least he had the excuse of being only nine years old.

Not today though.

No James.

No noise.

Nigel had snoozed through the alarm, snoring away happily in his new home. Next to him, Susan had barely *blinked* all night, let alone slept. In between bouts of drastic worrying, she had spent the time conjuring up various ways of outwitting, then battering, her captor. She figured that she just needed to get through today. Then she would have the whole weekend to keep her kids as far away as possible from Nigel and get back her husband. Somehow. The stress of it all was hurting. As if today - a school trip to a zoo - wasn't already going to be difficult enough without the added impossibility of a gun-toting maniac in the mix. She poked Nigel in the back to stir him. He merely grunted and shifted his body to face her.

"Nigel," she whispered, testily, and poked him again.

He jerked awake, startled.

"Blurgh," he burbled. His teeth fell out onto the duvet.

"Christ!" shouted Susan and leapt off the bed in a panic.

Nigel wheezed with laughter and thrust the falsies back into his mouth. Susan recoiled in repulsion, then spied the gun on the bed. Nigel followed her eyes to it, stopped smiling, and picked up the firearm.

"Right, we going to the zoo then?" he asked.

Susan shot him a look of pure contempt.

"I need to get dressed."

"Right," Nigel tutted. "I'll give you ten minutes."

"I'll only need two. Autumn and Jude need breakfast and lunches and coercing into their uniform."

"I can do that," Nigel said with a shaky confidence.

"No, just let me get dressed and I'll sort everything. Please keep away from my children as much as possible. They don't need to be part of whatever this is."

"But Susan," objected Nigel. "They're *our* children now." He smiled sinisterly at Susan. She thought about smashing that yellowing toothy grin from his face for good right there and then. But she remembered the gun, and opted to tell him to sod off instead.

Nigel leapt out of bed then opened the door. "Two minutes then," he warned as he stepped out onto the landing. Completely ignoring Susan's request, he banged hard on Autumn's door and bellowed for her to wake up. There was no response, so he tried again. This time a voice piped in from the adjacent bathroom.

"I'm already awake Dad!" shouted Autumn, through plumes of steam.

"Good girl," patronised Nigel.

He turned the handle on Jude's bedroom, then inched his head around the door. The boy lay in deep sleep on his bed in what looked like an immensely uncomfortable position. As if someone had just hurled a box of limbs onto the bed in a panic, Jude had all the dozing grace of a squashed spider. Nigel had no idea how anyone - even a contortionist - could rest in that position. He crept in and, needing to kill a minute, took a good snoop around his grandson's room. Toys of all description lay strewn about the shelves and cupboards, none of which looked particularly cared for. A desk on which something that looked like computer equipment sat, battling for space amongst papers, books, pencils, balls, and hastily discarded sweet wrappers. Nigel stared at a poster of a moustachioed cartoon man in a red cap dancing with a mushroom and wondered what the heck kids were into in this decade.

"Jude," he cooed softly. "Jude, are you awake?" Jude snored, ignoring the intruder. Nigel carried on rummaging through Jude's belongings.

What the hell is a Minecraft? "Guess what?" Nigel continued, as he thumbed through Jude's books about Star Wars and superheroes. "Your Mum's next door, getting naked."

"What?" asked Jude.

"FUCK!"

Jude sat up and giggled. "Dad!"

"Sorry son," said Nigel, gripping his chest. "Didn't know you were awake. You scare your old man like that."

"Is it school today?" asked Jude.

"Yes, get ready," ordered Nigel, still trying to calm down.

Jude threw the bedsheets back over his head and groaned.

"School *again*? I've already gone four times this week."

"That's life, mate," responded Nigel, matter-of-factly.

"What were you saying about Mum just now?" asked Jude from the muffled comfort of his bedsheets.

"Oh, er, just that I love her very much."

"I heard you swear. And you look really bad."

Nigel wrinkled his nose and flicked a V at the bed.

"Love you too, son."

He left the room, knocked firmly on Susan's door and entered without waiting for a response. Susan had just pulled over a jumper and was reaching frantically for a brush. Nigel, annoyed at missing nudity by mere seconds, tried not to show his disappointment.

"Coffee?" he offered.

"I drink tea," replied Susan.

"Suit yourself. I'm making coffee."

Nigel wandered downstairs to the kitchen to help himself to breakfast. He flicked on the kettle and popped some bread into the toaster. If it weren't for those two items, he wasn't even sure this *was* the kitchen. Everything appeared so sterile and featureless. Appliances blended into one another, united by anonymity. Where was the boombox and teasmaid? He explored some more.

Disarmingly, the front room had too appeared a little space-age for his liking; everything seemed to have lights that glowed threateningly. The large yet improbably thin television set, unusual looking boxes beneath, a variety of hand paddles with buttons, a strange small blinking box in the corner of the room, stereo equipment: all had illuminations that pierced the dark with an eerie hue. Nigel was a man of the analogue age; turntables and transistor radios stretched the limits of his technical prowess. Given an iPad he'd merely use it to snort coke off. He walked back into the kitchen, peered into the toaster and watched the bread slowly brown between the red-hot grills. He felt this era mocking his ignorance and contemplated leaving, letting the Harpmans get on with their lives. Then he remembered what drove him here, and why he was determined on revenge.

∽

Half an hour later, and considerably earlier than usual, Susan dropped off Autumn and Jude to their schoolgates.

"But why can't Dad do it?" Jude had protested.

"Your father's still recovering from yesterday's unpleasantness," Susan hastily explained, unable to reveal that their 'father' didn't have the foggiest where the school was.

"But Mum, we're thirty minutes early!" complained Autumn. "And since when did you call Dad 'father'?"

"Kids," Susan snapped, already regretting even engaging with their whining. "Just do as I say. Now it'll probably be Melody's Mum picking you up, ok? She's called Amy - tall, ginger, you've met her countless times. OK? Now repeat what I just said."

"Melody's Mum picking us up," repeated Jude (with a slightly mocking inflection, Susan noticed).

"Amy. Tall. Ginger," confirmed Autumn.

Susan then hugged her children extra tight before delivering them to the mercy of their teachers for the day. As she turned to leave she felt her eyes sting with the welling of restrained tears and pulse quicken. The parental urge screamed through her veins.

She had, of course, considered pelting to the police station to explain what had happened. But then what? In all likelihood, no one would believe her. Conversely, they would think her mad. Then she'd be carted off to the loony bin (or modern politically correct equivalent), whilst James' Dad inherited their life. Not a chance. She trudged back to the house to meet her new nightmare husband with all the enthusiasm of a dog being forced to eat salad.

She arrived back to find Nigel leafing through a family photo album as he chewed thoughtfully on a banana-flavoured chew bar. There certainly was a chimp-like quality to him, pondered Susan, as she stared at his bony arms and perma-furrowed brow.

"He does look a bit like you. But when he smiles, his whole face is an effervescent glow of warmth."

"Ooh, very poetic," said Nigel, jeeringly.

"Whereas you're some sort of malicious, dead-eyed Cheshire cat."

"Done alright for himself, hasn't he? My son, that is," opined Nigel, without bothering to look up. "I mean, here he is with this nice little home, very nice little wife." He looked up, stared Susan directly in the eyes, and licked his teeth.

"He has the love and support of his family, because that's what he gives us."

Nigel looked up and sneered. "You greetings card *wankers*."

"I'm sorry if a happy family is such an artificial construct to you, but it *does* exist. You'd have learned that if you put any effort into your own marriage."

"Shut your mouth-hole," ordered Nigel, and stood up, enraged. "You don't know the first thing about my marriage, and neither does my cumstain son, so butt out."

Susan flinched at Nigel's threatening demeanour, and cursed the fear he instilled in her. She felt best not pursue this line. "We need to leave at least five minutes ago. Are you ready?"

Nigel clapped his hands together in delight, grabbed his gun, then pulled the stetson on tightly around his head.

"Let's go feed some lions!"

CHAPTER 19

1984

Nigel Stanton fell back into the hallway, stunned by both a punch and the last five seconds of his life. An oddly familiar stranger had turned up at his doorstep and assaulted him viciously without a word of explanation.

"Get in," barked James. He jabbed a finger to Nigel and motioned towards his apartment. Still dizzy, and cradling a broken, bloody nose, Nigel did as he was told. This definitely wasn't the sex he'd imagined merely moments before. As he stumbled into the flat's cramped hallway, he launched a limp burst of retaliation, and swung a fist towards his oppressor. It donked lightly on James' head, who merely batted away the spindly limb and shoved Nigel to the floor with a grump.

"Get into the...living room?" James looked confused, clearly not familiar with the dingy layout of Nigel's squalid sex flat. Nigel picked himself up and slumped into a wiry brown couch. He knocked an ashtray onto the floor with a depressing flump of fag butts and ash.

"Look," began Nigel, "As you can see, I don't own much. But take what you want. Not the guitar, obviously," he added, his head bowed and whimpering slightly.

He gestured pathetically around the mostly bare room. His attacker took a withering peek at Nigel's possessions. A small coffee table with neatly arranged ashtrays and bar towels cowered beneath the room's dim lighting. Behind it sat a small portable television set, a tuning dial long since snapped off. A small record player shared floorspace with a sheepskin rug (the former owner of which looked as if it died giving birth). Then there was the surprisingly decent Gibson acoustic guitar.

James rolled his eyes, sighed, and dumped down a rucksack.

"We need to talk."

Nigel's brow furrowed rigidly. It was in danger of crushing his skull beneath it. Silence hung in the air awkwardly, as he licked his teeth. He brought a hand up slowly. James thought he might try to hit back again. Instead, he started scratching his nuts.

"So," began James.

"So what?" shot back Nigel, astonished. "You just punched your way in, and now you want a chinnywag? You're Radio Rentals, pal."

James winced at the slang, and dug his hands into his pockets. Nigel recoiled back, expecting his assailant to pull out a gun. He wasn't exactly sure why; he'd never been anywhere near a firearm in his entire life, though he suspected many an aggrieved husband would like to remedy that.

"So, I'm..." James halted, took a breath. "I'm your son. I'm James. I've come from the future."

Nigel pulled a face as if he'd just been asked to knit a woolly hat using only dead men's cocks. James produced what looked like a pocket calculator. Oh god, was he from Inland Revenue?

"If this is about the tax on the Allegro?"

"What? No, don't be ridiculous."

"I'm the ridiculous one?" deadpanned Nigel, at least partially relieved it wasn't a debt matter.

James held up the device for Nigel to see. "This is a mobile phone."

Nigel mouthed the words 'mobile phone' back to him, flummoxed.

"We all have them where I'm from," assured James.

"Which is the future?" affirmed Nigel, and whistled the *Star Trek* theme.

James nodded, then spoke slowly with an ice-cold assertiveness that bordered on militance.

"On this phone from - yes - the future I have photos that I would like you to see so that you believe me. Family snaps I keep on here. To scroll through just thumb across like this." He held up the device and demonstrated. Nigel nodded, unsure. James threw the phone across to him.

He inspected the device suspiciously and stared down at the smooth glass screen. The first picture he recognised instantly: it was him and Rose. His *wife*. It was taken just days after they met. They were in the backroom of a pub. He'd played a short set of blues standards to a polite if disinterested crowd. No change there then. Rose had dragged a fellow student nurse friend along to meet the man she'd accidentally fallen in love with instantly just three nights prior. She stood near the front politely tapping her feet, grinning throughout, and applauding over-enthusiastically after each number. The snap captured the two in a short embrace mere moments after he'd come off the "stage" (a short, raised platform affording the audience limited viewing capabilities). Nigel tottered on a stool cradling a pint glass in one hand. Rose was beaming up at Nigel, as he slung an arm lazily around her, already staring at another woman in the background.

"How did you get this?" asked Nigel.

"Keep scrolling, just like I said" ordered James.

Nigel did as he was told. He squashed his thumb awkwardly onto the screen.

"Just lightly, don't break it."

Nigel obeyed and brought up the next picture. It was Nigel and Rose again, but a little older and now with children. A young Nina grasped the neck of Daddy's guitar and gazed at the camera, as Rose cradled a newborn James close to her chest.

Nigel curled his lip and looked up at his man claiming to be his son.

"That was - what - eight, nine years ago? You've grown a lot in all that time. Who are you?"

"I'm James. I'm your son. Mother Rose, sister Nina. Born July 7th 1974. I'm forty-five years old and I have travelled back thirty-five years."

Nigel left this statement hanging. He looked down at the phone again and scrolled some more. Pictures of his children growing up through the years: playing in parks, building sandcastles, posing, falling off bikes, holding uncooperative cats, waving, smiling, laughing, dancing, singing. Each subsequent photo hit Nigel with a molecular tang of shame. He wasn't present in most, and didn't remember the pictures where he was. He kept scrolling. Suddenly, somehow, the children were older than they were now. They had advanced through the teens to their early twenties. The smiles had been replaced by sullen scolding glances or forced displays of affection. Then landmark footnotes of their lives: James off to university, Nina in her first car. James in a wedding suit, Nina's first born, Rose the proud granny.

Nigel dropped the phone in astonishment. His mouth dried completely, he reached for a cigarette.

"This is a joke, right? Is this *Game for a Laugh*? Where's Beadle?"

"No Beadle. No cameras. I'm your son."

"But how?"

"Time travel, I told you."

Nigel lit his cigarette and drew back a long lungful of smoke. "Do you all have time travel in the future then?"

"Very much not," replied James, tersely.

"Hang on, why did you hit me?" Nigel demanded, fuming.

"Well, for a start - exhibit A," declared James, and pointed with both hands towards the walls. "Never knew you had a minging shag pad. I'm sure my mum - *your wife* - would be very interested to know about this bijou bonk palace."

Nigel's face darkened. "What's it got to do with you?"

James' temper surged and he grabbed his father by the lapels. "Are you kidding me right now? Your wife works her heart out for our family. You sing a few songs, scrape in pennies and rent another property just to cheat on your wife?!"

"Piss off, you don't know anything," Nigel argued, back, and pulled away from his son's grip.

"I know that rather than support us financially, you suck us dry with dirty little escapades such as this place. Plus, unspeakable betrayal like this - exhibit B." James pulled an exercise book from his rucksack and threw it onto the floor. The polaroids Sid had handed to him scattered across the carpet. They formed a pattern of grot and filth, a mucky mosaic for perverts and wrong 'uns. One glimpse at the photos and Nigel's face filled with a crimson horror. He had no idea how James had this. Last he remembered he had hidden it away expertly inside one of Nina's ignored story books, never to be discovered. His little secret to revisit every now and again.

"A schoolgirl?" raged James. "My babysitter?! A child? Really?"

Nigel remained silent for a minute before whispering defensively, "She was seventeen."

James hit Nigel again.

James' Dad offered no resistance, and his head snapped sideways with the power of the punch. A left hook to the right cheek, his head pulsated with a sprawling mass of pain. Nigel really didn't like being punched.

"I'm sorry," he offered meekly to his son.

James cracked his knuckles and felt a rush of adrenalised satisfaction surge through his chest.

"Yeah, well, if it makes you feel any better, so am I." He spat onto the floor.

Nigel shook his head.

"James Stanton, I'm no saint, but you do your old man a great disservice, you really do."

"Harpman," corrected James. "I'm James Harpman."

"What? So, you're *not* my son?"

"Oh, I'm your child all right. But I took my wife's name - Harpman."

"You did what?" spat back Nigel, disgusted.

"We both thought it was for the best. Rather than stain her good nature with your legacy, a clean slate for mine."

"Of all the loony, disrespectful nancy boy nonsense..." muttered Nigel, perplexed. "Thank heavens you've kept James. I gave you that, named after the great James Brown."

"A musician who treated his wife terribly, wonder where you got that idea?"

Nigel sat up, vexed by his son's attitude. "So, what are you doing here anyway? If you hate me, why travel thirty-five years to be with me?"

James cleared his throat. He didn't want his father to know that *he* had forced him into this predicament. The less Nigel knew about him, the better. But he was already exhausted by the confrontation.

"I've got my own family now. An amazing, smart, beautiful, sexy wife, and two awesome children of imagination and intellect and fervour. It's just the best! But this, and you." He shot his father an accusatory stare. "This aches at my soul. You and your terrible parenting, or lack of it. Your cheating, your selfish behaviour, your bullshit excuses. Having my own family still hasn't helped me deal with *this*."

James wandered over to the window and peered through the nets. He watched an elderly lady struggle to control an Alsatian on a makeshift lead made from a skipping rope. He'd kill to be either of them at that moment. Instead, he was here feeling wretched in this stupid situation mostly of his own making.

"I don't want this hanging around my psyche anymore. I'm done being angry at a memory. It's not helping anyone. So here I am. I mean, hell, you're not making it easy, but we could start again, you and me. A completely fresh relationship. Not father-son, but *something*. What do you think?"

Nigel rubbed his bruise in thought.

"How sexy's your wife then?"

"For crying out loud, Nigel!"

"I'm joking! Sorry, couldn't resist. This is all so much, but yes of course. *Of course* I want to mend whatever it is I've broken as your father." Nigel eyed James suspiciously. "Though I must say they were pretty conciliatory words for someone who just punched me in the face."

"I owed you that. *Your wife* owes you that."

"Me and Rose..." began Nigel.

"Don't," warned James. "Just don't pretend that she is ok with any of this."

"James, you don't know us as a married couple. You know us as Mum and Dad."

"Mum and *Nigel*," insisted James. Nigel shot him a wounded look.

"Me and your mother, we have a very different relationship than the one you have in your head. *Very* different."

"So, I could just call her up, invite her round here, she'd be fine with this?"

"Not exactly," conceded Nigel. "But she's not the angel you think she is. She's come a long way from those innocent days when I first swept her off her tits."

James tensed up again.

"Cheating on you then, is she?"

"Your Mum? Ha! As if!" laughed Nigel.

"Well, how is she, 'a long way from those innocent days' then?"

"Well, she... She speaks her mind more. You know."

"Shit on a cauliflower, no! No, I don't! You think being assertive is the same as breaking your marriage vows? Or even, for that matter, a bad thing?"

"No, well, a bit. I don't know."

"And how about your lady from last night? You gonna see her again?" asked James, scoldingly.

"Doubt it, can't even remember her name. Lovely lady though, a gynaecologist I think."

"Knows a twat when she sees one then? No wonder she scarpered. Also, you bloody idiot, she works in the medical profession. So, at some point she could well bump into your wife."

"Shit," exclaimed Nigel. "Look, it's too late. Your Mum and I are over, and you obviously hate me."

"No!" protested James. "Well, perhaps I do a bit. Maybe a lot."

"I didn't hate my old man," said Nigel, and turned away from his son. "Barely knew him, mind."

Nigel harrumphed, stubbed out his cigarette, then stood up and strode over to the kitchenette.

"Tea?" he offered.

"Sure."

Nigel gently lifted a pan onto the stove then rummaged around his cupboards, rattling bowls and knocking over plates.

"Of course, I've got no milk. Or, as it turns out, tea bags. It'll have to be black coffee. You ok with that?"

"Fine."

Nigel pulled a jar of Maxwell House from the cupboard. It looked like it had seen better decades: the former red label had faded to a burnt orange and the granules congealed to a clump of dark brown. Nigel thumped the jar on the kitchen worktop, broke up the mush with a fork, then promptly served a mug of something vaguely coffee-shaped to his son. James blew on the piping hot liquid and took a sip. It was like licking a used nappy.

"Thanks," he stammered, then tried to rid himself of the bitter tang immediately.

Nigel sat back down, put his mug on the small table next to the chair, and rolled another cigarette.

"I'm not all bad, you know," said Nigel.

"No?" queried James, disinterested, and tapped on the mug impatiently.

"I once did a charity fun run for the Spastics. Plus, a mate of mine, Bobby Twang - he sometimes puts Winalot on his dick then gets his dog to lick it off. I'd *never* do that."

"Right," retorted James. "Just so we're clear; you're a good man because in your own words, you did a fun run for 'the spastics', and you're not into bestiality? Well, you're certainly a shoo-in for the George Cross this year."

Nigel glowered at his son and sipped his coffee.

"Never done anything bad then I suppose?" he asked.

"On the contrary, I stole the library manager's car the other day, but hey."

"That was you? I heard about that. The bloke's livid!"

James clamped his mouth shut, realising he shouldn't have said a damn thing.

James studied his father's features. He couldn't tell if he looked cruel, or if he was bringing his own prejudices to the aesthetics. Nigel reclined in his denim shirt, a small tuft of wispy chest hair bothering the open buttons and neck that sagged like a butcher's offcuts. James struggled to see how he had success with *any* women, let alone the seemingly endless line of married women and conquests he devoured weekly. Nigel finished a slurp and addressed his son.

"Look, I'm sorry that you feel this way about me, I really am. But have you ever considered just putting it to the back of your mind, and trying to forget all about it?"

"Great idea Nigel, because suppressing emotion has never caused anyone psychological harm whatsoever," James retorted, scornfully.

"Exactly," said Nigel, completely missing the sarcasm. He took another large gulp of the vile caffeine then put down his mug. "So, James, how about you start by calling me Dad?"

James blinked in disbelief.

"No, that's not how this starts. This is not on me, and you haven't earned the right, *Nigel*." Nigel nodded gravely in bitter acknowledgement. "How's your face?"

"Sore thanks, but I'll live. How did you get here then? Where's your time machine?"

James' legs jerked nervously.

"Currently working on it" was all he offered. "So now what?"

"Well James, we start again. Maybe not father-son so much, but Nigel and James? We can go out, get to know each other. This Saturday night, there's some music on and a buzz about town. We can catch a gig, have a few drinks and a laugh, that sort of thing. What do you say?"

James surveyed the room as he mulled over the offer. What with his father's slightly woeful pleading, the horrid sex pest decor of the room, and the photos of Nigel's erect penis scattered across the floor, anything was an improvement over this.

"Sod it, let's do it," he concluded. "What the hell have I got to lose?"

Nigel smiled broadly, even though it hurt his face to do so. He lit another cigarette in jubilation, drew a large lungful, and blew a smoke ring into the room.

James smiled back earnestly. Nigel clenched his jaw and winked, his eyes glinting in the dim light of the apartment.

CHAPTER 20

1984

Paul Kirkley had the sort of face that even a mother would struggle to love, and a haircut you could only get from handing over coupons. Despite these superficial setbacks, Paul Kirkley still thought he had a lot going for him.

After all, he ran his own pub. A horrible pub admittedly, but still. It didn't matter that the patterned carpet had worn to a thin gossamer thread, the seats offered less comfort than a bundle of razor blades dipped in lemon juice, and the beer tasted like pickled liver. He ran the pub. Well obviously, the brewery actually ran it. But hey - it was *his* name above the door. Yes, spelt incorrectly for the past two years, but they assured him they'd change it any day now. He could, at least, bar people from the premises; if they paid attention, which they rarely did.

Regardless, Paul Kirkley *was* the landlord of The Cloven Hoof, and no one could do anything about it.

"Paul, you're fired," declared Tabitha Kasterborous of The Sisters Brewery.

"I'm what?" he responded, astonished.

"You heard me, I'm not repeating myself."

"It would have been quicker to just repeat it," chipped in Tilda, the other Kasterborous sister. Tabitha stared hard into the wonky eyes of her business partner sibling and clenched her teeth in frustration.

"You can't fire me!" exclaimed a shell-shocked Paul.

"Can and have. Now piss off, we're taking this place back over." Tabitha strolled over to the bar and grabbed a glass from the shelf. She went to thrust it under an optic, but stopped to inspect the glass. Spotting several thumbprints around the rim, and a lipstick imprint so visible it looked as if it had been etched into the vessel, she threw the tumbler to the floor, enraged. Paul and Tilda winced in unison as it shattered across the cold stone tiles. Paul reached instinctively for the broom to clear the shattered pieces, but Tilda put a friendly arm out, urging him not to bother.

Tabitha chose another glass and again, inspected it. Satisfied, she thrust it beneath a whisky bottle and let the liquid drain into his glass. Without ceremony, she swigged back the alcohol and slammed the glass onto the bar. She motioned to Paul.

"You still here?"

"You can't just fire me!" protested Paul. "My name's above the door!"

Tabitha scowled, incandescent. She reached beneath the bar and pulled out a large, rusted hammer. Paul's eyes widened with fear. He *knew* he should have got rid of it, but Tabitha had always insisted he keep one behind in case, "shit kicks off", whatever that meant. It looked like he was about to find out. Tabitha pushed past Paul and opened the pub door.

"This is your name, is it?" bellowed Tabitha. "Pual Pertwee?"

"Well, no, but…"

Tabitha raised the hammer and struck the sign repeatedly in swift succession. The metal buckled and pieces flew off violently in all directions. Paul cowered and covered his eyes from the shrapnel. Tilda merely stared ahead blankly, not a hint of shock or surprise on her face.

Tabitha was always like this. Biologically, they might have had a lot in common, but in temperament, they might as well be different species.

Exhausted, Tabitha stopped hitting the sign, which was handy as she was about to smash through the wooden lintel beneath. The battered, sad-looking pieces of engraved metal lay on the pavement, nestling next to a curl of dog shit and a discarded crisp packet. Sums up my tenure neatly, Paul thought to himself, as he idly considered snatching the hammer from Tabitha's grasp and doing himself in. Instead, he ran back inside, grabbed his belongings, then emptied the till's entire takings into a drip tray and scarpered off out the back door.

Neither Tabitha nor Tilda pursued, they simply needed him out of their pub. Besides, it was easier to let him get away with his own cheeky bit of severance than let anything official run its course.

"Could we not have let him just stay?" asked Tilda.

Tabitha screwed her face up and let out a small malevolent chuckle.

"Holy Mary, Tilda, you really are too soft. He's a useless liability. Every local two-bit dealer was plying their wares here under his stewardship. Now we're in charge, that fucking stops. This is the perfect place to funnel through *our* funds."

Tilda chewed her fingernails.

"Besides," added Tabitha. "You run a decent pub, and you know you do."

A thin smile crept across Tilda's face.

Tabitha stepped across the threshold and bolted the door behind. Tilda lit a cigarette and pulled herself a pint of their own branded ale, Kasterborous. The pump angrily spat out a foaming brown sludge that flumped into the glass like dropped cake. Tilda lifted the glass to the light and inspected the yeasty soil with a grimace.

"Did he ever clean the lines?" she wondered aloud.

"You're holding the answer," Tabitha replied. She slung her handbag over a bar stool, then lowered her voice. "Besides, it's very different kinds of lines we're going to be dealing with from now on, eh?" She tapped her nose and winked at her sister.

Tilda threw the muck into the sink and put down the glass.

"We still need to operate as a functional pub. I better get these lines cleaned, change the barrels, open the curtains, and sort out the staff." Tilda squeezed her temples then picked up a crate of glasses. "Fuck's sake, it's a Saturday and we open in under an hour."

Tabitha checked her watch and tutted loudly.

"Where's our man? He was supposed to be here ten minutes ago."

"Ladies," came a nasal voice from a darkened corner of the pub. Tilda dropped the crate.

Tabitha withdrew a gun from her trousers and pointed it at the voice.

"Who are you, creep? Show yourself, slowly."

The creep emerged from the shadows: a tall figure with thick hair sprouting wildly from his large pate, a tidy goatee, and a pair of black thick-rimmed glasses perched on his beak-like nose. He wandered into the pub's poorly-lit bar area, casting a dim shadow onto Tabitha. The gun still trained at his head, she motioned for him to sit down.

"Tabitha, Ms Kasterberous. Colin Shatterem at your service."

"Tilda," said Tabitha. "You've not met Colin, have you? Librarian and regional drug dealer. Helping us out on the latter part of his job description."

Colin squirmed at the introduction, whilst Tilda's face relaxed a little. She smiled weakly at the new arrival.

"How did you get in?" demanded Tabitha.

"Paul gave me a key."

"Course he did. I'll have that back please."

She held out her other hand, expectantly. Colin complied reluctantly and turned to stare at Tilda.

"Are you joining us?"

Tilda rolled her eyes, ignored Colin, and carried on loading the dishwasher.

"Tilda's pub management only," explained Tabitha. "She'll cover the bars and brews. Just leave all the chemical needs to me. Speaking of which, I believe we're due our first transaction. How did it go?"

Colin shuffled uncomfortably in his seat. He felt the mole on his cheek twitch, and his head went light. He had been dreading this moment.

"We have a problem," he uttered, sheepishly.

Tilda stopped arranging the bar mats and looked up, concerned. Tabitha remained cool, but kept the gun pointed at her guest.

"Sounds like *you* have a problem," she corrected.

Colin nodded in acknowledgement, and felt wrath flare up towards his predicament.

"We have been robbed. The entire supply's takings! We sold the entire haul, but our dealer was accosted. We have got nothing left!"

"You're joking, of course?"

"No, I wish I was. Two jokers came out of nowhere and grabbed the entire profits. They must have had inside knowledge." Colin threw a conspiratorial heft behind his last sentence. He wouldn't put the Kasterborous sisters beyond stealing their own profits then needling him for it so that they get paid twice. It's certainly the sort of thing *he* would do.

"Shatterem," began Tabitha, her ferocity simmering barely beneath the surface. "You had our product. You have our money. Pay us up, or your miserable myopic arse will burn. I am deadly serious."

Colin gulped. "Tabitha my dear, I know you are, and believe me, I am going to do everything I can to make this right. This has not been a good week for me: my car was stolen, then this, plus I had to sack a brand-new member of staff."

"I couldn't care less about your banger or your book club you fucking nonce. You owe us three Gs. Find that money, or the supply, and I don't have one of your fingers removed. That's the offer. You've got two days."

Colin tapped his precious fingers on the table. Tabitha put the gun down, picked up the whisky glass, and slammed it onto the back of Colin's hand. It squashed hard into his skin and cracked across his knuckles. Colin yelped in pain as a vein burst and dark purple bruises formed immediately. He cradled his hand, mumbled an apology, and got up to leave.

"I will have your money, I shall see to it, I swear," he promised, unsure if he could actually make good on his words. He had the weekend to sort this unholy mess.

As he opened the door to leave, Bobby Twang pushed past him into the bar to start his shift. Colin didn't wait around any longer to see how the sisters might react to their dishevelled barman: he'd had enough conflict to last a decade.

Bobby smiled at Tabitha, unsure who she was or why there was a gun next to her on the table.

"Hello," greeted Bobby, cheerily.

Tabitha stared with utter disdain as the pot-bellied pond life stood in front of her, wiping crisp dust from his mouth. She turned back to Tilda.

"Who the fuck is this cunt?"

∽

A mile away a trembling hand pushed hard against open Hartnell Library's uninvitingly heavy doors. The entrant's other fist grasped a colourful book about cars. The tall figure strode with purpose past the fiction and straight to the hobbies and crafts section. Obscured by a bobble hat and suspiciously askew moustache, the man thrust the book onto the shelf, took a peek around him, then left the building immediately.

CHAPTER 21

1984

Bill pushed the spectacles up past his forehead and let them rest on his mop of curls. He peered into the circuit board then let out a gasp of delight. Grabbing his soldering iron, he teased a blob of liquid alloy onto the board, and fused back together the broken connection. He blew on the paste lightly, put it back down onto the bench, and smiled widely. He really was at peak contentment when fixing things.

Bill stood in an abandoned building at the edge of the industrial estate, just a short walk from the car. It had clearly been some sort of engineering workshop in its pomp, but had deteriorated badly since its last occupants had left. He was operating at a very worn carpenter's workbench, the vice missing its thread. Next to this was a large concrete space for fixing up vehicles, as a breeze block wall of rusted tools and spilled oil stood defiantly adjacent to a rotting wooden partition for an adjoining office.

Bill was about to take a sip of coffee when he noticed an impatient-looking shadow form over him from behind. He knew that twitchy silhouette.

"How's the book going?" he enquired, and turned to see James' puzzled face.

"Erm, what?" replied his friend.

"*Car Classics: the 1970s?* Have you hit your word count, set out your pages, et cetera?"

"Oh, that! Yup, just bought a couple of mags and books, read and didn't understand them, so copied most of it and cut out all the pics. Buggered if I was going over to Daimler or whoever to get the skinny on their latest model."

"Suppose we don't actually need it to be any good."

"Bit late for quality control now, it's in the library."

"WHAT?" exclaimed Bill, dropping his mug. "How on earth?"

"Did it yesterday. Took it to a local printer. Then just smuggled it in, added it to the database. Piece of piss."

"You weren't seen or recognised?"

"Turns out that underfunding libraries actually has an advantage; they're severely understaffed. And didn't see our man Shatterem. Amazing what you can get away with in a bobble hat and a false 'tache."

"James, that was an enormous risk," remonstrated Bill. "He could have seen you, apprehended you there and then, and called the police. Plus, there's a picture of you with his very car that we stole in that book. That doesn't strike you as a little bit reckless?"

"You worry too much," replied James. He pulled his fist into a shaka and laughed at Bill's concern.

Bill tutted.

"Looking sharp, by the way," said Bill.

James ran his hand through his buoyant hair and broadcast a pearly white grin to his friend. He straightened his silk red pencil tie, adjusted his crisp white shirt, and pulled tight on his blazer's black lapels. He looked like he had just stumbled out of a Robert Palmer video.

"Thanks, I do, don't I?"

"Suppose I better make another coffee. Want one?"

"No thanks," declined James, and sat on a rickety swivel chair. "This place is cool, glad we found it. Bit weird that it still has power though."

"Not my concern. Some poor sod is still somehow paying the bills on this place. Or maybe they just overlooked cutting it off. It's alright actually, just an odd homeless fella kipping on a mattress. He's pretty friendly, if a bit feral. I keep away at night, as I'm pretty sure others come here too."

James scanned the building with only a modicum of interest. A set of metallic steps to the far end led to a mezzanine level of storerooms, but their severely deteriorated condition prevented anyone but the most foolhardy or oblivious from climbing to the first floor. James' puppyish curiosity got the better of him, and he bounded upstairs.

"Heck James, be careful," warned Bill, flinching as the stairs groaned under James' heavy tread.

"Again, you worry too much," shouted James from above, as he started rifling through old boxes and documents. He found himself amazed at the audacity of a business allowed to leave receipts and invoices carelessly lying around for anyone to find. In 2019, this would be a fine-worthy data protection nightmare. He picked up the top item - a ledger book - and studied the list of names and transactions. It read like a bad joke book of comedy names - Willy Salmon, Mr R. Swiper, Jenny Tools, Arthur Itis, Claire Voyant, and so on. Alright, one or two alone wasn't impossible, but this many together seemed hugely improbable. Curiously, all the dates were from this year too, but this building couldn't have been occupied for nearly a decade. Seeing nothing else of interest or value, James put the book back and descended the creaky stairs. He made sure to pull an exaggerated face of fear, mocking Bill as he got to the ground floor.

"Happy now?" asked Bill.

"Nah, it's boring. How's the time machine coming along?"

Bill took a long gulp of his coffee and placed the mug onto the workbench.

"Surprisingly well. Parts all present and correct, and adapting to limited tech hasn't been the headache I was prepared for."

"And making the whole car a time machine? That's possible now?"

"Absolutely, yes. It's about redistributing the refracted optical beam of impermanence to absorb material. By which I mean the vehicle and everything in it. Quite straightforward really, surprised I hadn't thought of it till now. Plus, I can remove the unit should we need it mobile with a simple power source."

"You know I stopped listening after 'yes', right? Dare I ask for a timeframe?"

"You may dare. Tomorrow morning, tomorrow afternoon if I'm being kind to myself."

"Seriously? That's amazing! Make it tomorrow afternoon and come out tonight. Let's go to a pub or a bar or something. Experience the nineteen eighties in all its slightly miserable Thatcherite glory."

"No, I really should be cracking on with this. I daren't leave any of it here unguarded, lest it get nicked or destroyed."

"Put it in the car," suggested James, with an agitated air.

"What do you think I've been doing? But it's getting to the point now where I need the space to store certain bits and..." Bill stopped and waved his arms out like a frustrated politician. "It's just easier here, that's all."

"Oh come on, mate! When else are we going to be in the nineteen eighties together? I've not seen you for three days! Please, I hear *The War Machines* are playing The Inferno tonight. It'll be a laugh. Me and you - JH and BL giving this decade a bit of nu-skool love, yeah?"

"James, I really can't, ok?" Bill snapped. "And I thought you wanted to get back to 2019 as urgently as possible? What could possibly keep you from that?"

James ran his hand through his voluminous hair and pulled at the back of his head in frustration. He lowered his voice.

"Look, I wasn't going to say, but it won't just be us two," James paused, rigid with uncertainty. He was risking a bollocking from a mate here. "I've invited Nigel out with us."

Bill turned to James; his face had turned into a pallid smear in an instant.

"I beg your pardon?" he said, slowly and deliberately.

James picked up a clump of wiring from the workbench and pretended to be interested in it.

"Yeah well, I got talking to him, didn't I?"

"Did you? How the hell, James? *What* the hell, James?"

"He was just there, and I..." James trailed off, realising that this revelation had been a massive mistake on his part. Too late now. "I followed him. I followed him, OK?"

"No James, none of this is OK! I expressly told you not to go anywhere near the past. This isn't some vacation you know."

James continued to fiddle with the wires.

"I mean, you actually said it was. But there's so much I need to understand. I had to know what he's like, and why he left and all that. Look, I'm not saying this situation is perfect..."

"Not 'perfect'? Heck Harpman, what have you done?"

James put down the wires.

"I punched him."

"You did *what?*"

"I burst into his flat - he's got a flat here in Hartnell I never knew about. I followed him there and waited and then I punched him in his bastard face."

Bill cradled his head with both hands and massaged his temples.

"Wow James, great work," he said sarcastically. "Most time travellers worry about stepping on butterflies, but you throw fists at your father."

"We've already got over it. He accepted it. He knew he'd done wrong; knew he deserved it. Now I want to get to know him, maybe even accept him. I can't do that in 2019. But here in 1984 I can start again. Only, you know, as an adult. Can you see that I need to do this?"

Bill let out a guttural drawl of frustration.

"Yes James, of course I do. This is precisely why I have warned you away. Has it not occurred to you that this is how he was in the present forcing us back into the past? You are just putting into motion the events that conspired to trap us in this decade."

"No, it's the complete opposite. I'm not following your rules or instructions, I'm trying to make bridges *before* they're burned."

"By punching your dad in the face?"

"He deserved that! But like I said, we've got over that now."

"'We'? Are you sure about that? You see, that man we met very briefly a few days ago, albeit thirty-five years in the future - he seemed incredibly cross about something. Have you given any thought as to why? Maybe, just maybe, it was his future adult son who turned up inexplicably out of nowhere to attack him?"

"No Bill, honestly it's fine. I haven't even told him about you!"

"No James," shouted Bill, shaking with barely repressed ire. "It really is not fine. You have thoughtlessly thrown both of us into danger with your self-regarding nonsense. You have turned this scientific endeavour of mine into a Freudian melodrama of your own. Not once have you considered me in any of this, simply ploughed ahead with your frankly childish need for validation from a parent you openly admit doesn't care about you anyway."

"You don't know that," James argued, hesitantly.

"James, I cannot cope with your antics right now. Please do me the courtesy of fudging off very quickly as I try to work at double speed to get us the heck out of here."

James was stunned into silence; the mortal wounds of Bill's rage tore through his being as he stood open-mouthed in shock. He thrust his hands into his back pockets with such force he nearly tore the seams.

"Oh," was all he could muster. "I'll be off then."

Bill turned back to his workbench to fiddle with some wiring.

"Good," he responded, coldly.

James' soul stung. Perhaps he *was* just a massive, annoying distraction, a selfish friend, and a terrible human?

"Shall I pop round tomorrow, see how you're getting on, yeah?"

Bill didn't look back. "No."

James turned to leave. He slammed the door on his exit, his inner toddler having taken over.

Well, he was going out with Nigel tonight, and had now decided he was going to get absolutely shitfaced. Yup, that would definitely help.

James stomped his way through town towards his dad's flat. He scuffed his 9½ size shoes against the pavement, and barked at stray cats. He passed a lamppost to which a National Front poster had been stapled. He tore it from the pole, spat on the page, screwed it into a ball, and threw it into the nearest litter bin.

He arrived at the flat and hammered on the door. Nigel took too long to answer, which only exacerbated James' foul mood further.

"Where have you been?"

"Come in?" said Nigel, nonplussed by his son's attitude.

James strode through the hallway to the living room and slumped onto the sofa. He picked up the acoustic guitar and strummed hard. Two strings snapped just three bars in. James dropped the instrument onto the floor.

"Oi," shouted Nigel.

"What?" said James, stroppily.

"That's mine!"

"You probably stole it anyway."

"Who shit on your Frosties?"

"It doesn't matter."

"Come on," beckoned Nigel, attempting a smile. "You can tell your old man…"

"Don't!" warned James.

Nigel narrowed his eyes and reached for his tobacco pouch. He rolled a cigarette, and let the silence hang in the air, waiting for the frost to thaw. James reached for a can of Hofmeister lager on the coffee table. He pulled the ring pull, dumped it into the ashtray, then drank the entire tin's contents in one thirsty gulp.

"It's Bill," said James, with a burp.

Nigel raised an eyebrow. "Bill?"

"Bill my mate. He's here with me."

Nigel looked around the room expectantly as he fumbled with the lighter and smirked.

"Is he always with you, this 'Bill'?"

James tutted.

"No, he's not imaginary, or a ghost. I mean he's here in the 1980s. He's how I got here. He's my friend." James stopped, and chewed a nail nervously. "Or at least, he's supposed to be."

Nigel lit his cigarette and drew a lungful of vanilla tobacco smoke. He let it slowly curl out of his mouth and nostrils.

"Lover's tiff?"

"Great, casual homophobia, how very nineteen eighties of you. Bill and I are best mates. Have been since playschool. How do you not know any of this stuff?"

"Hey" shot back Nigel, defensively. "I know all your friends!"

"Name one."

Nigel took another long drag on his cigarette to afford him thinking time. It didn't work.

"Nina?"

"She's my sister!"

"You're always playing together!"

"It doesn't count! Face it Nigel, you have no interest in me whatsoever."

"I'm willing to learn," pleaded Nigel. "Tell me about Bill. Tell me about your life now. Tell me anything and everything you ever wanted to."

James' shoulders stooped gradually as he took a deep breath. He relaxed back into the armchair and stared at the Artex ceiling.

"Bill invented the time machine. Without him I wouldn't be here."

"Without me and your Mum you wouldn't be here," countered Nigel with a wink.

"A lovely image, thanks. Well, Bill's the brains, and I'm the, erm…"

"The sexy one in the cool suit?" offered Nigel.

"I'm the other one. Not special, no discernible talent. Just me." James leaned back and put his hands behind his head. "Do you know what I'm terrified of?"

Nigel put his cigarette into the ashtray and opened his arms out, statesmanlike.

"Tell me, son."

"I'm scared of my complete lack of skills. I worry that one day I'll wake up in the apocalypse and have to fend for myself and family by physically doing things and knowing stuff. Or I'm somehow back in dinosaur times, and it's just my wits versus a hungry Tyrannosaurus Rex. I can't *do* anything."

"Now hang on! Don't be so hard on yourself. Look at you - handsome, strong, forthright. Most men barely have one of these features, whereas you're bursting with idiosyncrasies and talents to die for."

James' eyes welled up.

"And do you know what really hurts?"

"Anal?"

"No, do you know what really hurts about all this?"

"Is it still anal?"

"You and anal! No. It's the fact that Bill's probably right about everything."

"Right about what?"

James shuffled uncomfortably in his seat and avoided his father's gaze.

"It doesn't matter. Got any stuff harder than, 'the bear'?" he asked, pointing to the empty Hofmeister can.

"Course James, just in the kitchen. Help yourself. Grab two glasses."

Nigel winked at his son and beamed encouragingly.

∽

Colin Shatterem approached the small, terraced house and knocked lightly on the yellowing door. He held his briefcase tightly and squinted through the cracked stained glass nervously. He stole a swift peep around the Root housing estate. He hadn't noticed anyone who frequented Hartnell Library, so was fairly confident nobody here recognised him.

He was ready to knock again but before his knuckles could clench the door swung open and a set of burly arms pulled Colin into the house. The librarian was thrust against the wall, legs spread apart, then subject to a clumsy pat-down. Satisfied, the occupant handed back Colin his briefcase and ushered him into the dinky front room.

"Thank you for that welcome Anton, though a simple 'hello' would be enough," said Colin, indignantly. "When I said to be careful of anyone entering your home from now on, I did not mean me."

The burly host lowered his hulking body into an armchair and invited his guest to do the same. Colin eyed the tattered nylon sofa and Nazi memorabilia suspiciously. Rather than take a seat, he perched his bony cheeks on the arm.

"What do you want?" said Anton.

"Anton, I am in trouble. Huge, cataclysmic trouble."

"I'm sorry to hear that, Col'. Is it about your cock?"

"I beg your pardon? No, where on earth did you get that idea?"

"I'm a milkman. All of my troubles are knob-related."

Anton pointed to his member to emphasise his point.

"Well, allow me the displeasure of introducing you to a non-penis-related crisis for once."

Anton leant forward in his armchair and tried to look thoughtful.

"Do you need a poo?" asked Colin.

"No, carry on," replied Anton, determined to listen for once. He massaged his giant sausage fingers across his thick, bald skull.

"We have to find that money. This is beyond serious. Can you tell me any more about the pair that plundered you?"

"They didn't bum me!"

"Plundered means stole from."

"Right, well, there were two of them. Not blacks. Or chinks."

"So, two men of non-black or Asian origin? Well, thank you Columbo, I shall get right onto that." Colin chewed his fingernails ferociously and spat them out onto the carpet. "We are nearly four grand in the hole, whereas we should have been making a tidy, easy profit from this venture. Can you not tell me anything about them other than they're not members of a jive band or cook a mean crispy duck?"

"One was tall with silly hair."

"Silly hair?"

"Wavy, light. Big forehead. Huge smile, though that could have been because he was laughing the whole time."

"Right, big forehead, big smile, big hair?"

"Yep, that's it."

Colin strained his eyes for a second as a candidate briefly entered his head. No, couldn't be. "What about the other one?"

"Bit bigger. Curly brown hair, glasses. He wasn't laughing. Much more serious. But he made away with the till, whilst the other one threw the milk bottles at me. I was stinking of full cream, the bastard."

Colin opened his eyes so wide his irises looked like pin pricks against the white. "Definitely those two? You are certain it was one big wavy hair and one with curly brown hair and glasses?"

Anton nodded like an obedient hound.

Colin felt a bolt of electricity surge through his veins as the full comprehension spread out like a picnic blanket in his mind. He fumbled excitedly with his briefcase and pulled out a colourful book.

Anton looked down, unimpressed.

"I've told you; I hate reading."

Colin ignored his business partner's protests and flicked through the book frantically looking for a specific page. He found it and held the double page spread up to Anton's confused face.

"Was this one of them?" asked Colin, his eyes dancing wildly.

Anton grabbed the book and inspected the picture. It was him. Standing next to a polished sludge brown Triumph Dolomite with thumbs aloft was the man who had thrown pints of milk about and laughed at his National Front stickers. Beneath the wavy hair and iron-strength forehead was James' huge cheery mouth, bursting with a slightly insincere joviality.

"That cheeky, chuckling bastard!" roared Anton. "Yes, that's him." He paused, and tried to process what was going on. "Why's he in a book? Isn't that your car?"

"Same day they robbed you, this 'cheeky, chuckling bastard' and the other one you described came into the library and stole my car. Yesterday I found that someone has added this abomination to the books. It is not a proper book at all. So, I took a look through and saw this. The thieving bastard has the audacity to openly mock me in print. Well, those two are going to regret dallying with Colin Shatterem."

"Why did you bring the book here?"

"The moron has given away their location in the photo. Recognise that building?"

"The old workshop at the Spooner Industrial Estate?"

"Exactly."

"But that's next to where we keep…"

"Precisely! I received a tip-off from a hopefully reliable source about who took the car. And now I know where they are hiding it and more importantly, the money. I thought you might be able to come along with me to add your not inconsiderable muscle to retrieve my Triumph, take back our earnings, and serve retribution."

Anton frowned slightly. "Serve what now?"

"Punch their lights out."

"With pleasure!"

"Two shits, one stone."

Anton grinned and cracked his knuckles.

CHAPTER 22

1984

James stumbled out of Nigel's front door with a tipsy confident swagger. A blast of thick summer air enveloped his semi-drunken stupor. He reached for the doorway to steady his legs, then carried on out into the street. Nigel followed, cigarette dangling from his lips. He pulled the door behind him and pocketed the key.

"Think I'll lead the way from here," he said, and pushed past his son. "I know where we're going, and you may need a breather."

"Bit warm, isn't it?" said James, and wiped his damp forehead with his sleeves.

"Yeah," agreed Nigel. "My scrotum's basically a puddle right now." He pulled at his trousers and tried in vain to waft a little breeze around his ballbag.

James turned a light touch of green and tried not to think about his dad's junk.

The pair made their way through the Hartnell streets towards the town's estuary. Along its bank sat a row of badly maintained fishing cottages, a poorly-stocked convenience store, and the father-son's first early port of call for the evening, The Cloven Hoof Public House. James recognised the building from earlier in the week. He flinched at the sign.

"Something the matter?" asked Nigel.

James wore a face of utter repellence.

"You take me to the first place I saw you copping off with another woman? Classy work, Nige'."

Nigel frowned, and James shook his head disapprovingly. He entered the building regardless.

"Come on," beckoned James to Nigel, and held open the door for his father.

With the daylight streaming in through the rarely cleaned glass roundels, James got a better look at the pub than the last time he was there. The dirty crimson walls boasted rows of cracked mirrors with painted adverts in peeling black lettering. A tarnished brass bell hung ominously over the long oak bar, above which a gantry in similar style creaked as the barman placed clean glasses into its shelving.

"You take your dates here?" asked James, pointedly.

"What of it?" said Nigel.

James raised his eyebrows.

"Nothing Romeo, you do you."

James took a cushioned bench seat close to the dartboard. He removed his jacket and loosened his top collar. His biceps strained against the shirt cloth.

"Hell, this fabric does not offer arse protection. They may as well have lined it with a Rizla," he complained, loudly. Another patron looked over to the raised voice, but on seeing Nigel turned his attention back to his vessel of brown liquid misery.

"I'll get them in, shall I?" offered Nigel.

James shrugged his shoulders.

"Sure. Pint of whatever awful thing it is that you guzzle please."

"Ah, hang on," said Nigel, and patted his pockets. "Forgot my wallet."

James shot his father a look of searing incredulity.

"You what?"

"Sorry, I must have left it in the flat."

James snorted gibingly, and handed his wallet across to Nigel.

"Don't spend it all at once, there's a good lad," sneered James.

Nigel nodded gratefully, stubbed out his cigarette, then sauntered off to the bar.

James drummed testily on the round glass-topped table then flipped the beer mats carelessly until he dropped them.

"Do you want a toy to play with instead, love?"

James looked up to see a woman standing at his table. She had a bar towel draped over one arm, a stack of pint glasses in her hand, and a face that didn't appreciate his puny huff of nihilism. James blushed immediately then scrambled to pick up the little cardboard squares he'd sent sprawling to the ground.

"Sorry, I was just, er, distracted."

The woman raised an eyebrow and took a closer look at the mat-flipper.

"Nigel?"

James was dumbfounded. He looked over to Nigel and felt a shiver of repulsion that they could be mistaken for one another.

"Been going to the gym or something?" continued the woman. "You look different. Sort of healthier, a bit bigger."

"I'm not..." began James.

"Pity your dick can't lift weights, eh?" she laughed.

James broke into a manic grin and put his hand out to stop her talking any further.

"I'm not Nigel. The name's James. Nigel is..." James hesitated. "Nigel is my brother."

The woman cocked her head quizzically and put down the glasses.

"Well, I never knew he had a brother."

Neither does he, thought James.

"I'm Tilda." She stretched across a long arm to James. He grasped her hand and shook it needlessly formally. "Well, you're definitely not like your brother. He'd have taken my hand and kissed up my arm by now."

James shivered with disgust.

"I'm very different from my sibling."

"Know the feeling," sympathised Tilda. "In town long?"

"Erm, probably not. Fleeting visit, you know."

Tilda took the cloth to the already clean table and peered intently at this mystery man.

"Just you and your brother on a night out then. The boys are back in town, eh?"

"Something like that."

"So, where do you normally live then?"

"Alfred's Valley, just down the road."

"I know where the Valley is, but thanks for the geography lesson. That's barely fifteen miles away; not exactly far, is it? You and Nigel tend not to see much of each other then?"

James leant back in his chair and sighed.

"Not really. Let's just say that when we do, bad things happen."

Tilda raised an eyebrow and stuffed the cloth into the top pint glass. "Bad things?"

"Oh, nothing out of the ordinary. Just the odd bit of armed robbery. Smashing glass and, er, breaking hearts." James had no idea what he was talking about.

Tilda tilted her head towards James and raised an eyebrow.

"Don't tell me it was you two who robbed that poor milkman?" she said with a laugh.

The blood drained from James' face and his heart pounded with panic.

"Milkman?" he stammered, trying to sound casual.

"Yeah, some poor milkman was done over. Did away with his takings and smashed up his float."

"They didn't smash up his float!" corrected James.

"Oh, you heard then?"

"Yeah, just on the grapevine, like," said James, desperately hoping this conversation would draw to a conclusion.

"What did you hear then?"

"Oh, nothing really," stammered James. "Just that two sods had done what you said."

"Two? I didn't know it actually was two," she said, fixing James with a stare that bore through the back of his skull.

He tried to look past Tilda towards the bar. He rapped his knuckles on the table again.

"Expecting many in?" he asked, disinterestedly.

"Who knows?" she said, and looked James up and down. "Well, have a good night, and nice to meet you, James."

"Charmed to meet you, Tilda."

Tilda returned to the bar with her empties and suspicions.

Nigel had pushed his way to the front of the bar. It wasn't busy in the slightest, but he hated hanging around regardless of how short the wait.

"Come on Twang, I'm dying of thirst here!" shouted Nigel to the podgy curly-haired barman as he handed a customer a dimpled pint glass of fizzy lager.

"Oh, it's you," said Bobby Twang, with all the enthusiasm of the condemned greeting his executioner.

"Two pints of mild please when you're ready, Twanger." ordered Nigel.

"Two straight off? Blimey, you must be thirsty."

"Not just me, Bobby. One for me, the other for James over there. He's erm," dithered Nigel. "He's my cousin. Yes, James is my cousin." Nigel pointed across to James, who was busy chewing his nails down to the quick.

Bobby nodded, grabbed the glasses, then began pouring as Nigel opened his son's wallet to pay for the drinks. As he unzipped the pocket, a thick wad of notes burst from the seams, and sprang out across the bar. Nigel's eyes widened as he scooped up the cash and tried to stuff it back into the wallet.

"Christ's cock Stanton, robbed a bank, have we?" said Bobby. Beer poured into the overflow drip tray as he stared at Nigel hurriedly gathering up the errant banknotes.

Nigel winked at Bobby, and waved a fistful of sheets triumphantly at the hapless barman. Bobby placed the drinks on the bar. Nigel peeled off two of the notes and casually flicked them across.

"Get yourself a half too, mate" he said, and packed the rest of the money back into his trousers.

Tilda pushed past Bobby behind the bar and grabbed the notes from Bobby's clutch.

"Feeling a little flush at the moment are we, Nigel? That's a lot of notes you're hanging on to."

"Tabitha?!" exclaimed Nigel, delightedly. "Long time, no shag, eh?"

"Tilda," she corrected. "Not to worry, I got your brother mixed up with you."

"My brother?" Nigel's forehead creased like a discarded dishcloth; the confusion reigned across his face.

"Yes, your brother James, you big idiot." Tilda laughed and rang the money through the till.

"No Tilda," said Bobby, ignoring customers. "James is his cousin, not his brother,".

Tilda cocked her head inquisitively.

"Cousin? No, James told me they're brothers. That's right, isn't it Nigel?"

"No, he said cousin. Said it twice, didn't you Nigel?"

Nigel took a sip from each pint to avoid answering the question.

"Sorry, wasn't really paying attention. What was that?" asked Nigel, his voice so high even dogs strained to hear it.

"James, over there," said Tilda, nodding towards James. "Is he your brother, or your cousin?"

Nigel flashed his gleaming white falsies in a disingenuous display of overconfidence.

"Why, he's my brother, of course."

"But you said," argued Bobby.

"No, you *heard*," countered Nigel. "Honestly, all that loud music you listen to must be playing merry hell with your hearing. Still, worth it though, eh?" He raised both glasses and made his way back to the table swiftly to avoid further questioning.

Bobby shook his head and cleared out an ashtray into a bin, hitting the plastic hard against the metal ridge.

"He definitely said cousin."

Tilda stared across to Nigel and James, and reached for the phone on the wall.

Nigel plonked himself down onto a rickety stool and wedged himself into the tabletop. James sipped then scowled at his drink.

"Good pint?" asked Nigel.

"It's as if Marmite had sex with some piss."

"Not all bad then?"

"It's horrible, that's why I said that."

"You liked Marmite when you were younger."

"Well remembered," said James. "Well, it would be, if it wasn't last week."

Nigel tutted, lit a cigarette, and blew smoke into his son's face.

James clicked his fingers and opened his hand out expectantly.

"Wallet," he ordered. Nigel reached into his trousers and flung the pouch across to his son. James weighed it up in his palm. It was considerably lighter than before. He tutted to himself then thrust it back into his pocket.

"That's a lot of money you have there. How are you funding this trip? Are you rich?"

James snorted with derision. "Rich? God no. Every month is a tightrope walk on the edge of our overdraft."

"Then what's well over a thousand quid doing in cash on your person? Looking to put a deposit down on a mortgage, are we?"

"Not exactly," said James, as he tried to wrestle with the mental arithmetics of how much 1984 property might cost.

"Well, take my advice - walking around with that much dough on you in this neighbourhood isn't the brightest of ideas, son."

James took a gulp of the revolting beer and ran his fingers down his pint glass thoughtfully. "Fatherly advice from Nigel?"

Nigel threw his hands up in submission and coughed mirthfully. "Don't say I didn't warn you! My friend Bobby over there seemed very interested in your wad, as did Tabitha."

"Tilda," corrected James.

"Only saying, flashing your cash is bound to attract scum to your money like flies to shit."

"*You* flashed my money, not me, you big bollock."

Nigel dove his face into his pint to avoid eye contact.

"Hang on, did you say Bobby?" asked James. "As in Bobby Twang?" He looked over to the bar, laughed, then waved at the vacant-faced bartender and motioned for him to join them.

"That's him!" said Nigel. "Nice fella. Likes a pie and a strum. Plays a mean riff here or there."

"Local music promoter too, yeah?"

"That's right. Though god knows how, he knows sod all about music. Thinks *Womack & Womack* is a solicitors."

"Didn't you tell me it's not just guitar 'licks' he's into though, is it? The other sort he enjoys would trouble the RSPCA, isn't that right?"

"Keep your voice down James, for Pete's sake!"

Bobby waddled over to the pair.

"Wotcha gents," he greeted.

"Bobby," nodded Nigel. "This is James. He's my brother."

"You sure?" chuckled Bobby. The comment rebounded off Nigel's stern brow in silence.

"Hello Bobby," said James. "Great to meet another musician. Nigel's told me *all* about you."

"I hope not everything!" said Bobby with a hollow, nervous laugh.

"Oh, I'm sure you two have secrets; you seem the best of pedigree chums. Great pals. Real couple of diamond dogs."

Nigel took a large gulp from his swiftly-diminishing glass as Bobby stood perplexed, a rigid expression welded to his face.

"Yeah, we get up to some scrapes, don't we Nige'?" Bobby elbowed his friend and winked. Nigel hunched his shoulders and shrank a little lower into his seat. "You two coming to The Inferno tonight? Got a great band on, *The War Machines*. I'll put their cassette on."

"Bobby my boy," said Nigel. "Is the kitchen open? How about some food?"

Bobby fiddled with his apron strings.

"Kitchen? I can do you a meat pie in the microwave?"

"Perfect. Two of those. With beans," ordered Nigel, and handed Bobby a small fistful of crumpled notes. Bobby took the money and scurried off to the optimistically titled 'kitchen',

Once he was certain Bobby was out of earshot, Nigel's face darkened.

"What do you think you're playing at?" he spat angrily at his son, who was amused by his father's discomfort.

"Enjoying myself for once," replied James with a smirk, and took another mouthful of beer.

The lo-fi dirge of a pub band's demo came booming over the pub speakers, bleeding into James' ear canals. He looked over to the bar to see Bobby Twang give him a thumbs-up. James waved back through gritted teeth. *The War Machines* sang a song about Divorced Love, or something. It had all the structure and melody of a one-man-band being chased through an assault course.

Nigel studied his son's face. The bloodshot, tired eyes overset by a strong, bowed forehead that wore resentment like a billboard advertisement. This surly, petulant forty-something man was far removed from the fidgety boy he'd largely ignored for the best part of the decade.

"So, tell me about the future," he asked, with genuine interest.

"Personally, or generally?" offered James.

"Well, for a start, how is it different?"

"Not sure that it is. Still wankers in charge and stupid haircuts."

"That's it?"

"Guess the internet's the biggest difference."

"The what?"

"It's a computer thing. Mostly arguing, cats, and pornography."

"Arguing cats? Blimey. I don't really go in for porn though, son. It just makes me laugh."

"Oh please. 'Porn makes me laugh'? Yeah, I'm sure the last time you looked at any you laughed so hard you spunked yourself."

Nigel rolled his eyes.

"And you've got a family?" he said, cajolingly.

James raised his head, and his eyes met his father's. His mouth turned upwards at the corners, and he leaned back on his chair.

"My family," James mused. "Yes, Susan, my wife. Autumn's the eldest, she's a girl, Jude boy."

Nigel's eyes brightened, and he stubbed out his cigarette. "Any pictures?"

"Well yeah, but I can't risk running down the battery on my phone."

Nigel sighed. "I get it son, don't worry." He stretched out his arms and blinked back what looked like tears.

"Sake," whispered James. He peered around the bar conspiratorially and reached into his jacket pocket. He turned on the phone and leant in towards his father. "Ready to see your daughter-in-law and grandkids?" he asked, his voice cracking.

"It'd be my honour, son."

James opened a digital album entitled 'Harpman Time!'. It started with a landscape photo of the four family members together, grinning at the camera held at arms' length by James. Each squinted towards the lens in the blazing English sun, a snapshot moment of raw, unfiltered happiness captured forever. The sea, a rare crystal blue, provided the backdrop as both children boasted ludicrous towers of ice creams that threatened to melt at any moment.

Nigel said nothing but gripped his pint glass hard.

"Nice family," he stammered.

James didn't react to his father's comment. He kept staring at the photo with puppyish adoration.

"That was this summer, just a day out at Alfred's Valley. Nothing special, but you know, everything special."

Nigel nodded in agreement, despite not really following his son's logic. James thumbed onto the next photo: Susan. His wife stood in a doorway, a mild hesitancy and nervousness in her smile, partially shielded by a cascade of dark treacle coloured hair through which the tips of her ears poked. She clutched a flute in one hand and a cup of tea in the other. Nigel raised an eyebrow and grabbed the phone from James to get a closer inspection.

"You've done alright, eh? Blimey, I can almost smell her."

James wailed in disgust and snatched back the mobile.

"Jesus Nigel, I am *so* glad you weren't around for Facebook."

"What's she like?"

"Susan? Clever, musical, cheeky. Very much not available," said James, as he flashed his wedding ring.

"Huh," huffed Nigel. "Well, let's hope she doesn't jump cock to another bloke."

"Why would you think or say that?"

"Hey James, I'm on your side. You're a charming catch to all womanhood, I'm sure of that." Nigel winked and took a sip of his drink. "You're a one in a billion. But you can't trust women."

"No," argued James. "*You* can't trust women. I definitely can. Especially my wife. And what right do you have to question a woman's loyalty, when you betray your wife so terribly?"

Nigel tore pieces from his beer mat, stuck for an answer. Bobby shuffled awkwardly to the table, carrying two plates of microwaved disasters.

"Oh, great timing Bobby my man!" exclaimed Nigel, and he clasped his hands together in gratitude.

"Two pies with beans," said Bobby monotonously, as he placed down the meals.

"Well, I'll be doggone if that doesn't look best in show, mate," complemented James. "You really are a man's best friend."

Bobby tilted his head inquisitively, then gave a curt nod to both men. Nigel poured a snowstorm of salt onto his dish, covering his entire dinner in a blanket of thick white dust.

"Great food and even greater company!" he declared.

"Well, none out of two isn't bad," replied James, as he picked up his knife and inspected the congealed ketchup blobs on the blade.

"Wotcha gents," repeated Bobby as he departed for the bar.

James leant across to Nigel and hushed his voice.

"Is Bobby a bit, you know, simple? Ignorant?"

"Ignorant?!" laughed Nigel. "He's Ignorant's older brother. He taught Ignorant everything he didn't know."

"Is he really into dogs?"

Nigel swilled his beer round his mouth, swallowed, then sucked the air into his teeth.

"Not really, I made it up. Good rumour though. Easy to believe, and hard to disprove. Keeps him in line."

James shook his head and got up to go to the bar.

"Another drink?"

"Sure!"

"Packet of peanuts? Unless you're allergic, in which case I'll get you two."

James left the table and headed straight for Bobby. He reached into his pocket, pulled out the Bobby's Twang Emporium plectrum, and smiled at the tiny guitar tool.

The pub filled gradually, as more customers piled into the saloon. Most patrons were ruddy-faced men, thirsty for oblivion. A few had gone to the trouble of splashing on cologne and tight fit tees to stir the interest of the town's womenfolk. Although, given the ratio of the clientele was skewed heavily in favour of blokes, it was unclear why they had bothered. Bobby and Tilda raced about the bar, taking orders and serving pints as Nigel and James swallowed down their sweaty if oddly satisfying pies.

With his full stomach bulging against both belt buckle and the table, Nigel rolled another cigarette then leaned back on his stool with his hands clasped behind his head. James smeared his final piece of soggy crust across the plate, mopping up the last of the tomato sauce. He gulped it back greedily and washed it down with a second pint of flat ale.

"Yeah, get it down before it has a chance to come back to life. How was your meal?" asked Nigel.

"I've had worse," said James, as he let out an astonishing gasp of trapped wind.

"See, a night out with your old man not so bad, is it?"

"Again, I've had worse," repeated James with a shrug.

As Nigel went to light his cigarette, he dropped the lighter onto the floor. He bent down to pick it up, affording James a swift clear view across the bar. He watched a dozen or so heads of different shapes and haircuts, all vying for Tilda and Bobby's attention, jostling for position and pushing into each other. One in particular took his interest. It was the tallest by some margin, a man with wild tufts of hair sprouting from each ear. James squinted at the figure to bring him into sharp focus. He recognised him instantly: Colin Shatterem. James' pulse quickened. His mouth dried like a cactus wrapped in sandpaper. The library manager leaned into the bar to have a closer word with Tilda, whose eyes darted over to James and Nigel. She nodded across to their table.

James ducked onto the floor and grabbed Nigel's hands as he fumbled with the lighter.

"Nigel!" hissed James. "We need to leave. NOW!"

"Nonsense! The night's just getting started," laughed Nigel through an unlit cigarette. He went to get up, but James pulled on his father's arm and held him beneath the table.

"Stay there and for god's sake don't get up," he ordered, petrified. Instead, Nigel took his lighter and ignited his son's hand. The small flame startled James who let go of his grip. Nigel sat back up to his stool and stared down at his cowering son, smiling.

"Nigel, didn't you hear what I said? We need to leave urgently!"

"And you didn't hear what I said. I did warn you that that much money would get you into trouble."

He lit his cigarette, crossed his legs, and gave James a sarcastic little thumbs-up.

James froze in horror as his jaw took a journey southwards. He didn't take his eyes off his father, still staring down smugly at his guppy-mouthed son. He looked across to the other end of the pub towards the door. There were dozens of feet blocking his exit and he could see the slender frame of Shatterem make his way across the bar to their table. He looked up again to his father who simply shook his head condescendingly.

"You knew?" James asked, incredulously. "You brought me here to meet him, *on purpose*?" James' vision blurred with a lethal cocktail of booze and shock. He slowly got to his feet but immediately fell back into his seat. He felt utterly powerless; his body had independently surrendered to fate as his mind shut down all functionality.

"James," said Nigel. "I believe you've met Colin? Mr Shatterem would like to know where his car is."

Colin Shatterem's lanky frame loomed into view.

CHAPTER 23

1984

James felt an icy chill of terror pulse through every nerve in his body. The gaunt figure of Colin Shatterem pulled a stool from beneath the table and sat down with robotic precision onto the chair. He pulled off a pair of thin silk purple gloves, finger by finger, and placed them down onto the table. He stroked his black beard as he stared ahead at his new nemesis. James noted the dark bruising on the back of his hand; as if someone had stapled a beetroot slice to his fist. If this whippet-thin nothing of a man had actually been punching someone, reasoned James, he certainly wasn't very good at it.

James glanced across towards the exit. The pub door was a good twenty feet away, before which was an obstacle course of tables and drinkers, scattered haphazardly around the room. No clear path to freedom. Even if he made the door, he couldn't be certain that there wasn't something worse waiting on the other side. Colin correctly observed James' mental decision making.

"If you are thinking of making an escape, I suggest you re-think. Anton will be here shortly, and he is very keen to meet you."

"Anton?" said Nigel, with a grin. "That bloke that looks like he eats professional wrestlers for breakfast?"

"The very same," confirmed Colin. "So, Mr Harpman, failure to be here is simply planning your own funeral. A friendly tip."

Colin's advice appeared anything but friendly. The library manager's fierce eyes danced with hatred, ripping through James as if he were damp tissue. James summoned his nerve and stared back with equal fervour. He knew Shatterem had him bang to rights, but sod it, he was this far in now - might as well make an enemy for life. Though at present, he really wasn't sure how long that life might be.

"Colin," welcomed Nigel with a deep, cheery bray.

"Norman," greeted Colin.

"Nigel," replied Nigel, irritably.

"Wait," piped up James. "You don't even really know each other? You two aren't even friends? You sold me out to someone you barely know?"

Nigel shrugged at his son and smirked.

James couldn't even look at his father. "You backstabbing son-of-a-bitch."

"Careful James, that's your Nan you're talking about there," laughed Nigel, as he folded his arms in glee at his little joke. Then his face darkened, and he leant into James, nose-to-nose. "Don't you ever punch me again, you disrespectful shit."

"Mr Harpman," cut in Colin. "As a thief, you have no moral vantage point from which to broadcast your sanctimony."

"Oh, talk properly, you panto-costume spindlewank."

Colin shook his head disdainfully, pulled his glasses an inch down his nose and peered over the frames at James.

"Your friend: where is he?" His acidic voice razored through James' skull.

"Like my luck, I'm all out of friends."

"It's Bill," said Nigel. "His mate is called Bill."

"Nigel, I am going to break your jaw," warned James.

"Such awfully violent tendencies. But then, what else am I to expect from a common thief?" said Colin.

"I don't know what you're talking about," protested James, badly.

"James, you and your friend - this Bill - are in *a lot* of trouble. I really would not want to be in your shoes right now."

"Why not? They'd be the only decent thing you'd be wearing," retorted James with a sneer.

Nigel stifled a giggle, as Colin rolled his eyes.

"We want this to be easy for you. We do not need to involve the police. I just want my car back, and my associates need my money back."

"Money?" asked James, in a high-pitched yelp. His eyes darted across to Nigel.

"Money?" repeated Nigel, and he turned to stare at Colin. "I thought this was about a car?"

"Oh, come now, James here knows what he's done. Not content with depriving me of my automobile, he and his friend managed to plunder several thousand pounds from my side business. Plus, they spilled some milk, over which I will not cry. Though Anton was most upset."

James' legs buckled from the hammer blow of reality. In one short conversation, he'd been rumbled for grand theft auto and daylight robbery. How in the name of Boy George's eyeliner did Colin know about the milk float? James flipped his mind's rolodex for a suitable answer or explanation. A blank smudge of featureless white whirred through his brain. Thinking was absolutely not on his side right now. He stared mute ahead at his bearded, beady-eyed accuser, then to his denim-clad father, who was examining his son with a detached if amused curiosity, an unlit cigarette dangling from his lip.

His father. That stupid, selfish, feckless sperm donor. In literally every sense, he was the whole reason James sat in the pub sweating pints of liquid guilt through every pore. How on earth could he have been so naive to think that he could rebuild a relationship that never existed? A relationship with a married man who shagged babysitters, spread vicious rumours about his friends, and had all the moral fortitude of a flan. This was Nigel's fault, thought James, and damn it, it was about to become his problem too.

James cleared his throat, cracked his knuckles, and leaned across the table towards his dad.

"Shit Nigel, looks like he's rumbled us."

Nigel's smile faltered in an instant and the cigarette fell from his lip. Colin Shatterem turned his head slowly to face the co-accused. He fixed him with a poisonous stare.

"Er, what," spluttered Nigel. "No, Colin, I don't know what he's talking about."

"Oh Nigel, don't play silly dickheads," continued James. "He knows about the milk float. We should never have robbed it," he added, melodramatically. (The drama teacher always accused him of overacting in school plays, something he was employing to daytime soap opera level effect now.)

"James, shut your mouth, and stop talking bullshit. Colin, he's talking crap, I don't know anything about any milk float or thousands of stolen pounds."

"Check his pockets," suggested James, calmly.

"Piss off!" snapped back Nigel.

"Nigel?" asked Colin, his eyes searching deep inside Nigel's own.

"He's trying to get out of it, clearly!" said Nigel.

"Except that he has admitted guilt," contradicted Colin. "He is merely asserting *your* part in this regrettable escapade."

He really does talk like a cunt, thought James.

"He's trying to throw you off the scent! Even a fruity twat like you must see that!" argued Nigel.

Colin thinned his lips and shook his head solemnly at Nigel.

"That is really not helping your case, Mr Stanton."

"Colin, I swear on my family's life," said Nigel, as he shot a withering look across to James. "Whatever this is - the milk float and the money - has nothing to do with me."

Colin flicked his eyes towards James, who was wearing the overplayed shock of a betrayed co-conspirator just a little too thickly.

"After everything we've been through Nigel," he exclaimed, and shook his head in childish dismay.

"Empty your pockets," said Colin.

"Why should I? I've got nothing to hide."

"Well, if you've got nothing to hide Nigel," began James.

"Oh, sod off, empty your pockets!" he shouted back to his son.

"Fine," agreed James. He pulled his wallet from his pockets and opened it. Completely empty. Satisfied, Colin turned to Nigel, whose jaw was barely hanging on.

"But you had hundreds..." Nigel trailed off, confused. James stood up and pulled out all his pockets. Empty.

"Mr Stanton," continued Colin. "I cannot and will not force you to display your pocketed items. However, my associate Anton will soon be here, and he is more than physically capable. It will be far less painful for all if you were to comply now, hmm?"

Nigel's already ruddy face turned a deeper shade of crimson. With cosmic reluctance, he slowly reached an arm into his left jeans pocket, pulled, and let the triangular cloth dangle for his interrogator's benefit. Nigel nodded patronisingly with a faint smile.

"See!"

"Now the other," ordered Colin. Nigel bared his false teeth in frustration and complied slowly. With a glacial sense of urgency, his right hand entered its corresponding pocket down to Nigel's hairy wrist. He pulled out an empty hand.

Then, in a flicker of astonishing speed, Nigel yanked his hand back out and thrust a fistful of tightly wrapped notes at Colin. The bundle of cash shot at his face with such swift ferocity, he fell backwards off his chair. The librarian flew back in shock onto the carpet, the money showering him in an autumnal flutter of pound notes, mocking his supine position.

Before the pub's patrons even noticed the commotion, Nigel bolted from his chair towards the door. He pushed entire tables over, and upturned stools in his path as he made his way outside. A chorus of jeers, furious swearing, and incredulous bellowing accompanied his chaotic trample across the lounge.

Stunned but wasting no time, James grabbed his jacket and followed in hot pursuit. He jumped up, then leapt across the tables that were still standing. Pint glasses and ashtrays went flying into the air, as James' shoes bounded across unsteady surfaces that wobbled precariously on the sodden carpet. Apologising as his legs narrowly avoided kicking his fellow drinkers in the face, James fell forward onto the barely-padded lounge bench, and collided with a small stag party of four friends. He landed on the groom, winding him in the process, and splintered a yard of ale that soaked shattered glass and sticky golden alcohol into his James' jacket. He rolled onto the floor and launched straight back up. He peered back at Colin. He was trying to get up, but he found himself at the mercy of a small group of boozehounds scrabbling desperately at the money strewn about him, clawing at the floor for a chance at sterling. The two men locked eyes for the briefest of nanoseconds. James narrowed his gaze, regretted every life decision he had ever taken, and let out a guttural bellow of frustration. He turned back to the door, muttered an apology towards the groom, and pushed his way out in the street, his heart hammering like a thunderclap on shuffle.

Colin bellowed in a nasal rasp of apocalyptic exasperation. "Anton!"

CHAPTER 24

2019

Sue Harpman pinched her thumb and forefingers together tightly, digging her nails into the skin. As the index finger closed in on puncturing the tip of her thumb, she withdrew back and instead unscrewed a water bottle to take her seventh unnecessary gulp of the morning. Nigel stood next to her at a leafy bus stop, a self-satisfied grin plastered across his face.

"You alright?" asked Nigel, a distinct lack of concern in his voice.

"What do you think?" said Susan, despondency etched into her soul.

"I think you're misunderstanding me, and that's sad and wrong."

"A selfish would-be rapist is telling me I'm wrong. OK Nige'."

Nigel's face darkened in a brief thunderclap of anger. He breathed in deeply and replaced it with an oleaginous simper.

"Selfish? No, no no, Susan, I don't want you thinking that of me."

"Well, I do, and of the many things you currently control in my life, my thoughts aren't one of them."

Nigel bristled with genuine irritance. "I'm not enjoying being in this position, you know."

"Then leave! Leave me and my children alone and give me back my husband. Reject selfishness. And maybe don't force your daughter-in-law to go on a school zoo trip with a loaded gun."

James' father shook his head in fervent disagreement.

"Susan, you worry too much."

"No, I just live in a world with consequences. I don't flee to another time zone when it all gets a bit too much."

"You could say the same for your husband," said Nigel, and stubbed his cigarette out on the pavement.

Susan's stomach dropped as she realised the implications of Nigel's statement. Had James run away from his family? Since his Mum had passed, he had been distant and distracted a lot of the time, rarely present in the moment.

She packed the thought away in the, "things to worry about later" folder of her mind's well-stocked athenaeum as the bus arrived. Susan's colleague Barbara stared through the smoky glass of the vehicle's front window. Her face changed from welcoming to confusion as they pulled up next to Susan and Nigel. The children cheered as the door opened. Nigel waved.

"Mrs Harpman!" greeted Barbara. "And Mr Harpman?"

Susan hoped Barbara wouldn't question whether it *was* Mr Harpman. Her colleague had only met him a small handful of times so relied on her memory making up for any differences. He looked like he was under the bus, not trying to board it.

"Sorry Barbara, he was attacked yesterday," Susan explained. "I didn't want to leave him on his own."

"Attacked? My god, is he ok?"

"Yeah. No. Sort of. He'll be fine with the pupils; I'll keep him out of the way."

"You should have rang in, we'd have understood."

"And leave you alone with Callum Agnew? What if he eats your tights? Besides, who else would do it? We'd have to cancel, it'd be illegal without proper cover."

Barbara nodded in acknowledgement, though bit her lip awkwardly.

"Speaking of legal, is he…" She left the question hanging, hoping Susan would join the dots.

"Police checked? Not really, but he's my responsibility. Just pretend he's not here. I try to."

Barbara attempted an encouraging smile but couldn't hide her bewilderment. The three adults boarded the bus. Rows of excitable, restless children turned their faces to the front to greet their teacher.

"Good morning children," announced Susan. "Hope you're all ready for a good day. This man is Mr Harpman. No need to talk to him, or even look at him, ok?"

"Are you a boxer?" piped up one of the children from the back.

"Callum, what did I just say?"

"But he looks like a boxer, Miss. All bruised up."

"I'll take this Miss," said Nigel, laughing.

Susan huffed.

"Are you a boxer, Mr Harpman?" she asked wearily.

Nigel shook his head, then knocked the children back with a wide and monstrously toothy smile. He addressed Callum.

"Regrettably no, the pugilistic artform is not one I have mastered, young man."

"Don't talk like that," said Susan through clenched teeth. "No one talks like that."

"My Dad could have you," shouted another boy.

"Your Dad had a lot of men then?"

The bus hummed with a mixed response from the children; a light giggling from the senior year and a baffled murmur from the youngest.

"So, what's your name then?" asked Nigel, ignoring Susan's pleading gestures for him to stop engaging.

"Trevor," replied Trevor. "But my friends call me Trevor."

"What?"

Susan dug an elbow into Nigel.

"Trevor it is then," he announced. "A fine name it is too."

"Can we swap seats?" asked Trevor. "My seat's uncomfortable and smelly because it's next to the toilet."

"Well, we can't have that then, can we Trevor? I'd happily take your stinky seat if it'll make you feel better."

Susan surreptitiously stepped on Nigel's foot.

"There'll be no swapping seats, Trevor," Susan decreed.

"Sorry Trevor! Was just trying not to be, you know, *selfish*." Nigel looked squarely into Susan's eyes as he made his apology. She turned to see that most of her pupils were now actively interested in Nigel. Years of dedicated teaching meant nothing compared to a minute of crowd-pleasing populism.

"Right," said Susan. "We should get…"

"I'm called Felicity" interrupted Felicity.

"Well, that's a very pretty name, Felicity," replied Nigel.

Felicity blushed and made a love heart symbol.

"My name's Warren," said Warren.

"Right, shall we get going?"

The bus pulled out of the bus stop as the teacher and her fake husband took their seats.

"My name's Warren" repeated Warren.

~

At the zoo, Nigel had been disappointed to find just how lowkey the whole park was. It was mainly rows of glass enclosures containing cute mammal after cute mammal, shivering in bales of hay. The occasional exotic bird, some shit-flinging monkeys, and lion's den aside, this was basically a pet shop that charged for entry.

He was still stung by Susan's accusations of selfishness. He could have gone anywhere in time, yet here he was trying to forge a relationship with his son's wife. What was selfish about that? Nigel stared gloomily into a marmoset enclosure. The miniature simian gazed back at its latest onlooker with an impenetrable pall. It scratched its head lazily and blinked at Nigel. The momentary break made Nigel concentrate instead on his reflection in the glass. He eyed his battered visage in revulsion: he barely looked like himself anymore. His bruised, bloodied head was a palette of purples, greys, and reds; a smorgasbord of clashing colours onto which a face had somehow gate-crashed. Susan entered the reflection and peered ahead at the marmoset.

"Ugly fucker, isn't he?" she remarked.

Nigel raised an eyebrow, and turned to face his son's wife.

"Dunno, I find him quite a cute little scamp," he replied.

"I was talking to the monkey."

Nigel tutted and took his hat off.

"What do you want?" he asked, with a rasp.

"My husband back and for you to get lost. What do you want, Nigel?"

Nigel narrowed his eyes then took a tobacco pouch from his pocket and went to roll a cigarette before Susan immediately slapped his hands.

"Don't you dare," she snapped.

Nigel protested grumpily and stuffed his hands and the tobacco back into his pockets.

"Shouldn't you be making sure the kids aren't screwing each other or whatever?"

"They're seven and under. Barbara's just holding the fort for five minutes whilst I'm checking *you're* not, dunno, holding up a flamingo for a few quid. I haven't seen you for the best part of an hour. What have you been up to? Where have you been?"

"Here and there. Enjoying the molluscs. Look, I'm bored, I want to feed something. Give me some money."

"I gave you a stash of cash this morning!"

Nigel shrugged. Susan hesitated but for a quiet life she reached into her handbag and grabbed a small fistful of change. As she poured the coins into Nigel's cupped hands, he grasped her fingers and stroked them firmly along to the tips. As if a live wire had been jammed into her spine, Susan jolted backwards at the touch and dropped the remaining change. Nigel curled his lips into a grin and bent down to pick up the coins.

Susan's shock turned to ferocity in a heartbeat.

"I don't know what you think you're doing, but don't you ever touch me again, have you got that?"

Nigel blinked in silent frustration as he put the change into his jeans' back pocket.

"Really Susan, you're stressed, I was just trying to be nice. Not selfish! I'm really not the monster your husband made me out to be, you know."

Susan was about to retort, when a shrill cry for help shattered the frosty air between the two. Instinctively, Susan ran towards the noise, away from her sorry excuse for a father-in-law. The yelp came again, and Susan followed its sound to a large wooden building next to the concrete block toilets - the mollusc shed. She pelted into the room to find an elderly lady comforting Callum Agnew. He was sitting on the floor rigidly. His legs were bent, the knees nearly touching his face, and his hands clasped together interlocked. Most troubling was his breathing, which was wildly excessive. Susan recognised the crude signs of a panic attack, though Callum's Jurassic gulps of air did seem somewhat theatrical.

"This lad's not well, call an ambulance," instructed the elderly lady. She took a tissue and tried to blow his nose, bizarrely. Callum stopped breathing heavily for a second to mutter something. It sounded suspiciously like, 'sod off' but Susan couldn't be sure, and was more interested in making sure the child was ok.

"No need for an ambulance, thank you, I'll take it from here," said Susan, firmly. "Callum, it's Mrs Harpman. Have you taken anything, or eaten anything you shouldn't have?"

Callum looked confused and stopped his breathing for a second. His eyes darted about for an answer. Not finding one, he simply shook his head, wobbling his jowls as he did.

"Right, what we need to do now is to control that breathing of yours. First, I want to, erm…" Susan hesitated, immobile in an instant.

"Oh piss!" shouted Nigel as he barged into the room.

His obscene outburst interrupted Susan's flow entirely. Flustered, she threw daggers at the hapless idiot, and went to continue her treatment. But much to her surprise, Nigel strolled over to the child with a cocksure confidence she found unsettling.

"I'll take over from here, Susan."

Callum broke into a smile upon hearing his teacher's first name. Then, almost mechanically, he returned to gasping for air.

Nigel pushed aside Susan and sat cross legged in front of the boy. He reached across and took his palms in his. Susan put her hand to her mouth in disbelief. *What was he doing?*

"Callum, is it?" Callum nodded enthusiastically. "Well Callum, I need you to be a big brave boy, can you do that for me?" Callum smiled wanly. "OK, can you slow down your breathing? In through the nose and out through the mouth." Nigel paused, unsure. "Actually, maybe try it the other way round."

Callum stopped breathing entirely to ask, "What?"

"That's right, Callum, good going," said Nigel encouragingly, and he squeezed the boy's hands tightly. Callum winced at the tight grip, but nevertheless slowed his breaths down to a regular pace within an unlikely thirty seconds of Nigel's medical assistance.

"It's a miracle," commented the old lady, and with a wink, nudged Susan in the ribs.

"Yes, it certainly is," agreed Susan, the cynicism dripping from her tongue. She stepped forward to help Callum to his feet and pulled the overweight lad up by his hands.

"How do you feel now, Callum?" asked Susan, kindly.

"Much better Miss, thanks to Mr Harpman. Thank you, Mr Harpman!"

Nigel tipped his hat to the boy and bowed his head.

"The honour was all mine, young Callum. Call me James."

"Thanks Mr James Harpman, you are my hero," said Callum as he charged both fists to the air.

"Right, with me, Callum," ordered Susan.

Nigel exchanged nervous glances with the old lady.

Susan took Callum by the hand and led him to the corner of the room. They stood next to a large plastic tub containing damp clumps of earth and half a dozen African land snails. The creatures nonchalantly rippled their feet across the clear sides, leaving a smear of mucus in their wake. Callum took a large chocolate bar from his pocket, tore open the wrapper, and started gobbling at it.

"Callum, what just happened there?" asked Susan.

"I had a panic attack, Miss."

"Right, and what is a panic attack, Callum?"

Callum stopped chewing and gave his mouth a moment off duty so he could fully concentrate on the question. His jaw slackened to show globules of brown, frothy saliva slowly trail from his teeth to his chin below. Even the slugs were disgusted. Susan had seen her pupil's revolting table manners countless times though, and was too incensed by what she suspected to give a damn about it.

"It's like a heart attack, Miss." His eyes flicked over to Nigel briefly, who winked at the boy. Nigel took his cue and began to stroll over to him.

"Stop!" ordered Susan, and held a hand out to warn off his advance. Surprising himself, Nigel did as was told and froze mid-step. "Callum, empty your pockets."

"But Miss!"

"Just do it."

The child reached into his trousers and reluctantly pulled free a fistful of sweets, a few chocolate bars, and several banknotes totalling a good fifty quid or so. Susan raised one eyebrow and stared deep into the boy's fretful eyes.

"Where did you get all this, Callum?"

Callum's eyes darted frantically between his teacher and Nigel, as warm chocolate goop dribbled from his chin and pooled onto the cold concrete floor. Susan muttered under her breath and crushed her fingers together into fists.

"Mr Harpman," she said, pointedly.

"Mrs Harpman?" answered Nigel.

"You bribed a child?"

"Just wanted to prove I'm not…"

But before either party could begin to discuss Nigel's stupid ruse, the couple were interrupted by yet another scream. A bellowing, ear-piercer that filled the crispy winter air and shook the birds from the trees.

This time, however, the fear sounded legitimate.

A school child burst into the room, arms flapping in a terrified hysteria.

"Felicity lovely, what is it?" asked Susan, feeling her chest tighten. Felicity opened her mouth to speak, but the words wouldn't form. Her lower lip wobbled, and tears formed in her eyes as she tried desperately to stop her teeth chattering in terror. She stuttered out several syllables before finally settling on the one sentence no one in Uncle Rusty's Petting Zoo ever wanted to hear.

"The lion's escaped!"

CHAPTER 25

1984

Nigel fled The Cloven Hoof with Olympian speed, belying the physicality of a middle-aged chain smoker with a drinking problem. His feet barely touched the pavement as his bony legs stampeded through the Hartnell streets. He ran from James, he ran from Colin, and he ran from whatever other dramas his increasingly complicated life might cook up. He took a sharp right turn into Wilson Walk where his shoulder smashed into a streetlight. He cried out in pain.

"Pisslamp," he roared angrily, and paused just long enough to deliver a couple of swift kicks to the blameless inanimate object before carrying on down the alley.

James followed a crucial twenty seconds behind. On any normal day, the fitter and leaner next generation-born Stanton could probably outrun his dad with his feet tied together.

This, however, was no normal day.

Virtually teetotal, he was completely unused to drinking pints of lukewarm yeast. Consequently, a belly full of beer and a head full of intoxicants made him virtually useless at running. His legs swerved from side to side, his feet abnormally heavy with each step. Propulsion made him feel dizzy and sick, and his limbs simply refused to cooperate. He was used to the svelte pelt of his regular daytime jogs. Now he was moving at the pace of a confused crackhead who'd just woken up to find his trousers on fire. His body felt dense and sluggish. He kept turning backwards to check for pursuers. Wheezing with all the athleticism of a clubbed seal, he took a wide right into Wilson Walk, and tripped over a bin. The filthy metallic cylinder crumpled beneath him, and spilled its contents onto the small, cobbled walkway. Empty crisp packets, used tissues, and broken bottles scattered across the street. James cursed and lifted himself off the strewn debris. He stumbled back to his feet and carried on down the alley.

"Nigel!" he shouted at full-throated volume. He needed to find out what else his dumbo father had told Colin, and protect their time machine at all costs. If it meant silencing Nigel forever, then so be it.

Resting outside a Rumbelows just around the corner, Nigel heard his son's call and groaned loudly. James recognised his father's voice. His eyes widened as an extra burst of energy pushed him further onward.

He screamed his father's name again, this time in a low guttural rasp. Nigel turned to run, but he suddenly realised that he could barely breathe, never mind sprint into the night. The intensity of the last few minutes had suddenly caught up with him, and his clothes clung to his body thanks to a thick layer of warm sweat.

James turned the corner to see his father bent over in exhaustion. Nigel was breathing excessively in a desperate bid to get more oxygen into his tired lungs. Only he found that sucking the hot summer air deeply was making him feel worse. His hands tightened, the fingers curled into an uncontrollable fixed clench, and his breathing became more erratic and shallow. His eyes bulged and reddened as he reached out towards his son. James knew the drill: the stupid sod was having a panic attack.

A blanket of ambivalence descended onto James: pure inner turmoil plastered across his face as his conscience staged a battle of moral obligation. Help the horrible bastard? He was, after all, just a human struggling to breathe. That's the most basic right of any living creature. Why should James deny anyone that? On the other hand, this was all his fault: a little panic attack wasn't going to kill him and hey, may even provide the git with a little humility. Though the lava coursed through his veins for the man, he couldn't just leave him.

With a sigh of resignation, James moved towards his father.

"Oh, come on then you daft twat," he said gently, as he cradled Nigel's convulsing body into his. "You need to focus and relax." He softly clasped his parent's hands and smoothed them with his fingers, drawing out the jitters. "Stop trying to breathe ten-to-the-dozen. Slow it right down, OK? In through the nose, and steadily out of the mouth. Can you do that?"

Nigel nodded wordlessly, his head shaking as he did. His eyes watered and he slumped gradually against the shop front, supported by James. He sat with his father as his breathing shed its frenetic urgency and eventually calmed.

James urged Nigel to his feet, and let him rest on his shoulder as they shuffled on. The still evening air hung heavily as each avoided looking at the other. James clicked his tongue impatiently and whistled tunelessly. *Anything* to fill the silent void. His full, stretched stomach felt awful; a gurgling mess of fear, regret, and hops. He wanted this nightmare to end.

Thanks to his son's intervention, Nigel had regained self-control; the sense of helplessness and surrender had all but completely dissipated. He pushed off James, resisting his help and limped on next to him. But the uncomfortable ground and the awkwardness of what had just occurred was needling his temper. The dexterity to roll another cigarette had returned, so he duly obliged his craving, much to James' ire.

"Really?" said James, finally breaking the silence.

Nigel lit the cigarette and coughed immediately.

"How do you feel?" asked James, reluctantly.

"Yeah, fine," replied Nigel, sheepishly.

"Right."

James wiped the sweat from his face and took a long look at his dad. Except to take a drag on his cigarette, Nigel's lips remained tightly shut.

"Fine, next time choke on your panic attack, see if I care," said James.

Silence resumed its position as the bitter soundtrack to the frosty air between father and son. James stopped, as Nigel took a moment to lean against the doorway. James' spine stretched out; he felt a pinch of power, towering over his pathetic father.

"You set me up, your only son. To Colin? What for? And did you know about the milk float, and what's that lanky twat got to do with it? Well, now it's backfired on you, 'cos I've convinced them that you're part of it. And you're going to get your head ripped off."

Nigel played dumb and kept on smoking.

"Oi Nigel, I'm talking to you, why did you do it?"

Nigel threw the cigarette onto the pavement and leapt to his feet.

"You punched me in the face. Your own father. What do you expect? A hug and a ruffle of the hair?"

James pushed his father back against the door forcefully. Nigel's body slammed against the glass like a ragdoll.

"You cheat on my Mum, you parent like it's an inconvenience, and you spend our family's money on a shagpad. What do *you* expect? Forgiveness and a fishing trip? You're a lousy father who never gave me or your daughter the time of day. Never threw me a ball to kick, took me to the cinema, told me about - I dunno - cars. Just nothing. You know, when you suggested a night out I genuinely thought you had changed, and wanted to make amends. More fool me for thinking you were anything other than a self-regarding failure of a decent human being."

"Oh, grow up you whining little shit. I didn't know anything about you robbing a milk float, you stupid wazzock. Stop blaming me for your failures. I 'didn't tell you about cars'? I don't know anything about cars. Pick up a book, learn for yourself. I gave you independence, the greatest gift of all. Fuck off and leave me alone."

"Gladly," yelled James. "Oh, by the way, once I heard what you did to him, I told Bobby Twang to take your guitars, equipment, and gave him the keys to your flat. You're welcome."

"What?" bellowed Nigel. He patted his pocket for his door key, but it had disappeared. The father and son glared at each other. James turned to leave. He stopped immediately.

At the far end of the alley stood two figures. One wiry and impossibly tall, the other short and improbably wide. Stood together they formed the silhouette of the number 10. James peered at the figures with a growing sense of unease. He recognised Colin's withering frame straight away, and the realisation crept up swiftly that the other fella was the milkman he'd robbed only days ago.

"Shit," was his one word.

Nigel didn't wait to exchange pleasantries. He pushed James aside and charged down the alley as fast as his tired legs would carry him. The librarian and the milkman made their way towards James, who took a step back in rigid dread as the vast spectre of Anton's enormous body advanced upon him. James looked right to see the diminishing speck of his father's disappearing act as he ran out of sight. James bunched his hands into fists and prepared himself. He ran towards Anton, his arms windmilling. Upon contact, Anton repelled his attack with ease, pushing James back as if he were a bothersome kitten. James flew backwards several feet. His coccyx smashed against the cobbled street, and he cried out in pain. Anton laughed, drew back his gums, and rubbed his mighty meat hooks together. They were the size of Christmas turkeys.

"I'm warning you," said James with a flicker of a smile, as he clambered to an upright position. Anton stormed over. James thrust his foot out and kicked his opponent hard in the shin. Anton looked down, unimpressed, and again, swatted James back several feet like a minor inconvenience.

James picked himself up and glanced down to see a pile of rubbish strewn across the cobbles. Sticking his leg out he rolled a bottle neck over his foot then punted it with full clumsy force towards his attackers. The glass flew with considerable gusto at Anton. It struck his brow and shattered upon impact, the shards razoring through his skin. The burly racist clutched his head and howled in pain as blood poured from the wound.

"Anton!" cried Colin in shock and moved immediately to assist his friend. Anton writhed in agony, clawing at the embedded splinters from his forehead. A few had lodged into his cheek but miraculously, none had punctured his eye. Colin reached for a hanky and began the painstaking process of trying to wipe powdered glass from his companion's face. At the far end of the street stood James, hand covering his mouth in sheer disbelief at the carnage he had just created. Colin took a nanosecond from his caring to shoot James a look of purest detestation, which James took as his cue to finally flee the scene.

At the far end of Hartnell town, Bill Lambert was fighting with neither his father nor a pair of angry drug dealers. He was, however, wrestling with some errant wiring that had freed itself from his overhead projector. He had balanced the box precariously onto the edge of the workbench, beneath which he lay poking into the apparatus with an impossibly thin screwdriver and a pair of nail scissors. There were better ways around this, he thought, but most involved being in the right decade. He pulled the earth wire from its entrapment, but no sooner had the thin tube become free than Bill's fidgeting fingers dropped the scissors. The sharp jaws plummeted down onto the stone floor, narrowly missing Bill's temple by mere millimetres.

"Oh, carob drops!" exclaimed Bill in frustration. He waited patiently for his temper to subside then carried on calmy fixing the time machine merely seconds later.

After sealing the box back together by blowtorch, he slid himself free from the workbench and stood up to admire his handiwork.

"Not bad, Bill," he said aloud, awarding himself a moment of praise. His brief celebration ceased however; he noticed the smashed coffee cup he dropped earlier and thought of James. His stomach lurched and his blood fizzed with anxiety. He *loathed* fighting with his best friend. It felt so alien and uncomfortable, threw his life upside down, and infused even the sweetest moments with a dollop of sour. For two people who usually went out of their way to avoid confrontation with anyone else, they were unusually regular scrappers as pals. Bill literally wore the scar to prove it.

He trudged over to the time machine and lifted the box hesitantly, then carried it out to the Triumph, parked to the rear of the building. He rested it gingerly on the bonnet, unlocked the vehicle then leant into the passenger's side. He positioned the machine inside as it had been when they first stepped into the vehicle. The same vehicle that had since been left to rust under a bush for the ensuing decades. Bill's head was firmly ensconced within the footwell as he fixed the power cable into the cigarette lighter when an unknown voice broke Bill's concentration.

"'Ello 'ello 'ello, what's going on here then?" boomed the voice sternly.

Bill smiled, assuming James had returned to apologise. He lifted his head from the car to greet his best friend. He instantly recoiled upon seeing the voice's owner. Stood in front of him was the unmistakable sight of a British Bobby. The officer was resplendent in a tall custodian helmet and black buttoned-up uniform with black tie and white shirt. Bill's eyes danced nervously over the walkie talkie radio nestled snugly between his jacket, and a small row of shiny numbers on the law enforcer's epaulettes. Bill's mouth dried and his heart smashed through his ribcage in a thud so hard he thought the copper would be able to hear.

"Can I help you officer?" he whimpered, screwdriver still in hand.

"It looks like you can," informed the officer. He took a small white notebook from his breast pocket and flipped the pages. "This car has been reported stolen. Anything you wish to tell me sir?"

Bill started crying.

CHAPTER 26

1984

The copper dropped his notebook in surprise. He wasn't used to dealing with crying suspects. In fact, he wasn't used to dealing with suspects at all. He reached out a hand to pat Bill on the head.

"There there," he cooed soothly. "No need to cry. I'm sure we can straighten all this out." Bill's whimpering turned to wailing. He scrunched up his blotchy eyes and covered his face with his palms in shame. Great soggy sobs burst from his soul. It had been a trying week, all told.

The police officer picked up his notepad, pocketed it, and turned away from Bill. With his back to his perp, he radioed into the station.

"Pccch!" heard Bill. "I'm in the old mechanic shop at the Spooner Industrial Estate, next to the former cheese factory. Have a suspect in the custody. Yes, he's in the custody right now. Male, curly hair. The stolen artefact is present. I will be bringing him in for questioning. Over. Pccch!"

The policeman turned back around to face Bill. He was still weeping, sniffing back mouthfuls of tangy snot that now lined his throat. His face was red raw from crying, each new tear an abrasive scour against his cheeks. He sat upright in the Dolomite's passenger seat and caught sight of his blotchy face in the wing mirror. This wasn't how he saw his first foray into time travel going. If he was Doctor Who, he decided, he'd definitely be one of the crap ones.

"So," began the copper, uneasily. "Do you want to tell me about where you got this car?"

Bill pulled an embroidered hanky from his breast pocket and blew his nose. He exhaled deeply and raised his head to face his questioner.

"I don't know where to start. Or rather, when to start."

"Just tell me about how you stole this vehicle."

"Well, it's tricky. You see, we already had it. Sort of. We took it with the very best of intentions."

"I'm afraid intentions and the law aren't good bedfellows, sir. Also, your name."

"My name?"

"What is your name?"

"I'm…" Bill paused, determined not to give everything away. "My name's Peter Cushing."

"The film actor?"

"Oh yes, no, obviously not."

"Look sir, I know you're nervous, but you need to be honest with me. Save you getting into any more silly bother."

"No fine, my real name is Doctor Emmet Brown."

"A doctor, eh? Would have thought that a medical man would have enough money to buy his own motor car."

"What can I say? I'm an academic Doctor, not a medical practitioner." *What on earth am I saying?*

"Well, it must be nice doing what you want to do."

"I guess."

That was an odd thing for a policeman to say, thought Bill. (Though for all he knew, it was a perfectly normal thing for a policeman to say. He was so unused to being interviewed by the police, the law enforcer could have asked him the best way to boil potatoes and he'd be none the wiser.)

The policeman strolled around the workshop, inspecting Bill's tools. He picked up wires and circuit boards and buttons, turning over each with methodological scrutiny. Bill shivered in fright at what he might deduce from all this. Rarely had he felt so utterly powerless.

"And what are you doing here, Dr Brown?"

"Science, sir," answered Bill, meekly.

"For what purpose?"

"To extend our knowledge and understanding of the world."

"Don't get smart with me, you're in a lot of trouble already!" snapped the copper. Fear seized Bill.

"I wasn't trying to be funny, I promise!"

The policeman put down a lightbulb he was studying and calmly walked over to the car. He ran his hands over the smooth caramel-coloured bonnet and lightly kicked the tyres. He removed his helmet and clutched it in front of him right at Bill's sitting height. Bill stared at the badge. Given his fear of authority he'd never taken the time to take a proper look at a policeman's helmet before. First thing he noticed was how cheap and silly it looked. Like a kid playing dressing-up.

"You said 'we' earlier," said the policeman.

Bill's heart sunk into his bowels. He hadn't meant to drop his friend in this, even if they were currently fighting.

"Did I?"

"You know you did, Dr Brown. And you were seen with another man at the scene of the crime. Who is your accomplice?"

Bill scrambled to think. An intensely intelligent man, this wouldn't usually present a problem. But nothing about any of this was usual. "Marty Mc…Fox?" he answered. He wasn't sure that was right; he hadn't watched *Back to the Future* in over twenty years.

"Marty McFox?"

"Yup, that's him," said Bill with all the self-assurance of a dog kennel made from sausages.

"Took it from the library, didn't you? Did you know it belongs to Mr Shatterem, the manager?"

"We're very sorry for the upset, and will pay for any damage," Bill found himself saying. He thrust his wrists out, expecting to be handcuffed for his crimes. No cuffs came. In fact, Bill couldn't see any.

"It's a nice place, Hartnell library."

"Yes, I agree." agreed Bill.

"I didn't expect a car thief to be a learned man. If you are as you say you are - a doctor - you must have done a lot of reading."

"I've done my fair share," said Bill, unsure where this was going.

"I like reading," said the copper.

"Well, that's.."

"Actually, I don't like reading," interrupted the policeman. "I *love* reading. The printed page brings nothing but unfathomable joy to me. To absorb stories, characters, plots, and drama. The creative power of the author brought alive by simple black ink on white paper. Beautiful bound editions, softbacks, all neatly stacked. The arrangement of imagination. What a thrill. A building for the sole purpose of education via the published language. What a treasure, what a treat for all."

The copper had become fully animated, salivating at the thought of a fully stocked library, much to Bill's confusion. He paced the workshop, gurning at his own soliloquy and waving his finger around, pointing at thin air.

"Well, that's nice," said Bill, wondering what on earth this had to do with his arrest.

"Nice? *Nice*? It's the ultimate. Imagine you had a fraction of that passion for *your* job. Now imagine that it was whipped away from you at the very first hurdle not by your own hand, but by the actions of a pair of thoughtless bastards!"

Bill's mind suddenly switched on. He looked again at the helmet, the radio, and the - now evidently - toy truncheon. He could even make out the seal on the vacuum-formed plastic. A wave of relief was replaced instantly by a cold sweat that molested Bill's entire body. If he wasn't a copper, who was he, how did he know, and what did he want?

"You're not a real policeman, are you?" he asked, gingerly.

"You got me!" he said and reached for the inside of his tunic. "But this is a real gun. I really didn't want to use this, I thought the policeman ruse might last a touch longer. Still, it's amazing what souvenirs our grandparents brought back from the war, isn't it?

He pulled out a thick black metallic hand pistol, and pointed the firearm directly at Bill, whose hands shot up immediately.

"My name is Simon Colenutt, and you cost me my dream job at the library."

Bill mouthed "sorry" at Simon. Simon grabbed his plastic radio and made the pretend buzz noise Bill had heard earlier.

"Pccch! I'm just going to hold the suspect here for questioning."

Bill squinted in terror, and held his hands out cowering, expecting a bullet to pass through his skull immediately.

"I'm sorry I'm sorry I'm sorry I'm sorry," he repeated, terrified.

"You will be," replied Simon, and struck Bill firmly with the gun's butt, knocking him out cold.

CHAPTER 27

1984

James' brain took a backseat as an almighty surge of adrenalin powered his body through the streets of Hartnell. Screw Nigel, he simply had to get back to Bill and leave this rotten year behind. A failed, backstabbing father, a crooked librarian, and a giant racist were enough to convince him that time travel really wasn't for him. None of this shit had happened to Marty McFly. Where was his moment on stage playing Chuck Berry to a crowd of mind-blown admirers? At least when he was in the present everything fucked up in the right order.

A severe ache stabbed through James' chest. He clasped a hand to his hyperactive heart as he carried on running through the town. His dry tongue lolled from his mouth to which the evening's sickly mugginess clung. He daren't look back in case Shatterem and the Big Unfriendly Giant were closing in on him. He knew it was pretty unlikely, given Anton's face was currently dealing with a Glasgow kiss from a beer bottle. James still felt a smidgen of shame about that, regardless of his own peril. He hadn't meant to cause harm, just slow the guy down. Still, James counter-argued with himself, Anton *was* a massive racist. So, in a way, absolutely fuck him four times over.

He headed for the Spooner Industrial Estate. With any luck, his pursuers had no idea where the car was being kept. He could hide out there until Bill had finished the time machine. He'd simply have to apologise to his friend earlier than he'd planned to. (He *always* said sorry first. Largely because it was always his fault, but still.)

James was fairly sure he was heading the right way, but confidence wasn't exactly at full capacity. Thanks to the beer in his belly and decades of development in his hometown, he felt as if his internal compass was being trolled by an industrial magnet. Panic dulled his senses. So many streets, buildings, and pathways were completely different from his childhood. The town still retained a similar basic template as before, but the changes threw his gyroscope into meltdown. The high street remained largely intact, but the entire shopping centre was missing, replaced by a grand, almost needlessly ornate red brick building of unknown purpose. A few metres on a badly scuffed sign revealed it to be the local printing press. No wonder it was gone, James rued, thinking of all the magazines that had folded over the last fifteen years. He briefly thought of periodicals that had served his youth - *Mean Machines*, *FHM*, *Melody Maker*. How all had gone to die in the cutthroat world of dead tree publishing. Then he suddenly remembered his unfinished *Fear of Beans* review and added it to his list of worries.

The enormous superstore and its unnecessarily complicated traffic system was absent. In its place stood a vast furniture factory which had seen better centuries. Large sections of concrete were missing entirely, windows absent, and plants growing through the neglected roof. It looked to James as if the asbestos was the only thing keeping it up. How he had forgotten any of this was a mystery to him. Perhaps life had a way of deleting this inessential nonsense once it learned more important things, like the Heimlich manoeuvre or your wedding anniversary?

James' pace slowed down as he reached the edge of the estuary towards the industrial estate. He allowed himself a moment of respite with a small lean against a telegraph pole. As the dizziness descended, he realised he wasn't just tired, but *exhausted*. With any luck, he could simply crash onto a mattress and snooze until it was ready to leave. He let out a grim chuckle as he realised the best he could hope for now was a piss-stained discarded clump of springy fibre.

In 1984 the estate stretched out to the town's outer edge, with just fields behind. By 2019 entire neighbourhoods, cul-de-sacs, and luxury housing developments had since sprung up, extending Hartnell by at least another mile. James tried to remember which way they had driven in so that their return journey would avoid crashing through both shrubs and wanky apartments.

The sun was finally settling on Hartnell as he approached the workshop. Parked over the road were a couple of cars he hadn't seen before. James' stomach dropped: who came this far into a deserted industrial estate for the views? Cautiously, he crept up to the door, listening intently. He heard raised voices inside. None of them belonged to Bill. Shit.

He edged the door an inch and cupped his ear to the door. He heard barely one word of discussion before a hand reached from inside and pulled him by the hair into the building.

"Ow bollocks!" James shouted, as Anton's meaty fist threw him onto the concrete floor. He tripped over his best friend's body, lying prone next to the Triumph. James brought his hand to his mouth in shock and checked Bill's face. Semi-conscious, breathing lightly, and eyes half closed, Bill drooled a little and attempted a half-smile at seeing James' panicked face. A small spatter of blood trickled from the back of his head.

"Bill, I'm so sorry," said James, and for once, meant every syllable.

Bill burbled some incomprehensible gibberish and attempted a reassuring smile.

It didn't work. James could feel their time travelling adventure coming to an incredibly sticky end.

CHAPTER 28

1984

James looked up to see Colin, Anton, and an odd-looking policeman all staring down at the pair. None looked pleased to see him. The policeman held a pistol in his right hand. Colin clutched *Car Classics: The 1970s* with a rigid sneer plastered across his face.

"So *that's* how you knew where I'd be," said James, unnecessarily.

"If you are going to steal the library manager's car," explained Colin, "Maybe do not supply the victim with proof of your crime and location."

James raised his eyebrows in acknowledgment. "Yup, good point." He turned back to Bill. "You don't need to say you told me so, ok?"

Through the haze of his concussion, Bill simply glared disapprovingly at his friend.

"Now gentlemen," began Shatterem, pacing around the room rubbing his gloved hands together. "You are in the rare privilege of having a choice in tonight's proceedings. Firstly, you pay me every last penny of what you stole, then return my car to its original condition, and we say no more about it. For that I will let you off by having Anton lightly beat you for, say, five minutes?" Anton nodded reluctantly towards Colin. Holding a large wad of tissues to his bleeding face, five minutes would barely scratch the surface of what he felt he was owed.

"Let's hear option two," said James, hopefully.

Colin laughed mockingly. "Oh, my dear James, you are such a wag!"

Twat, thought James.

"Option number two then. Well of course, this is a free country. And in this wonderful free market economy emboldened by the even more wonderful Mrs Thatcher, you have freedom of choice."

"So, you and the milk monster over there are part of a drugs racket? I'm not sure dealing coke is part of the free market economy," said James.

"You think I can afford a Triumph Dolomite on a librarian's wage alone?" spat Colin, venomously. "And you can stop looking down your nose at 'supplying'. It's entrepreneurship without boundaries. No income tax, no VAT!"

Fear prevented James from singing the *Only Fools & Horses* theme.

"We are beholden to no one. No paper trail, no accounts."

"Well, we do keep logbooks and receipts, Col" countered Anton. "They're upstairs."

"Anton you imbecile!" roared Shatterem.

James raised his eyebrows and checked on Bill again, worried for his friend. Bill tried lifting himself up to a sitting position. He wanted to show James that his injury wasn't as bad as it looked, but his sore head wouldn't allow him to complete the task. James fumbled around in his coat surreptitiously.

"Option two then?"

"Ah yes, thank you," said Colin. "Option two - Anton beats you to death."

"Right," said James. "So, die or not die. Real head-scratcher that one. I guess option one then?"

Anton advanced on the pair.

"Wait!" begged James. Colin held out a velvet finger to Anton. The hulk stopped reluctantly. "It's just, before we get to the pummelling, I'm genuinely curious. How does a librarian get to be a drug dealer?" James reached inside his jacket and fumbled with his mobile phone.

"Businessman," corrected Shatterem.

"But your business *is* cocaine?"

"What is your point?" confirmed Colin.

"You deal cocaine. You're a drug dealer. Why can't you just own it? Admit it, be proud!"

"The nomenclature of my business is hardly important; I wonder why you push this matter?"

"Just want you to say it. Admit that Hartnell's finest librarian is actually a master criminal."

"Oh, 'master criminal', I like that!" Colin's fingers danced with delight. "Well, if it will satisfy your whining, then fine." Colin cleared his throat dramatically before he continued. "I, Colin Shatterem of Hartnell Library, am a master criminal. I take in vast shipments of cocaine and other substances from my suppliers. Then, using a network of contacts such as Anton here, distribute them around the local area for large profits and gain. Does that satisfy you, Mr Harpman?"

The corners of James' mouth turned upwards. "Thank you, yes it does."

"Hang on, 'Mr Harpman'?" interjected the policeman. "Doc Brown here said his name was Marty McFox!"

James turned to look at Bill. He raised an eyebrow disingenuously.

"Great Scott Doc, 'Marty McFox'?" James withered sarcastically. He turned back to the policeman. "Some copper he is. What is it with Dickhead of Dock Green anyway? Have you got the fuzz on your side?"

Colin smiled, revelling in James' unravelling.

"My dear Mr Harpman, you have been naive. A police officer? Alas no, but a fledgling librarian with a penchant for, shall we say, the theatrical. Allow me to introduce Mr Simon Colenutt."

Simon beamed with delight at his boss.

"Librarian? Am I back in the library, Mr Shatterem? Really?"

"Of course, dear boy! You have played your part with excellence."

"Bananarama!" shouted Simon, and waved his gun in celebration.

"For Christ's sake!" bellowed Anton. "Are we going to get to the beating or what?" The gargantuan racist clenched his fists tightly, and his face flushed a shade just shy of royal purple. Simon cowered immediately from the angry brute.

Colin Shatterem folded his arms, and tutted.

"I'm sorry, she gets like this," he explained to Simon. "Anton, be patient. You will get your pound of flesh. And more importantly, there is still the matter of my car." He turned again to address James and Bill. "What have you done to her?"

James looked at Bill and shrugged. How was he supposed to explain this?

"I'll show you," Bill muttered, quietly.

He pulled himself from the floor and yelled out in pain. He reached for the back of his head and rubbed his bulbous wound. The blood had dried slightly and matted his curly hair. It was as if a ballbag had been caught mid-detonation.

"I'll do it," offered James.

"Yes, you do it," ordered Colin to James. "Curly top, stay right where you are,"

James mouthed 'fuck you' to Shatterem.

"And Harpman, I advise you to be very quick about this. Anton will land a punch on your friend for every ten seconds you take. Anton, would you do the honours?"

The burly monster stepped over Bill, who buried his head into his chest, protecting as much as his body as possible. His skull still rang with muffled white noise and a grogginess that crashed repeatedly into his synapses. James panicked into the vehicle.

Anton took a swing at his prey. A fist like a granite loaf smashed into the side of Bill's head. He had never felt anything like it before. The brutal force shocked him to vomit spontaneously, as pain exploded onto his right ear. Coldness spread throughout his head whilst his heart rate tripled in a matter of milliseconds. Oddly, the agony seemed to subside almost instantly, replaced by a fuzzy numbness. Bill lost all feeling in his fingers, then arms. His head bowed to the ground, and the rest of his body followed. Double vision faded in and out of black. All he could hear was counting. But he didn't know who was counting, or why, or even what numbers were anymore.

"Seven. Six. Five. Four."

James scrambled about the car, grabbing bits of the time machine. He fumbled with a screwdriver and dropped it in the footwell.

"I would get a move on if I were you," warned Colin.

"Please!" begged James. He used a valuable microsecond to check on Bill. His friend was tucked into a foetal position, convulsing.

"Three."

"I'm going as fast as I can, I'll have all the explanations for you."

"Two."

"Please don't hit him again. You'll kill him!"

"One."

CHAPTER 29

1984

Anton smiled malevolently, clenched his fist tighter than before and drew back his arm as far as it would go. With colossal effort, James commanded every last milligram of his fading strength and wrenched the unwieldy lightbox from the car. He pointed it towards Anton and hit a switch with a final gasp as he fell back into his seat. A searing light emanated from the apparatus and blasted Anton with full force. The violent thug screamed in shock as a dazzling burst of ultrabrilliant white enveloped his hulking frame.

Within seconds, he was gone.

The room returned to its former light; summer dusk poorly illuminated by a fluorescent strip with no diffuser. James finally exhaled, and clambered out of the car to check on Bill. He cradled his friend's almost immobile body.

"Bill," he whispered. "How are you feeling?"

Bill unwrapped himself from the foetal position and merely blinked.

Colin Shatterem stood open-mouthed in disbelief, bewildered. He glanced over to Simon, who was still holding the gun shakily.

"Keep it trained on those two at all times," instructed Colin.

Simon did as he was told and aimed the weapon towards the two friends.

"Where is Anton?" demanded Colin. "What did you do?"

James snorted dismissively.

"Gone. Gone for good."

"What have you done to him? What is that?" He gestured towards the time machine that James had dumped down in the car seat.

"Anton is not mine or your problem anymore. He is in…" James paused, uncertain. He took a swift reading of the box. "He's in the year 459AD, to be precise."

"I beg your pardon?"

"I sent him back in time. Around the Jutes invasion, I think. Should suit a racist like him."

Simon tentatively pulled the hammer back on the pistol, and motioned for James to get away from the car. James put his hands in the air and shuffled away from the Triumph.

"I do not know what on earth the pair of you are up to," continued Colin. "But it stops right now. I demand my car and money returned, Anton or no Anton."

He motioned to Simon, who pulled back the hammer on the gun.

A new voice entered the conversation.

"God, are you trying to use up the world's supply of boring? Leave some for the rest of us."

Colin Shatterem span round to face this intruder. Nigel Stanton raised a hat to the room.

"You!" fumed Colin.

"Me," agreed Nigel. "Hello James."

James' jaw slackened as he took in the image of his returning father. Nigel winked at his son, then shot a finger gun salute to Colin. Colin snatched the firearm from Simon, furiously. James saw his opportunity and inched towards the vehicle.

"How did he get in? You are *fired*, Simon Colenutt. I'll see to it that you never work in literature again."

Speechless, Simon reached for his plastic truncheon, before immediately placing the toy back into its flimsy holster, his face flushed with shame.

"Nigel?" said James.

"James," replied Nigel. "You ok?"

James thinned his eyes and opened his arms to present the scene before him.

"Not really," he mithered.

"Has he hurt you?"

"No, but Bill…"

Nigel looked down at Bill's sorry state. The battered time traveller pulled himself up on James' legs and leant against his friend, fatigued.

"I'm fine, thanks," Bill spluttered, in a manner that suggested he was very much not. He perched himself against the workbench and sucked in air, maniacally.

Colin retrained the gun on Nigel.

"What are you doing here?"

"I'd be happier if we could have this conversation without a weapon pointed at me."

"I bet you would," smiled Colin. He kept the line of fire directly towards Nigel.

"OK, gun on me it is. I've got a deal for you."

"You are in no bargaining position, Mr Stanton." Colin turned his gaze to James and Bill. "Stay away from the car, the pair of you. I have no desire to be on the receiving end of your vanish ray."

James shuffled a few feet away from the Triumph. He had hoped for a repeat blast of time travel attack on their captors.

"Speak now of this deal."

Nigel adjusted his hat and straightened his shirt collars.

"Firstly, you must be aware I had nothing to do with any of this."

"What?" said James, aghast.

"Stay right there," threatened Colin, waving the gun.

"Colin, I would never double cross you," continued Nigel. "This pair of idiots have branched out on their own, they think they're the fucking A-Team."

"Who?"

"It doesn't matter. The point is, I'm offering you a once-in-a-lifetime opportunity here. And we can make *millions*."

"Go on," said Colin, intrigued.

"Time travel!"

"Time travel?" replied Colin, incredulously.

"Real, bonafide back and forth throughout history. Plundering the past to your wallet's content. Make sure fire bets you know that will pay out. Be at the right place and time of famous heists. Steal arts and treasures from whichever period you choose. Forget drug dealing, you can fill your boots from the annals of the olden days. Centuries of jackpots to be won. Have any woman, or probably man in your case, that you choose. Ultimate piracy across the decades. What do you say?"

"Time travel?" repeated Colin.

"That's what they've done to your car, it's a time machine! Think about it. These two robbing bastards are from the future."

James tore his coat off and slammed it down on the floor. His final thread of attachment to his father had been severed for good.

"Time travellers?" he laughed. "I've heard everything now. We're just souping up your motor to sell it on. Illegal parts from Bulgaria."

Colin thinned his eyes at Nigel quizzically.

"Colin, he is taking you for a mug, mate," continued James.

"Shut up," said Nigel.

"Let him speak," ordered Colin.

"This was all his idea. Every last plan of detail. The car, the coke money, even luring you to the pub under the pretence of ratting me out. It was a ruse to see if we could shake you down for even more. Me and Bill were more than happy with the car and the cash. But Nigel here wanted more. He wanted to *destroy* you."

"You lying wanker! Colin, you can't possibly believe this!"

"Oh, but time travel? Much more likely, eh?"

James stuck a middle finger up to his father. Nigel wanted to launch himself in fury at his son, but was aware Colin still had a loaded weapon aimed at his head.

"Colin, I can explain, he's my son from the future, and he hates me. This is his revenge. You've got to believe me!"

Colin inhaled deeply, strolled calmly over to Nigel, and smiled. Nigel smiled back. Colin took his gun and smashed it against Nigel's face, pistol-whipping him to the floor.

"You take me for a fool?" he bellowed, as he rained down blows onto Nigel's cowering body. Without the gun, the spindly weakling would have no power at all, but the solid steel butt struck again and again into his forehead.

As his father was beaten mercilessly by a deranged librarian, James dived into the passenger seat of the car and plugged the time machine back into the cigarette lighter. All he needed was a semi-conscious Bill to work the machine and he'd do the rest. The former part of the plan appeared nigh-on impossible though, as Bill leant against a workbench, sleepily sucking his thumb.

Colin stood back from his handiwork, and gasped at what he had done. Fresh bruises and welts had scattered across Nigel's face, the physical imprint of his rage. Nose bent and blood streaming into his mouth, Nigel looked across to James thinking he might offer help. To Nigel's intense disappointment, his son was too busy fiddling with a car to even notice.

Colin raised his gun and aimed at James in the car.

"I told you not to move!"

He went to fire a bullet into James, but a small fist thumped him on the back and caught him off guard. The librarian cried out in surprise, and dropped the gun. Simon kicked it away, then jumped onto the back of Colin and began peppering his head with little rabbit punches. Irritated, Colin shook off his now ex-employee and tried to subdue him with his own underwhelming brand of measly blows. The pair had the weakest fistfight Bill had ever witnessed. It was like two blades of grass swaying gently into one another.

"I just wanted to be a librarian!" screamed Simon. He slapped at Colin with open palms, pulled off his glasses, and poked him in both eyes. Colin Shatterem fell to the floor, clutching his peepers in horror. His head hit the concrete, and he slumped forward, dazed. Simon spat at his former boss, then ran from the building wailing into the sweltering summer night.

"Bill, get here now!" yelled James to his friend. Bill stumbled over to the Triumph and looked into the open door. James sat in the passenger seat, almost in near tears trying to fathom which wire was which. His eyes pleaded for Bill to take over. James rued the day he had decided to give up paying attention in physics in favour of learning to draw perfectly his favourite bands' logos. To be fair though, his command of the *Iron Maiden* font was impeccable.

Bill opened the driver door and grabbed the lightbox. He pulled a mass of wires and cabling, crossed over the colours to disentangle them, and jammed the connector into the cigarette lighter port.

"Thermo alternator," he slurred to James, who had no idea what that meant. Bill turned the key in the ignition and the car roared into life.

"Let's get the heck out of nineteen eighty..."

CLICK

The cold, hard barrel of a Webley Revolver pressed against Bill's head.

"Not so fast boys," croaked Nigel, spitting blood onto the dashboard.

CHAPTER 30

1984

James sighed loudly. They had been *so close*.

"Out of the car, now," screamed Nigel, slamming his fist on the Triumph's roof.

The pair got out of the vehicle. Inexplicably, Bill giggled a little, as he waddled over unsteadily to the workbench.

"What's he laughing at?" said Nigel.

"Beats me," shrugged James.

"Good idea," replied Nigel, and struck his son across the face with a right hook. "Should have done that a long time ago. I am your dad, after all. That's my name, it's my title. I'm your *dad*."

The warm tang of iron flooded into James' mouth. He reached for his swollen lip then laughed in defiance along with Bill. He wasn't even sure why he was chuckling, but it made just as much sense as anything else right now.

"You'll never be my dad, *Nigel*."

Nigel shook his head and waved the gun at the two giggling idiots.

"Right, here's how it's going to be. You're going to set this thing to where you came from. 2019, was it? Let's say two days before you left. Then set it for one million years for a return journey - dinosaur times."

He shot James what he thought was a menacing look. James rolled his eyes. "But lock out the controls for that return journey. You can do that, can't you, curly top?"

James grabbed Bill by the arm. "Bill, don't."

"Or what? We get shot?" replied Bill. "I don't want to get shot, I've already been hit very, very hard tonight. I'm no scientist, except I am, and I think a bullet through the head might just finish me off."

James let go reluctantly. Bill winked as he climbed into the vehicle.

"No funny business. Set the dates, or whatever it is you do."

"Just two journeys? 2019, then a million BC?"

"Dinosaur times, yes!"

Bill punched in the coordinates as he muttered, "moron" under his breath.

As Bill fiddled with the car's machinery, James took stock of the carnage around the workshop. His father grasped a gun as he tended to a deep gash in his forehead. A concussed Bill, a faraway look on his face, his head soaked in blood. Colin, a stationary lump of tangled velvet. James thought he could hear him whining, but it could just be the faint whistling of the trees. The massive racist milkman was missing entirely, having just been sent hurtling back several hundreds of years. He was effectively dead, about which James didn't feel all that comfortable. Comparatively, James thought he had done quite well as injuries go. Just a single sucker punch from Nigel, and a creeping fatigue from tonight's events. Plus, thanks to *The War Machines*, a newfound appreciation for *Fear of Beans*.

This time travel business had *really* gotten out of hand.

"What are you doing Nigel?" asked James. "What do you hope to achieve from this?"

"My boy, I am going to fuck up your life the way you've fucked up mine."

"What happened to your 'get rich' scheme?"

"Oh, I'll do that afterwards for dessert. And don't think about fucking me over." Nigel pointed at Bill. "As insurance, curly top is coming with me."

"No!" cried Bill and James in unison.

"It's that or I commit spermicide right now," said Nigel, and cocked the gun at his son's temple.

"James mate, don't be a silly pudding. Don't worry. I'll be fine," assured Bill.

"That's good to know mate." James paused. "I am also a bit worried about myself being stuck in the past. Perhaps selfishly I know, but still."

"If you're done, close the door, Bill," commanded Nigel.

Bill reached for the handle. He put his hand on the rubber pull grip, and began the motion to pull it to. But he didn't close the door. Instead, he closed his eyes and let out an enormous guttural moan.

"Close the door," Nigel repeated.

"I am so sick," he drawled, a lilt of pique in his inflection. "I am so Bakewell tart sick." Bill raised his head, which was juddering with a crackle of fizzing energy.

James backed up from the car and allowed himself the beginnings of a smile. He shook with excitement and his eyes blazed with anticipation. It was *this* Bill. He knew this Bill. He didn't come around often. He had been on the receiving end of it before. Nigel had no such intel.

"Close the door and let's get going you massive spaz!" ordered Nigel.

Bill turned to face Nigel, head on. The two were close enough to kiss.

"I am so custard sick to death-by-chocolate cake of doing what I'm told by people like you."

"People like me?"

"People like you." Bill's tired eyes shone fiercely.

Nigel scoffed. "Silly puddings?"

"No. Ignorant *cunts*. Ignorant fucking cunts who don't even fucking know when the fucking dinosaurs fucking lived!"

Bill lunged at Nigel and buried his forehead deep into James' Dad's face. Bursting on impact, Nigel's bridge bone splintered, blood exploded from his nostrils, and his eyes flooded with tears. Bill leant across, turned on the ignition, leapt out of the car, grabbed a remote control from under the seat, then slammed shut the door.

He hit a button and waved goodbye to a shocked Nigel, who was nursing his mess of a schnozz.

"Get back," warned Bill, and hit a button on his big box of tricks.

The car screeched into life, reversing out of the workshop, smashing through the garage door and into the deserted estate.

"Better buckle up, Nigel, you silly pudding," he shouted, as the car's panicking inhabitant couldn't decide whether to shoot his way out of the vehicle or try to steer it. As Bill hit another button which made the car careen off into the night at petrifying speeds, Nigel opted to try to steer it to avoid instant death.

The car flashed a blinding white and disappeared from 1984.

James pulled a hand up to his mouth.

"What just happened?"

"What was always going to happen," replied Bill, with a big dopey, slightly brain-damaged grin.

"Remote control?"

"Remote control!" laughed Bill.

"Has he gone to dinosaur times?"

"No James, 2019."

"What? But that's how all this trouble started!"

"Precisely, we can't change our past, even if it is in the future."

"But he's just sodded off with our only time machine."

"Oh James, you really think I spent my time here building just one time machine?"

Bill picked up a torch and led James outside to the rear of the workshop. Barely visible beneath a mess of foliage was a corner of tarpaulin. Bill pointed the flashlight into the trees and pulled the canvas away. Beneath stood the impossibly inelegant sight of a Lada saloon car, resplendent in unremarkable cream.

"What's that?"

"Russian engineering, given a fourth dimensional spin."

"You built two time machines?"

"Why would I have spent all that time making just one time machine, knowing that your dad was going to take it anyway? We might as well have tried to make a getaway on an exercise bike. Also, the clues. Remember 'Double your efforts to do over fate'?"

"Oh yeah, didn't think of that. Shitting heck, you built two time machines whilst I made a shitty scrap book and screwed everything up with Nigel. You're brilliant. You're bloody brilliant, Bill."

"Apology accepted. By the way, 'The Jutes'?"

"*Horrible Histories*, obviously. How are you feeling?"

"Terrible, thanks. Groggy. Very groggy."

"Same. We should get going. But a little housekeeping first."

James strolled back into the workshop and crouched down next to the woozy frame of Colin Shatterem.

"Oi, bookkeeper," he said and lightly slapped Colin's face.

The shock of being manhandled jerked him into life. He glowered at James, no less incandescent than he had been all week.

"Bookkeeper means accountant," he corrected.

"Yeah, whatever. Right, first things first. For what it's worth, I *am* sorry about taking your car. Nothing personal. It was kind of fate, if you can believe in such things. Secondly, you're going to stop drug dealing."

Colin tried to scramble away, but James grabbed his collar roughly and forced him to stoop back down.

"But Mr Harpman, you put me in the most awkward position."

"Not the first time I've heard that, and no complaints yet."

Bill tutted loudly.

"You're going to ditch the drugs, concentrate on your lovely library, and leave us alone forever. No vendettas, no vengeance. Maybe even, if say, one of our kids loses a book on loan, such as *The Gruffalo*, you overlook charging us?"

"What?"

"Alright, forget the last bit. But definitely no more charlie, no more beatings, and keep your trap shut about us."

Colin snorted derisively.

"Or what? What, pray tell, can you two oafs threaten to keep my silence?"

Bill nodded in silent agreement, completely in the dark on what James was proposing. James reached into his pocket and pulled out his phone. He swiped it open, pressed on the photos app and hit play on something. Colin's face fell harder than an acrobat on meth. In crystal clear high definition, he watched a video of himself declaring his drug dealing secret directly to James' phone. His shrill nasal pitch cut through the air like lemon juice in a wound.

"I, Colin Shatterem of Hartnell Library, am a master criminal. I take in vast shipments of cocaine and other substances from my suppliers. Then, using a network of contacts such as Anton here, distribute them around the local area for large profits and gain."

James stopped the video.

"If anything happens to us," warned James, "This video goes straight to the police. And I plan on keeping this safe for the next, let's say, thirty-five years at least. Also, there's all those incriminating receipts and invoices upstairs, which we'll hang onto for safekeeping."

James dragged himself upstairs, opened the boxes, and stuffed the paperwork into his backpack.

"Plus," added Bill, "and this is very important. That book, *Car Classics*? That has to go back on your shelves indefinitely."

"And make sure this photo stays in its inner sleeve," said James. He handed Colin the photo of Nina and Nigel dressed as Father Christmas. "Don't let anyone actually borrow it. You see to that, or the cops see that."

"My suppliers will take my finger!"

"Then you better keep those lovely gloves of yours, eh?" said Bill.

Feeling faint, Colin immediately wet himself. James and Bill stared down as piss soaked into the trousers, causing a dark patch to spread out onto the librarian's crotch.

James patted Colin on the shoulder.

"Point made; we're going."

"Yeah, we're pissing off now," added Bill, and smirked at Colin as he grabbed his belongings.

The pair headed off out of the workshop. 2019 felt tantalisingly close.

CHAPTER 31

2019

Susan Harpman had only ever wanted three things from life. She really didn't think she was asking too much.

Firstly, Susan Harpman had always longed for the gift of children. Life had delivered those. Or rather, she had delivered those, and earned herself the indignity and sting of vaginal stitches as a result. Still, children. So, yay to that.

Secondly, since she was old enough to scour nature books, she had always dreamt of seeing the northern lights in person. Just three years ago, James had come through with a holiday in Norway, and Susan had seen for herself nature's very own light show in all its gob-smacking glory.

Thirdly, and perhaps the humblest and perfectly reasonable of all her requests, she wished not to be eaten alive by an escaped lion. Given her predicament, she felt that life was only delivering at sixty six percent capacity right now.

In single file, the small group of two adults, an elderly lady, and two children snaked their way round the building in brisk fashion towards the 'simian experience', which was one more exhibit closer to the exit. Susan had, possibly foolishly, asked Nigel to lead the way so she could see both children at all times.

"If we keep together, we're all moving safely and surely towards the exit," Susan mumbled with insincere authority.

"All together in one clump? To the lion, that'll be like eating a prawn salad," hissed Nigel, as he crept along the outer wall of the mollusc shed.

"Am I going to be a prawn salad, Miss?" whimpered Felicity. "I don't want to be a prawn salad."

"Nah, you'll be a toothpick. When he's had his fill eating the rest of us, he'll use you to wipe the guts off his gums," gloated Callum.

"No one's being a prawn *or* a toothpick, we'll be fine," assured Susan.

"Bollocks to this," said the old lady, and broke free from the group to waddle off on her own.

"Excuse me!"

"Let her go Miss," said Callum. "Let the lion pick her off first and give us a chance to leg it."

"He's got a point," agreed Nigel.

Susan shook her head and carried on, bringing up the rear.

"Are you sure that there are no other pupils here, Felicity?" she asked.

"No miss, they're all in the cafe."

Susan was mostly assured of their safety in the optimistically titled Yum Barn. (In reality a giant windowless shed with benches and the option of chips or starvation. Except in winter, which it was, when the staff were absent and the kitchen closed.) Susan tried ringing Barbara again, but it went straight to voicemail.

"Can you just go over it again, Felicity, if you don't mind?" she asked.

"I went to the toilet, Miss, but came out of the wrong door. It had a bar across it."

"An exit, right."

"Yes. So, I got out and the door shut behind me. Then I saw the lion's den, which had a big hole in the fence."

"How big?"

Felicity pulled her arms as wide as they would go and as high as she could point.

"And you sure you saw the lion leaving?"

"Its giant head with its furry mane popped out. It sniffed the floor, then walked out, like a massive pussycat."

"How far away were you?"

Felicity pointed to a picnic bench about four metres away.

"And he didn't see you?"

"No, Miss."

"I'm not even scared of lions. I hope we see it, I can do my judo on it," said Callum.

Susan ignored him.

"You've been a very brave girl, Felicity. Thank you. Right, just pass the monkeys, Nigel."

"Nigel?" interjected Callum. "I thought his name was James?"

"And I thought you suffered from panic attacks," said Susan, sick of his shit. Callum shut up. "How the hell did the lion get out in the first place?"

"It's a mystery, isn't it?" said Nigel, avoiding eye contact and biting his lip.

"You?!" whispered Susan, in a demonic fury.

Nigel said nothing and carried on.

The group moved towards the simian experience house nervously. Nigel's eyes darted left to right, anticipating a big cat attack any second. He quickened his pace as they approached the line of monkey cages. He put his back flat to the back of the enclosure, inching along sideways, and encouraged the group to do the same. The four edged their way across the containers like a row of paper chain people.

A chimp reached through the bars to grab Nigel's hat, but he managed to rescue it before giving his would-be primate thief a two fingered salute.

"Don't teach you that at school, do they, eh?"

"Actually, we do," said Susan. "Obscene Gestures towards Primates is a core topic at Hartnell Primary, isn't it children?"

Neither child responded.

Just past the playpark with still no sign of the furry predator, the foursome made it to the cafeteria. Susan practically shoved all three into the front door. The room was abuzz with excited children, all munching on their packed lunches, blissfully unaware of the danger they faced if they stepped outside. Barbara looked up from her neglected sandwich, which had startled to curl at the edges. She was surrounded by three children in various states of upset.

"Mrs Harpman, finally! And Callum, Felicity, and, er, you."

"Hello Miss Wright," replied Susan, her eyes stretched wildly. "Quick word?"

Barbara told her pupils to busy themselves for a couple of minutes, so they tore into their teacher's lunchbox and helped themselves to her Jaffa Cakes.

Susan pulled Barbara aside and the two huddled in the corner of the barn.

"OK, don't freak out, but we're ninety nine percent certain the lion got out."

Barbara's face remained perfectly still. As if caught in time, not a single tic of emotion registered.

"Barbara? Did you hear what I said?"

"Sorry yes, I just thought you said the lion had escaped!" She tittered, and grabbed Susan's arms playfully.

"That's exactly what I said, Barbara."

Barbara's mouth dried instantly, and she felt her bowels loosen.

"A lion? On the loose during a school visit? Please tell me you're joking."

"It's ok," reassured Susan. "We just need to make sure all the kids stay locked in here, whilst we call the park ranger or police for help."

"Miss! Miss!" shouted a child.

"Yeah," agreed Barbara, mildly comforted by Barbara's plan. "You're right. As long as no one leaves here, there's no way for the lion to get in."

"Miss!"

"In a minute, Roman." shushed Barbara. "And if the enclosure sign is right, it's an elderly male, so chances are it's looking for a snooze rather than dinner. OK?"

"Yeah, it's scary, clearly but really not the disaster it could be."

"Miss!"

"Just keep everyone here and we'll be telling future year groups about today with a smile on our faces and relief in our hearts."

"Miss!"

"Roman, you really need to wait for the adults to stop talking before you interrupt. Now what is it?"

"It's Callum, Miss. He's left the cafe. Reckon he's gone looking for an escaped lion. Wants to do some karate on it. Miss. Miss. Did you hear me? Miss!"

CHAPTER 32

1984

Bill and James grabbed their belongings and stuffed them into the Lada's poky boot. Quite how the Russians managed to smuggle dissidents and chopped up traitors inside them was anyone's guess, Bill mused. He flicked on the projector and jabbed his control panel with fusty precision.

James leapt into the driver's side and adjusted the seat. Bill stared at him incredulously.

"You're not actually going to drive, are you? Aren't you drunk?"

"Maybe a bit, but you're concussed!"

"That is true. Concussion is really dangerous. I think I should retire from professional wrestling."

"But you don't do professional wrestling."

"Well, all the more reason I should retire."

"I'm not sure either of us should drive," said James, and stumbled out of the car onto his face.

Bill shrugged then shuffled over to the driving seat, adjusted the mirrors, and started the ignition. The Lada's engine spluttered into life. Bill crunched the gear into first and pulled out very slowly from the car's leafy hiding place. As the car juddered into second, its twin occupants illustrated the dictionary definition of the word, 'concerned'.

"Couldn't you have got a better car?" James asked.

"I spent all the money on the time machine bit. Where was your half of the dosh?"

"Gave it to Bobby Twang, long story. Actually, it's not, I presented him with that inscribed plectrum. He thought I was joking at first, but managed to convince him it's his destiny to establish Hartnell's number one guitar shop. So, I helped him on his way with Nigel's guitars and a starter loan."

"Loan?"

"Well, I mentioned that one day in 2019 a Bill Lambert will come into the shop and ask for a Gibson Les Paul. As repayment he'll give it to you for free. My apology."

Bill's eyes clouded over, and he shook his head.

"Well, that's, erm…"

Bill pulled out the car's choke valve; the engine just shied from stalling with an encouraging growl. Bill steered into the large stretch of concrete that made up the vast majority of the industrial estate's rear. He pulled the gear back into first and slammed his foot onto the accelerator. The little engine yelped like a rodent with its tail trapped. The car shot forward at an impressive speed as Bill climbed the gears. Despite his injuries, he felt the tingle of triumph start to itch his skin.

"When I say go, hit that button there," instructed Bill, and nodded towards a control panel resting on the handbrake. James looked aghast at the box. There were about fifty buttons on the display.

"Which one?"

Bill rolled his eyes and glanced sidewards at his travelling companion. Why couldn't James have at least a passing interest in science?

"The biggest one with ENTER written on it," Bill replied, with a weary groan.

"Gotcha."

The car picked up more traction and belted across the tarmac towards Hartnell town. The windows rattled in the doors, as the unforgiving suspension juddered up their backsides, melting James and Bill's spines.

"You ready?"

"Ready!"

"Go!"

James punched the button, an orgiastic smile stretched across from ear to ear. Bill cheered wildly as the car filled with light, blinding its occupants. An almighty bang rang out across Hartnell's mid-eighties dusk.

James and Bill finally left 1984.

The tyres skidded across the ground obstinately as Bill slammed on the brakes. They spun round, until the vehicle came to a stop. James clutched his head in pain. Bill squeezed even harder his already tight grip on the steering wheel. The pair took a long minute to calm down before either turned to face the other. James spoke first.

"Did it work?"

Bill grabbed the box and studied the readings.

"Oh, jellybean sandwiches, no!"

James shrank into his seat a little.

"Good news?"

"Well, we've moved."

"Good start," said James, optimistically.

"We're in 1994," sighed Bill.

"What? I need to save my family, not live through Britpop and the death of Kurt Cobain again."

"Maybe the required negative energy density can't be sustained by the confinement of this primitive vehicle?"

"Parklife!"

Bill stared at his friend in surly silence.

"Sorry, couldn't resist."

Bill punched in some coordinates again. He reached into the back seat, pulled his backpack into the front, and removed the laminated document. He read the same sentence several times - BUNNY HOPS TO THE WARREN - before his tired synapses finally cracked into life.

"We might have to do several smaller leaps."

"Fine, let's do it," agreed James, resisting the urge to hum the *Quantum Leap* theme.

The car flew forward, and the pair repeated their flight procedure again. The balding tyres burnt into the concrete as the Lada sped off again.

With another bang, the car left 1994, and catapulted five years into the future.

CHAPTER 33

2019

Susan juddered as Roman's words reverberated around her head.

"Miss? Miss?"

"Roman," croaked Barbara. "That's very interesting news. Could you please take a seat back in the cafeteria, there's a good boy."

"Yes Miss," replied Roman, and skipped happily back to his seat.

Barbara tapped Susan on the shoulder.

"Susan, we need to phone the police *now*."

"You do that," agreed Susan. "Phone the police then phone the park. Seems to be the only way we can get them to notice that their biggest, most threatening exhibit has gone walkabouts. I'm going to get Callum."

She strode off back to the cafeteria to find Nigel. She found him at the till trying to pry it open.

She pushed him back hard against the counter and hushed her voice. She leant into his ear.

"Still got that gun?"

"What?"

"The gun? The gun you threatened me with, do you still have it?"

"Maybe..."

"It's a binary question Nigel, is it still on your person?"

"Yes," said Nigel, sheepishly.

"Good. Get out there and hunt down that lion."

Nigel laughed maniacally.

"Piss off!"

"Callum is out there with a wild lion on the loose. He might get killed or, at best, severely mauled. You are the only person here who can tackle that problem and save that child. You want to be less selfish, here's your chance."

Nigel trembled as he fumbled inside his coat for the weapon.

"You have to come with me," he said, and looked pleadingly into his son's wife's eyes.

"So, you can push me in the way as you make your escape? No thanks."

"This is a two-man operation. I need someone to grab the boy whilst I take care of Leo. Strength in numbers and all that. You know it makes sense."

"We're not supposed to leave children at a twenty to one adult to child ratio. It's dangerous and illegal."

"So is a child being mauled by Africa's finest."

Susan squeezed her temples between her thumb and forefingers. Not for the first time in her life, she wished her husband had been grown in a lab.

"For pity's sake, let's be quick then."

Susan turned to address the whole room as Barbara hovered outside the toilet door, discreetly calling the police.

"OK children, listen in. Mr Harpman and I have to pop out, so again you will be left with Miss Wright. You are under strict instructions not to leave this room. If you even think about leaving here, Christmas *will* be cancelled."

A strong wail of discontent flooded the room. Miss Wright came back in, ashen-faced. She muttered in hushed tones to Susan.

"Police marksman on his way. I tried ringing the park but incredibly, the line's engaged."

"The lion's enraged?" said Nigel.

"The phone's busy, you numpty," seethed Susan. "Can you keep the children here for a while longer please? Know it sounds insanely dangerous, but we're going out there."

Barbara slapped on a disingenuously broad smile and clapped her hands together.

"Right class, twenty questions. What am I - animal, mineral, vegetable and all that."

"Miss, are you a cow?"

Nigel and Susan made their exit.

Running around the perimeter of the park, Nigel held the gun handle with a fervent grip. Susan grabbed onto his coat jacket for dear life. She wasn't letting go of the one thing that stood between her and a lion's jaws.

"Shouldn't we go to the entrance first?" asked Nigel and nodded back towards the direction they were heading. "That way we can cover the whole park from top to bottom."

"Callum said he was going to tackle the lion himself. He knows it was last *past* the mollusc shed, not at the entrance."

"Bloody Callum, he knew the risks when he wandered off."

"He's eight years old."

"Thought you said the oldest were seven."

"Callum's special."

"Too right," agreed Nigel.

For a zoo that didn't boast an awful lot of attractions, Uncle Rusty's Petting Zoo covered a lot of ground. As well as a paltry gift shop, which sold mouse mats with pictures of shrews on them, the exhibits were spread across acres of poorly maintained grass that were more mud than lawn. The cafe was situated just past the rodent displays, mostly a collection of malnourished rabbits and shivering guinea pigs.

The pair crept around the playground, Nigel's gun cocked ahead, ready to fire. Susan hoped she wasn't being filmed. She really didn't want to be the subject of a badly-spelled Facebook rant on some local concerned parents' group.

Nigel made a dart across the roundabout, then dived between the swings. Crouched down, Susan kept hold rigidly onto his hips, like the world's laziest pantomime horse.

"What are you doing?" hissed Susan.

"Ssh!"

Nigel pointed ahead. Susan followed his finger towards the bushes. Spreading out beneath the bush was about a foot of lion tail, complete with sprouting black tassel. The sandy coloured rope-like appendage swished erratically from the ground. Its owner spread flat out beneath the bush in a prone position. Susan had seen enough wildlife documentaries to know that the tail behaviour meant *something*, but couldn't remember what. Was it happy, horny, hungry, playful, or pissed off? Maybe all five at once?

Susan felt the adrenaline power through her veins. Nigel aimed the gun vaguely towards the big cat. Susan pinched Nigel's sides. He turned round and threw her a face of purest genocide. She shook her head and mouthed, "no" at him. He mouthed "why not?" back. Susan pointed to the left, as the shrubbery ended next to a path leading back to the lion's den.

Sat cross-legged on the path a few feet from the giant furry carnivore, was Callum Agnew. He chewed messily on a toffee bar as his beady eyes surveyed the feline with bewitched fascination. The big cat glared back at the tubby boy, its mighty paws outstretched in front, almost within swiping distance.

Susan and Nigel crept backwards to the outer perimeter of the playpark, then shuffled around the railings towards Callum. The pair were mere feet from both feral creatures.

Nigel turned round to face Susan.

"I'm sorry," he whispered.

"About what?"

"Firstly, I shit myself back there, so being behind me must have stunk."

"Not the time, Nigel!"

"Secondly, this."

Nigel pointed the gun directly at Susan and took a huge breath.

"OI LION," he bellowed. "COME AND GET YOUR DIN DINS RIGHT HERE."

Susan went to scream, but no sound came out.

The lion's head jerked into life. He raised his mighty mane and prowled towards the commotion. Nigel grabbed Susan and clinched her writhing body in front of his own. He pressed the gun to her ear and kissed her head.

The lion roared.

CHAPTER 34

1999

James and Bill had barely moved a quarter of a mile, but had so far managed fifteen years into the future.

"We're in 1999?" James asked. He rubbed his eyes, and yawned so loudly Bill covered his ears.

"Yes, but clearly not ready to party like it."

Bill chuckled at his own joke.

"Balls," muttered James. "So, we keep driving here in short bursts a few years at a time?"

"Looks like it. Says so here."

Bill grabbed the laminated document and pointed to the final clue - BUNNY HOPS TO THE WARREN.

James screwed up his face and wound down the window for some air.

"You know I hate these bloody clues."

"You have mentioned that, yes. But they've served us well and I've got them on a floppy disk ready to go. Just one more to crack - PRINCE'S BUG DELIVERS THE MESSAGE."

"Prince Charles?" suggested James.

"Has he got a bug?" pondered Bill.

"Dunno, he's got big sausage fingers. Sausages equal bangers, like this car is a banger? Does that help?"

Bill screwed up his nose. "We'll keep guessing."

Bill pulled at the lightbox and dodged a flying spark. It wasn't looking especially grand. The bulb fizzed and the usually ultra brilliant white light glimmered dully.

"Really hope we can bunny hop home today."

"Please say you can. I've no idea what my vengeance-fuelled father is likely to do. Remember him in 2019? He was a pair of horns away from being an actual demon."

Bill gave a non-committal murmur as he took a wire cutter to the box and stripped some copper bare. He jammed the metallic strand back into the box and screwed tightly a loose panel. The electricity hummed pleasantly.

"That should do it, let's get back to the..."

Bill stopped mid-sentence, his attention ensnared by something he glimpsed outside the car. He pressed his face against the window so his breath smeared across the glass. James tapped the dashboard impatiently.

"Bill?"

Laughing, Bill lunged at the door and gripped the handle, jumped out of the vehicle, and ran with lightning speed towards the estuary. James had never seen him move that fast, and that included the time C&A were giving out free waistcoats to the first five customers.

He dashed over to the water's edge, following a barely perceptible colourful line that became more visible with each stride. James climbed out and jogged gently to catch up. As he approached, he caught sight of his best friend pulling desperately on a multicoloured dog lead that led into the flowing river. A young woman was screaming at the side of the bank, her face a blotchy mess of terror and tears. James stood paralysed in confusion.

"You gonna help or what?" shouted Bill, as he struggled to hold on to the taught lead. The rainbow patterned cord quivered from the strain. James ran down to the water's edge and grabbed the slack behind Bill. He pulled with considerable might and the pair fell backwards onto the muddy bank. A metallic snap sounded out as a dog collar chain popped under the force exerted on it. A small whimper escaped from the water.

"John, no!" shouted the lady, and she ran towards the river.

"John?" said James.

Bill scrambled to his feet and dived into the water. He flailed about in the estuary and launched himself towards what looked like a discarded towel. Bill reached out, grabbed the object, and stomped his feet onto the gravelly riverbed to halt his flow. Spluttering mouthfuls of rancid river water, he made his way towards the woman and handed her what James now made out to be a small brown dog. The creature trembled in his owner's hands and shook its fur. A yelping bark of what Bill could only hope was gratitude sounded out across the gully.

The woman cradled the sopping wet pooch and fussed at its miniature ratty face.

"Ooh John, who's a naughty John? Getting all stuck in the river, John? That'll learn you for chasing the seagulls, John."

Bill smiled at the woman, through painful bouts of shivering. He coughed up a lungful of untreated river. James ran at Bill and covered him in his jacket.

"Thank you so much," said the lady. "Are you ok? You saved John's life. Anything I can do for you, anything at all."

"Well, actually Martha," replied Bill.

Martha's spine stiffened at the mention of her name. She went from overwhelming gratitude to rigid alert in a matter of nanoseconds. Bill clenched his teeth then removed his glasses to wipe them on the jacket sleeves.

"Martha? This is Martha?" asked James. "Martha from the library Martha? Clues Martha?" asked James, delighted. He stopped to point at her working legs. "Hang on, I thought you said…"

"Not now, James."

"You know me?" puzzled Martha.

"Well, sort of," explained Bill. "It's a bit complicated. We're from the future."

Martha backed up and reached for her rape alarm.

"Nine eleven," said James, flatly. "It's a terrorist attack that occurred/will occur in New York in the year 2001. It's bloody horrible."

"What are you doing?" said Bill, horrified.

"She needs convincing, so here's the proof. Reality television show *Big Brother* will start next year, America will welcome its first black president in 2008, and best of all, a member of pop group *East 17* will run over himself whilst being sick from eating too many baked potatoes."

"What?"

"Hello Martha, I'm James."

Martha waved one of John's paws at the pair, unsure what these dog-saving weirdos were doing.

"So, this is 1999, yes?" asked James.

Martha nodded slowly. Her eyes darted about the bank for possible escape routes. She regretted not buying a bigger, more ferocious dog.

"In twenty years' time you two will meet again. At the library. By then you've already met Bill, because of this, but he won't have met you. See?"

Martha took a small step back.

"You're scaring her, James," said Bill.

"How did you know I'd be here?" Martha asked, her voice an octave lower.

"I recognised the dog lead! You still own it twenty years later! You don't get many like that across the decades."

"John's still alive in 2019?"

"I, er, recognised the lead."

"Oh."

James cut in.

"Right, firstly don't worry about the millennium bug, it's a load of nothing. Hang on! Millennium bug, 'Prince's bug', Prince's 1999, and here we are delivering the message. I actually got another one of those bloody clues."

Bill gave his friend a patronising little round of applause.

James continued, filling in Martha with a few choice pop culture spoilers - "*Doctor Who* comes back and eventually there's a lady *Doctor Who*!" - as well as a highlight reel of forthcoming notable atrocities to prove their authenticity.

Over the next ten minutes, he and Bill convinced Martha that everything they said was true. He included a short tour around the Lada, a swift swipe through James' phone, and the promise that generally the world would get both better yet somehow worse at the same time. Bill handed her the floppy disk and promised he would see her in twenty years.

"Sorry, but we have to get back to 2019," he said. "But we will meet up for that coffee, yeah?"

"In twenty years? I won't put the kettle on just yet then."

James slapped the roof of the Lada impatiently.

"Sorry, but we really have to go," he insisted.

"I'll be back," promised Bill.

"Alright Arnie," Martha giggled. John barked at the departing time travellers.

The car started and ambled away slowly from its stationary position. James and Bill waved goodbye to Martha and John, their barely-open palms unsteadily circling the air in confusion.

"This is weird," said James.

"No more or less weird than all the other stuff we've done this week."

"I was talking about the age difference. She's, what, twenty?"

"She's our age in the future!"

"Tell it to the judge, mate."

Bill put his foot down and sped off away from Martha. The Lada accelerated towards Hartnell, leaving Bill's encounter a mere speck in the distance.

The car flashed bright white and disappeared.

CHAPTER 35

2017

Bill and James raced through the next two decades, a few years at a time. They saw for themselves the industrialisation and build-up of the town's outer edges, as new buildings and developments appeared around them. As they landed at the penultimate year, 2017, the accumulation of half a dozen time travel journeys had taken its toll on the pair and their vehicle.

A flustered, red-faced Bill fanned himself with the laminated document. James simply stared ahead, near comatose with heat exhaustion and dehydration. The almost completely dilapidated car's paintwork had melted away. The tyres sizzled; the tread worn through entirely.

"I'm not sure how roadworthy this is anymore. Or timeworthy," said Bill. "Structurally speaking, Lada's weren't made to drive through wormholes."

James shut tight his eyes and smoothed his head. He tucked his skull between his knees to heave large dollops of air and stop himself throwing up.

"After this, no more bloody time travel. Even if I get an invite from John Lennon himself to jam with *The Beatles* at Apple studios in 1969."

"How likely is that exactly?"

"It's on the lower end of possibilities, I'll give you that. But hey, the drummer from *Elastica* watched one of my gigs once."

"I know James, you tell me at least once a month."

James crossed his arms and pouted.

"Let's just get back to stopping Nigel, eh?"

"One more trip, and we're home. We should get there the very day we left, Thursday November 28th, 2019."

"Can we hit a specific time? Ideally just after we left."

"More or less," said Bill, hiding his crossed fingers beneath the seat. "Your Dad got there two days before we met him."

"Which I'm guessing is how he spread yet another rumour about Bobby Twang's dog fetish."

"If we can head him off before he gets to your family then minimal damage done, yes?"

"That's the idea."

Bill wrenched at the steering wheel for what he hoped would be the car's final journey. The wheel's former circle shape had warped into a mush of spokes and offences against geometry. Bill manipulated the clump of metal to face the car towards town one last time. He turned the key in the ignition.

Nothing.

Not even a click.

He tried again. And again. And again.

James looked sharply to his right, and caught the panic in his friend's eyes.

"No," he exclaimed. "No. No no no no please, not now, we're closer than ever."

Bill shrugged.

"Maybe push?"

"Right."

Still dazed, James walked to the back of the car. He pressed his palms against the piping hot metalwork. He immediately pulled them back and screamed in agony.

"It's molten fucking lava!" James waved his hands about, trying to fan air onto instant-formed blisters. Bill got out, pulled down his trousers, and threw them at James.

"They're still wet, use them like a sort of damp oven glove," he suggested. James nearly burst into tears, but did as he was told.

Wrapping his hands in his friend's sopping chinos, he pushed as hard as he could against the wrecked vehicle. He gritted his teeth and grunted like a madman as rivers of sweat poured down his head. The car rolled forward, picking up speed. Bill flicked the ignition in an obsessive frenzy, determined to start the stupid bloody Lada he very much regretted buying. His foot smashed the acceleration pedal hard, and he jumped up and down in his seat, pumping the vehicle for a sign of life.

A tiny spark ignited, and the whimper of an engine returned to consciousness.

"Come on!" yelled Bill, punching the roof.

The car's combustion kicked in, and the Lada mewled back to pootling along. James leapt into the passenger seat and joined in the boisterous celebration. Bill put his foot down and James hit the enter button like the professional co-pilot he now considered himself to be.

The gleaming white blinded the passengers again, as Bill and James finally landed in 2019.

Bill didn't take his foot off the accelerator. He kept driving on into and through Hartnell. A small fire had started in the dashboard, and the gearbox began to smoulder too. Bill kept his foot on the pedal and zipped through the town's back alleys as fast as his regard for other road users and pedestrians would allow. James laughed maniacally as he stuck his head out of the window away from the wilting speedometer and flame-licked time machine.

"2019, I love you!" he bellowed to the outside.

"We'll be at your house in seconds, mate," assured Bill, as he narrowly avoided taking out a hissing cat.

The car screeched to a halt outside James' house, but Bill kept the engine running. He threw his jacket onto the fire, smothering it instantly. James ran to his front door to find it locked. He pulled at his hair in a desperate attempt to make his sleep-impoverished brain work. It did the trick.

"She's at work! Of course, Susan's at work! Maybe Nigel's not even here yet."

Bill looked up from the remote control in alarm.

"Oh shit," he exclaimed.

"What?"

"It's not Thursday the 28th."

"What is it?"

"It's Friday the 29th. We've overshot by twenty-four hours. I mean, it *is* only one day, but you know, your dad could have burnt down Rome by lunchtime."

James punched himself in the head then pulled his hair again. Then lightly tapped his skull for inspiration.

"The zoo! She's at Uncle Rusty's, come on!"

He leapt back into the car and Bill thrust the gear into first and hit the gas with all his might. The Lada thrust forward, and the pair zoomed towards their destination.

"Do you think he's with her?" asked James, as he fiddled with his fingers.

"I think it's a very real possibility. He was livid, and swore to screw up your life."

"Oh, bloody hell Bill, he's got a gun!" James cried. He grabbed his friend by the arm and shook him.

"I know James, I'm sorry. But hey, there's more of us, erm, and…"

"You're not wearing any trousers?"

"See? Feel better already?"

James' stomach lurched in agony.

The pair approached the leafy stretch of woods in which Uncle Rusty's Petting Zoo largely hid from the outside world. The Lada swung into the wildlife park's small weed-infested gravel drive. Bill slammed on the brakes, churning up the stones. The rear tyres finally burst, relieving the wheels of their thin strip of perished rubber.

James fumbled clumsily with the door handle and freed himself from the car. He hurried to the boot and pulled out his rucksack.

"Bill, grab the time machine, and put it in this bag!"

Bill pulled the projector's connection from the Lada, slammed a battery pack brimming with three dozen D batteries slammed into its side, then placed the machine carefully into the bag. James slung it over his shoulder and strode to the entrance. Ideally, Bill would have liked just another thirty seconds so he could put some clothes on, but it didn't seem like the highest priority right now. He waddled over to his friend in just his wet pants and tee. James turned towards Bill, anxiety crippling his face.

"I just hope nothing mental's happened and we're not too late."

The piercing sound of a bullet being fired ricocheted across the valley.

CHAPTER 36

James' broke into an instant run towards the gunshot. He vaulted over the meagre turnstile to the park, his heart thudding against his ribcage. Bill followed behind, proffering an apology to the pay booth, a gesture wasted entirely on the snoozing employee.

Nearly slipping on the muddy grass, James followed the sound. He sprinted past the cafeteria and simian experience and headed towards the mollusc shed. Wriggling the backpack free from his shoulders as he ran, he held the bag in one hand and bound over a hedge that led into the playpark. The zip opened, spilling the contents onto the grass. Bill scrambled to scavenge the lightbox from the sodden ground as James carried on to the outer edge of the lion's den.

Without warning, James' journey came to an abrupt finish; his legs had stopped moving before his eyes could assess what he was even looking at. Just behind, Bill finally dawdled breathlessly onto the path. He dropped the lightbox in surprise.

In front of the two friends stood James' father. His face awash with pure, distilled loathing, he clutched Susan hard against his chest. His left arm extended into the air, pointing the pistol skyward. Behind them a chubby boy in a rain mac stood quivering. He looked so frightened he could barely eat his second Mars Bar. To their right, close to a torn hole in the chain link fence, a mighty male lion bared its fist-sized fangs at the humans, its eyes focused and back legs poised to pounce.

James could hear his own shallow gulps of breath.

"Nigel," said James, in a voice barely above a whisper.

Nigel and Susan looked across to James' dishevelled husk. James tried to smile at Susan, but it was little more than a faint muscle twitch. Nigel's eyes bulged with incredulity at his son's appearance.

"James," said Susan, hoarsely. "Take it you've met your father?" Every inch of her trembled as she struggled to free Nigel's clutches.

Nigel tightened his grip around Susan and pressed the gun against her head. His right hand squeezed lightly around her throat. He stared his son directly in the eye as his dirty fingernails caressed her neck.

"Please Nigel," begged James. "Let her go."

Nigel held her against his body again and waved the gun.

"Or what, James *Harpman*? I've got a gun, and you've got a big cat problem."

"James!" shouted Bill, and threw the lightbox towards his friend. James caught it and aimed the lens towards his father. He glimpsed the lion, just a few feet away from the most important woman in his life. The beast blinked and shook its mane, unsteady and thanks to the big loud bang, nervous on its paws.

"Shoot the gun again!" shouted Callum.

"No Callum, we won't be shooting the gun again, will we?" said Susan, unconvincingly.

"Yes Callum," added James. "No shooting."

"Son," spat Nigel. His resentment teetered on insanity. "You simply had to come and mess up my life."

"You messed up your own life."

"I didn't ask for any of this, I didn't ask for you to barge into my apartment as an aggrieved adult. I thought I had a young son who looked up to me, who could follow in my size ten footsteps, who enjoyed my company. A son who calls me DAD!"

"You *earn* that, Nigel. And you're lying to yourself. You weren't there, *ever*. Not for your wife, nor your daughter, and definitely not for me. I tried to look up to you, really! Satan knows I tried. But how can you look up to someone who simply isn't present?"

The lion growled a bassy rumble of discontent. Callum jumped back on hearing its deep, mournful grunt.

"But I'm here now?" continued Nigel, a faltering crack in his voice.

"Yeah," agreed James. "And look at what you've become."

Nigel's eyes faltered slightly. His eyelids hung low, and his face crumpled.

"I just wanted to..." Nigel looked shamefully towards the floor, unable to finish the sentence.

"Wanted to do what?"

Nigel sighed ruefully. "I wanted to be the hero."

"So, you bribed a child to fake a panic attack and set a lion on the loose?" said Susan, appalled.

"I don't know," Nigel retorted softly. "I just wanted a family."

"You *had* a family. And you could have been my hero. Just by being my dad," said James.

Nigel stared at the gun and felt his grip loosen.

"I've got poison in my heart, and shit in my pants. I headbutted Susan. I hit your wife." A tear trickled from his swollen eye.

"What?" James tensed his shoulders and felt the hairs on his neck rise. "You hit Susan?"

"I'm sorry Susan," bleated Nigel, pathetically, and let his arms fall by his sides, releasing his son's wife.

"Men don't hit women, Nigel," said James. "Real men don't *ever* hit women."

"Oh James," said Susan. "I've already told him; no *man* has ever hit me."

With those words, Susan turned to face her captor, and brought her arm up fiercely between his legs, crushing his testicles. Nigel gasped for air, dropped the gun, and collapsed forward onto his knees. Susan kicked the gun away and ran. She pulled Callum by the hand, but the boy resisted. He pulled sharply back and ran towards Nigel.

"Callum, no!" shouted Susan.

Bewildered by the commotion, the lion leapt towards the boy. Nigel grabbed Callum and thrust him to safety, himself curling up into a ball as the lion batted him with an almighty paw. Nigel walloped the path hard as the lion began a frenzied attack on Nigel. It tore through his clothes and scratched at his skin, tearing through his flesh.

"Dad!" shouted James. Nigel looked up, a glimmer of a smile. James fired the time machine directly at his father. A force of luminous dazzle hit Nigel. The lion leapt out of its beam. Swaddled in white light, Nigel's frame burnt into the background as he started to disappear. James could just about make out his father's eyes blinking back in gratitude at his son, which then twinkled out of existence.

Bill grabbed the gun and fired a shot into the air then pointed the weapon directly at the lion. Fed up with today's events, the huge cat retreated gratefully back into its den.

James finally gasped and dropped the lightbox. He felt his eyes sting a little. He looked down at the spot where Nigel had just been mere moments ago. A small wisp of black smoke drifted into the wind, whilst his dad's right foot still in its shoe stood on the concrete. Its bloody ankle stump crisply smouldered.

"What?" said James, peering at the appendage.

Bill looked over from the lion's fence and came to inspect the lone piece of Nigel still remaining.

"You didn't cover every part of him then?"

"Clearly not. Will he be alright?"

"Well, it looks like the light cauterised it immediately, so he won't bleed out. Though, you know, the lion attack. Where have you sent him?"

"I don't know, there wasn't a set date. He could be anywhere."

Bill picked the shoe, pulled the foot out and threw it over the fence. The lion sniffed then gobbled it up immediately. James grimaced as the cat tore strips from his dad's bone and chewed down his flesh.

"I am going to need so much counselling after this," said James.

"Oh look," said Bill, peeking inside the shoe. "Size nine and a half." He showed it to James.

James exhaled again.

"Hello," said Susan.

James' heart leapt and he embraced Susan with a hug that nearly crushed her ribs.

"Fucking hell, it's good to see you."

"It's not so great to smell you," laughed Susan.

"Oh, thought I might look like a bit of a roguish rock star, you know."

James raised an eyebrow, winked, and clicked his tongue.

"No, you're like a bin bag full of piss. Where have you been?"

"Somewhere awful."

"Swindon?"

"Close enough. How are you? How are the kids? What happened? I am so unbelievably sorry about everything."

"All fine, and no time for mega apologies now, but believe me, you *will* need to do them."

"I know, I know."

"So, what's time travel like?"

"Mixed. At first, it's like 'wow!'. As if you're being offered a free milkshake. But then once you're drinking it you realise the only flavour they had was semen."

"Interesting analogy. Hey, I finally got to meet my father-in-law. He seemed nice for a man you wouldn't want to spend any more than no minutes at all with. James, are you ok?"

"Not really. But maybe I am. I just can't help wondering if what he said was true. What if I hadn't shown up, none of this had occurred. Would he have gone on to be a decent father? I don't know. But then, he forced *me* into the past, which set the whole chain of events in motion. Although from his point of view, we were already there? I really don't understand what just happened."

"It's an infinity loop," explained Bill. "A time schism caught in an endless replaying of events. It has no real beginning, but you can't change it, not a whisker. Laws of physics, mate."

"Really?"

"I've absolutely no idea, I just made all that up. But whatever happened, it was his choices that got him to where he ended up, not yours. By the way, hello Susan."

Bill waved to his best friend's wife.

"Going for the wet underpants look, I see?"

Bill blushed, only just realising for the first time that afternoon that he was almost completely nude.

"Anyway, we should probably seal this fence back up before the lion gets any more ideas," suggested Bill.

"How?"

"Use the lightbox. Melt the steel, forge it back together. Should be easy enough, just turn the power right down."

"Let's do it. I've got just enough time to get home, write about *Fear of Beans*, send it off, then hug my kids all evening before I probably die of a heart attack once this last week has caught up with me."

"That's the spirit!"

"I'm going to see Nina too. Even if I am *clearly* right about our dad, there's no need to shut her out."

"Proud of you mate," mumbled Bill, and gave his pal a friendly pat on the back.

"Dude."

"Dude."

James and Bill picked up the lightbox and set to repairing Nigel's vandalism. As they soldered the chains back together, Susan took Callum aside and sat him down.

"Bit of an exciting day for you, yeah?"

Callum took a sweet from his bulging pockets and chewed messily.

"I won't tell anyone Miss, if that's what you're worrying about."

"Why do you say that?"

"Because you look really worried. But don't worry, no one will believe me anyway. But I do like sweets, Miss. I really like lots and lots of sweets."

Callum winked. Susan stood and winked back. He really wasn't so stupid after all.

"Deal," she said. "Come on, we need to get back to the others."

"Sure."

The four took a brisk walk back through the zoo towards the entrance. As they reached the cafeteria, Susan put a hand out and stopped Bill from entering.

"Bill, please don't come into the cafeteria undressed like that."

"Oh yeah, sure," he agreed, and he headed to the car park for a change of clothes.

"Hey, that reminds me," James suddenly said in delight. "Look what I've got."

He reached into his backpack and pulled out a small bundle of children's clothes. James beamed smugly and handed them over to Susan. She took the clothes and looked them over, inspecting the togs with a critical eye.

"Where did you find these?" she asked.

"Bouchers Clothing! Just as we remembered it! Well, obviously."

"Not bad, James. Not bad at all. A plain white pair of shorts, and a red and white striped tee shirt. Exactly as specified."

"Nailed it," said James, confidently.

"They're the wrong size though, way too small." She thrust the clothes back at James, shook her head, and walked back into the building.

James looked down at the shorts, crestfallen. He scrunched them up in anger then went to stuff them back into his backpack. He unzipped the bag and shoved the lightbox aside to pack in the clothes next to it. The lightbox glowed with a faint glimmer of residual power.

It gave James an idea.

A stupid, irresponsible idea.

"Bill?"

THE END

ACKNOWLEDGEMENTS

Thanks to Shaun Baines for his invaluable editing skills, Daniel Morgan for the exceptional job on the cover art, and most of all, to Lisa, Willow, and Elijah. Incredibly, not only do you put up with me, but have actively encouraged this endeavour every single stumble of the way. I wouldn't have typed a damn word if it wasn't for you three. (So, readers, if you hate the book, blame them, ok?)

ABOUT THE AUTHOR

Miles Hamer has written for Total Film, SFX, Horrorville, XBox World, SciFi Now, and loads more besides. He has also crafted copy on subjects as far ranging as holiday insurance, food packaging, and, er, pig farming. He lives in Devon with his wife, two children, and cats. This is his first novel.

mileshamer.com

COMING SOON!

Bill's jaw plummeted to the ground. A glassy mist came over his eyes and his chest trembled.

"James, have you lost your fudging mind? A kidnapping?"

James sucked in his gums and blinked rapidly at his friend.

"It'll be a cosy kidnapping," protested James. "A friendly abduction!"

"There's no such thing! Just like you don't get a cheery murder, or a jolly molestation."

"Oh, come on, he probably won't even notice."

"Yes, how silly of me," said Bill. "It's so hard to detect when you're being held against your will, isn't it?"

James dropped his shoulders, and let out a lungful of air.

"Bill, I have to do this. There is no other way. We have tried every other available non-kidnappy option, trust me. None has worked. This is the last resort. Admittedly, it's a terrible, dangerous, and ugly resort that no one actually wants to go to."

"Cleethorpes?"

"Steady on Bill, it's not entirely without hope."

Bill frowned, as James flashed him an uneasy grin.

TO BE CONTINUED…

Kidnap to the Future, landing Summer 2025

Printed in Great Britain
by Amazon